BAD

Don't miss the next book in the
BAD UNICORN trilogy:

Fluff Dragon

BAD
unicorn

BY *Platte F. Clark*

ALADDIN
New York   London   Toronto   Sydney   New Delhi

ALADDIN
An imprint of Simon & Schuster Children's Publishing Division
1230 Avenue of the Americas, New York, NY 10020
First Aladdin paperback edition March 2014
Text copyright © 2013 by Straw Dogs, LLC
Cover illustrations copyright © 2013 by John Hendrix
All rights reserved, including the right of reproduction in whole or in part in any form.
ALADDIN is a trademark of Simon & Schuster, Inc., and related logo is a registered
trademark of Simon & Schuster, Inc.
Also available in an Aladdin hardcover edition.
For information about special discounts for bulk purchases,
please contact Simon & Schuster Special Sales at
1-866-506-1949 or business@simonandschuster.com.
The Simon & Schuster Speakers Bureau can bring authors to your live event.
For more information or to book an event contact the Simon & Schuster Speakers
Bureau at 1-866-248-3049 or visit our website at www.simonspeakers.com.
Cover designed by Jessica Handelman
Interior designed by Karina Granda
The text of this book was set in Bembo.
Manufactured in the United States of America 0214 OFF
2 4 6 8 10 9 7 5 3 1
The Library of Congress has cataloged the hardcover edition as follows:
Clark, Platte F.
Bad unicorn / by Platte F. Clark. — First Aladdin hardcover edition.
p. cm.
Summary: Max Spencer is an underachiever but when a carnivorous unicorn,
Princess the Destroyer, and an evil wizard, Rezormoor, bring him, the only one who
can read the legendary Codex of Infinite Knowability, to their magical realm,
he must find the courage to save himself, his friends, and the entire human race.
ISBN 978-1-4424-5012-7 (hc)
[1. Magic—Fiction. 2. Adventure and adventurers. Fiction. 3. Books and reading—Fiction.
4. Unicorns—Fiction. 5. Wizards—Fiction. 6. Humorous stories. 7. Fantasy.] I. Title.
PZ7.C55225Bad 2013
[Fic]—dc23
2013001877
ISBN 978-1-4424-5013-4 (pbk)
ISBN 978-1-4424-5014-1 (eBook)

To the entire Clark clan: Aidan, Allie, Hunter, Kennidy, Hailey,
Platte Christian, Kiaya, and my sweetheart wife, Kathy

ACKNOWLEDGMENTS

WHEN YOU ANNOUNCE THAT YOU'RE WRITING A BOOK ABOUT A carnivorous unicorn, you quickly find out who your friends are. Thankfully, I had many allies who stuck around, starting with my wife Kathy, who never gave up encouraging me to write a novel, and my daughter Kennidy, who read new chapters of Bad Unicorn as quickly as I wrote them. More help came from my son Platte Christian and daughter Hailey, as well as from my mini focus group: Allie, Hunter, and Aidan. And without the assistance of my in-house equestrian expert and daughter, Kiaya, I might not have ever resolved whether or not unicorns had eyebrows. I also want to thank my awesome agent, Deborah Warren, and everyone at East West Literary Agency, as well as my amazing editor, Fiona Simpson. A special thanks goes out to the team at

Aladdin, from publisher Bethany Buck to the brave soul who suggested putting an impaled squirrel on the front cover. I also benefit greatly from an amazingly talented writing group, composed of E. J. Patten, David Butler, Eric Holmes, and Michael Dalzen. Thanks to Russell Jolley for help with the Judo moves and terminology, as well as to beta reader Jessica Powell. And finally, my love and appreciation goes out to my mom, who has always been my biggest fan.

Foreword to the
Codex of Infinite Knowability

✢

IF YOU'RE READING THIS PAGE YOU'RE probably not a wizard and most definitely not my blood descendant. Stop! For this is the *Codex of Infinite Knowability*—"codex" because it is a very old book, and "infinite" because the words herein are not bound to any page numbers or table of contents (for that reason, it's *not* recommended that you use the *Codex* as a citation source for book reports). I suppose congratulations are in order, for you managed to get past the first level of electric shock protection (perhaps by opening the book with a stick or by wearing insulated gloves). However, don't be too smug about your accomplishment. The *Codex of Infinite Knowability* contains the fifteen Prime Spells—the very foundation of all the magic in the three realms. Just drawing close to them is so dangerous that my team of lawyers requires me to tell you that at any moment you may be electrified, frozen, torn asunder, flung into the air, incinerated, or cast across time and space into the dark regions of the umbraverse. As the *Codex*'s author, I recommend you close the book now and run away—preferably with screaming and arm flailing. Sure, it might be socially awkward for a while, but it's way better than experiencing total physical destruction.

Okay, you've ignored my warnings and are reading anyway. Fine. Please note that copyright violators will not only be prosecuted to the full extent of the law, but tied to the Tree of Woe and licked by fire kittens.

Also, if the final battle for earth did not go well, to our squirrel overlords let me say "well played"— you were a worthy opponent. If humans still survive, take heed and remember two very important things: First, never turn your back on a squirrel with a nut. Second, the *Codex of Infinite Knowability* is the most magical book ever written. Just having it in your possession will not only put your life at risk but will make you the target of the powerful and power-hungry. These are not creatures to be trifled with, believe me. My recommendation is that you abandon this book to whence you found it and wait for my long-lost ancestor to claim it—for only those of my blood will be able to read further and unlock the mysteries I have so carefully hidden away. And if you happen to find this great descendant of mine, please tell him or her *not* to bend the *Codex*'s pages—is it so hard to use a bookmark? A little courtesy goes a long way.

Maximilian Sporazo
Arch-Sorcerer and Regent of the Wizard's Tower

╬

PROLOGUE

PRINCESS THE UNICORN WAS HAVING A BAD DAY. PROBABLY NOT AS bad a day as the happy-go-lucky frobbits she'd eaten—but a bad day nonetheless. First of all, the frobbits weren't very satisfying. As a whole, frobbits were short, moderately salty creatures with big ears, hairy feet, large eyes, and bodies that were roundish as the result of long days of eating, drinking, and making merry. Frobbits had always been considered tender folk—both emotionally and when slowly roasted. But the frobbits of late were just . . . bland. And then there was the frobbit musician chained to the nearby tree. Sure, he was playing all the right notes on his little frobbit mandolin, but he wasn't really *feeling* the music—perhaps because Princess had eaten his band mates. And if there was anything Princess despised it was bland frobbits and music without soul.

Magar approached Princess. He was a thin human with gray-flecked hair and a dark goatee of the evil henchman variety, but now his head hung low in the proper attitude of respect. As Princess's designated wizard he was required to serve her until released by the Tower's regent—and that wasn't likely to happen soon given the current state of things. Unicorns were among the most powerful creatures in the Magrus, and Princess was a particularly nasty one, especially when on a rampage. Nevertheless, he had resigned himself to making the best of it—at the very least he'd try not to get himself incinerated. "Your Highness," he purred, casting an annoyed glance at the frobbit musician, who immediately stopped playing. "I hope you found these ones more to your liking."

Princess sighed in a way that sent shivers down Magar's spine. "No, they're not to my liking at all. Honestly, Magar, everything in this whole realm is either bland or tainted."

"True enough," the wizard answered, straightening as he tried to work the kinks out of his back. "Everything in the Magrus is tainted with magic. But it's magic that makes us what we are."

"Maybe. But that isn't the case everywhere, is it? Not in the upper realm—not in the Techrus."

"The human world?" Magar replied, wiping ash from his robes. As a wizard he never quite understood why he had to wear what amounted to a dress adorned with moons and stars. Mages didn't wear long dresses. Mages wore armor and rode into battle swinging swords and casting spells. They were the star spell casters in the Magrus—wizards were conjurers in pajamas and pointed hats. Not that Magar really wanted to be a mage, especially with all their in-fighting and challenging one another for position. Being a wizard was generally a safer line of work, and that suited Magar just fine. "The Techrus is a tiresome place devoid of magic," he continued. "And besides, unicorns there have a certain . . . reputation."

"Reputation? What kind of reputation? As blood-thirsty conquerors?"

Magar knew he had to tread carefully here—he'd seen Princess do bad things to those who delivered disappointing news. "Uh, not exactly," he finally answered.

"Then as devourers of flesh . . . destroyers of cities?"

"Well . . ."

"Creatures of nightmare and flame?"

"Uh . . ."

Princess frowned, stamping her hoof on the ground.

"Well, at the very least, I'm sure we're known as stabbers and gorers?"

Magar thought better of answering. He'd seen the strange pictures drawn by human children—pictures that showed happy unicorns leaping over rainbows, many with ribbons and tassels twisted about their horns. The wizard could only offer a halfhearted shrug in response.

"No, not even as stabbers? Then why do humans suppose we have horns at all?"

"Perhaps for picking delicious fruit from the trees and sharing with friends," the frobbit musician offered in as helpful a tone as he could muster.

Princess smiled—as much as a horse-based creature of evil could smile—then lowered her head. Suddenly a bolt of lightning erupted from her horn and zapped the frobbit into dust. "Not helpful," she said.

Magar made a mental note: Avoid future fruit-pruning references.

Obliterating something, however, did seem to lighten Princess's mood. She moved to where the mandolin lay on the ground and casually stepped on it with her hoof. "Well, everyone in the Magrus knows that in addition to stabbing things, a unicorn's horn is like a wizard's wand, only much more powerful. That's why we're so feared."

"Undoubtedly so, Your Highness."

"Then here's the situation as I see it," she continued, stepping off the smashed mandolin with a final twang of a broken string. "The human realm is stocked with delicious nonmagical creatures to eat and it has a certain under-appreciation for what unicorns really are."

Magar didn't like where this was going. As part of his training in the Wizard's Tower he'd learned about the human realm. Specifically, that it was a place full of strange machines, loud noises, and a substance called *twinkee* that never aged.

"The only way to the human realm is through the monks of the Holy Order of the Tree of Attenuation—and just filling out the release form takes two years."

"Perhaps."

"And besides," Magar continued, "ever since the Great Sundering, most magic won't work there. So even if we could make it you'd be . . ."

Princess raised the patch of hair over her eye (the term "uni-brow" had been summarily rejected). "I'd be, what?"

"You'd be unable to use the full extent of your impres-sive and powerful magic," Magar said, swallowing. "Your Highness."

"There are different kinds of magic, Magar. I thought your Tower would have taught you that. Anyway, I think I want to talk with Rezormoor Dreadbringer. I've heard he's obsessed with the Techrus these days."

Rezormoor was the regent of the Wizard's Tower. Even as a student, Magar had thankfully had little contact with him. Not only was Rezormoor the most powerful spell caster in all the realm, but he was notoriously boring at parties. This was due in large part to his singular obsession with finding the legendary *Codex of Infinite Knowability*. He tended to drone on about it, even when people yawned, tried to steer the conversation in another direction, or *accidentally* stabbed themselves with dinner forks. The thought of some kind of unholy alliance between Rezormoor and Princess was enough to put a knot in Magar's stomach. "I will take you there, if that's what you wish."

"Didn't I just say that? Yes, Magar, I want to go to your drab Tower. And if Rezormoor's disagreeable, maybe I can at least trade you in for an upgrade—that way the trip won't be a complete waste."

Magar bowed, feeling the old twinge returning to his back. You at least had to be alive to be traded in, he thought. And that was a good thing.

CHAPTER ONE

MAX FINDS A BOOK
THE TECHRUS—PRESENT

IN THE HUMAN REALM, WHERE LIFE WAS SO DREARY MILLIONS OF KIDS tweeted messages like, "eating breakfast," "it's Friday!" and "☹," Max Spencer was riding the bus to Parkside Middle School and reading a book. But not just any book—he was reading a book that had been a part of his life for as long as he could remember. The fact that the last time he'd opened it was six years ago wasn't important. What *was* important was that he'd found it under his bed (hidden beneath a dinosaur-themed swimsuit) just in time for his book report, which was due today. Max was used to having luck—just not the good kind. And that made him slightly nervous.

Max lived in a small house in a small town. He was expected to do chores like beat the weeds back once a week and unclog the toilet if it wouldn't flush. But he didn't mind as long as he earned enough allowance to pay for his online games. In the virtual world he was someone impressive—unlike in real life. In PE, for example, Max was always picked dead last (even when Tina Eubanks had two broken arms and a broken leg). And during football season Max had to stay on the sidelines and practice "imaginary jump rope" because the school counselor said competitive sports were damaging his self-esteem. Max was pretty sure middle school was hard enough without becoming known as the jump-rope kid.

As the bus pulled away from the next stop and the kids hurried to find their seats, Max kept his eyes on the pages of his book—partly because he had his English assignment due, but mostly so he wouldn't make eye contact with Ricky "the Kraken" Reynolds. The Kraken was not only the bane of all nerds, geeks, dorks, and the great mass of unclassifieds that wandered the halls of his school, he was also the captain of the wrestling team. He'd earned his nickname after crackin' the bones of two different kids during a regional tournament. The fact that there was also a terrible mythological creature by the same name was simply a bonus.

The key to riding the bus safely was to not be different. If you were a jock, or popular, you were generally safe. But if you were a little pudgy, had a big nose, wore braces, played a reed-based band instrument, or stood out in any way, you were no longer riding a bus—you were a passenger on Ricky's private yellow torture chamber on wheels. Just last week Max had witnessed Ricky deliver an atomic wedgie, a frontal Melvin, a purple nurple, and the dreaded two-handed monkey scrub. The best thing to do in situations like these was to keep your head down and hope Ricky stayed focused on someone else. And that's what Max did, staring intently at his book.

He was reading a section about unicorns. Not that he thought unicorns were especially interesting, but the book had a strange habit of choosing whatever topic *it* wanted. For instance, if Max wanted to read about something other than unicorns he could grab a handful of pages and flip ahead, but there he'd find exactly the same thing he'd been reading previously. After several attempts, all with the same result, Max finally decided that you didn't actually read the old leather-bound book; instead it allowed you to read parts of it. He knew that didn't make much sense, but a book was a book and he had an English assignment to do.

Someone yelped from the backseats where Ricky and his friends were, so Max hunkered down even farther and continued reading: *In addition to being ruled by a queen, unicorns are highly magical creatures capable of speaking to humans. Occasionally, a unicorn gives up on its diet of grass and oats and goes for a little variety, perhaps by eating the human it was previously talking to. Unfortunately, once a unicorn gets a taste for meat there's really no easy way to stop it from plundering, pillaging, and devouring whatever it wants. This includes frobbits, who happen to be a bit of a delicacy, are easy to catch, and come in at around six hundred calories each.*

There was a picture of a unicorn standing defiantly on a hilltop next to a human wearing a robe with moons and stars on it. The unicorn was white, with a long mane accented with pink streaks. On its head sat the emblematic horn, shaped like a tall ice cream cone swirled to perfection. The whole thing reminded Max of a poster a young girl might hang on her wall next to her kitten calendar. Beneath the picture the caption read, *Princess the Unicorn, also known as Princess the Destroyer. Pictured here with her faithful wizard, Magar the Tolerated.*

"Dude!" a voice exploded near Max, and he looked up to see his best friend Dirk dropping down in front of him. Dirk was wearing his favorite "Wang Computers" T-shirt as he leaned over the back of the seat, completely oblivious to the Kraken or anybody else. "The online raid last night totally rocked! I was like, 'You want some of this?' And they were like, 'Yeah, we want some of that.' So I was like, 'Then that's what you're gonna get.' And they were like, 'Good, because that's what we want.'" Dirk paused, noticing what Max was holding. "Hey, isn't that the old book you used to read?"

"Codex," Max said a little too loudly. "So another raid, huh? Sounds . . . epic." Max had lost count of how many times they had had this exact same conversation.

"It was. I totally destroyed this noob elf. Then I did the whole 'chicken' and 'laugh' dance over his dead body. It was awesome."

Max could picture Dirk's character doing the chicken dance and then laughing—two of the commands at the ready for online gamers wanting to add a little insult to injury. "Didn't that happen to you once?" Max asked. He seemed to remember a large party of orcs dancing around Dirk's mangled corpse.

Dirk frowned. "Yeah, well where do you think I got the idea?"

"Figures. So anything else happen?"

"Just the usual, except the elf was part of some humongous guild and they all came after me. Then they danced around my dead body and mocked me for like an hour or so—all two hundred of them."

Having an entire guild chasing Dirk through the game was also something Max had seen before.

"So where were you? I didn't see you log on at all."

"I told you I got busted after staying up all night. I can't play until the weekend."

Dirk shook his head. "Smacked down by the man! Or should I say the woman." Max had made a deal with his mom that if he got a B average he could play online games on weeknights and weekends, and if he got a C average he could only play on the weekends. Max had just barely missed getting all B's last term, so he figured that getting close should count for a couple of extra game days. But when his mom returned after her night shift and found Max still awake and online, he'd discovered what "letter of the law" truly meant. Unfortunately, his mom had an administrative account that locked him out of the game. Banished from all known forms of fun, Max decided to look for lost comics under his bed, and that's when he'd rediscovered the book.

"So what's up with that . . . *codex*?" Dirk asked, motioning toward the odd book and unconsciously rubbing his fingers. When Dirk and Max were little, Dirk had tried to open it—but every time he touched the cover he got shocked. Max laughed hysterically as Dirk tried over and over, grabbing his fingers and yelping with each failed attempt.

"I found it in my room," Max said, wiping some of the dust from the cover. Although it was very old, the book was in remarkably good condition. It had a reddish tone to it, which Max thought looked a bit like the color of dried blood. The edges appeared to be outlined with three rows of ornate symbols, but on closer examination it could be seen that the symbols were actually tiny, intricate dragons that interlocked with one another. In the center was a gold, eight-pointed star that split the cover in half. On one side of the star a number of people in colorful robes were crowded together, and on the other side there was a mix of fantastical creatures. "I'm going to use it for my book report. Except right now it's talking about unicorns."

"Unicorns? Unicorns are lame."

"I know, except these unicorns cast spells and eat people."

Dirk nodded, getting the gleam in his eye that Max

knew well. He and Dirk had been best friends since the second grade. It had all started when eight-year-old Ricky Reynolds had taken Max's glasses and taunted him to try to get them back. Max stumbled along, everything blurry, trying to make a grab for them, but he was way too slow and clumsy to even get close. That's when Dirk showed up. Apparently, Dirk had just learned a new "your momma's so fat" joke and decided to try it out on Ricky. Soon after, Ricky forgot all about the glasses and was chasing Dirk— but Dirk happened to be the fastest kid in the entire town. After that, Max and Dirk became best friends.

"Okay, a carnivorous man-eating unicorn might be cool. Too bad they're not vampires," Dirk said, his head bouncing as the bus hit a pothole. "Vampire unicorns would be awesome." For Dirk, any creature plus being a vampire equaled something awesome. Unless that creature was a love-struck human running around with his shirt off.

Max hurried to put the book in his backpack as the bus made the last turn leading to Parkside Middle School— Home of the Eagles! But for some reason Max couldn't get the image of Princess the Destroyer out of his head. It wasn't a particularly cold day, but a strange chill crawled up his spine.

⁓

Mrs. Lundberg's seventh-grade English class was always too hot. It was as if the administration had decided that sitting through English wasn't hard enough, so they decided to crank the temperature up and see who could stay awake. After thirty minutes it was almost a relief when Max heard his name called. He made his way to the spot just under the READING IS FUNDAMENTAL banner. "I'm going to read from a book that I've had for a long time," he said, pushing his glasses up. "It's called the *Codex of Infinite Knowability*—and I think 'codex' basically means book, but its fancier or something." Max looked up at Mrs. Lundberg, who's raised eyebrow signaled that he should keep going, so he held the *Codex* up for everyone to see. "The part I'm going to read is about unicorns," Max continued, opening the book to the spot he'd marked earlier. Several of the boys started snickering.

"Did you say . . . *unicorns*?" Mrs. Lundberg asked in a husky voice.

"Yeah," Max answered, looking down. But this time the page he'd marked didn't show a unicorn. Instead it had a drawing of a small creature with oversized feet, a large head with round eyes, and a curly tuft of hair. In its hand was a small stringed instrument. The title of the page read "On Frobbits."

"I mean, no!" Max blurted out, seeing now that his unicorn page had disappeared. "I mean, not unicorns. I'm going to talk about . . . *frobbits*."

"Frobbits?" Mrs. Lundberg asked, raising her infamous eyebrow again.

"Yeah. They're way better than unicorns." Or so Max hoped.

Mrs. Lundberg stared at Max with a look that almost made him confess to having no idea what he was doing, but instead she waved her hand in the universal gesture for "Let's get going."

Max cleared his throat and began to read . . .

ON FROBBITS

⧉

OF THE VARIOUS LIFE-FORMS LOCATED in the middle realm—or Magrus as it's formally called—the peace-loving frobbit is a must-see for any traveler. Frobbit culture is based on the unwarranted trust of strangers, moving slowly when chased, and taking baths seasoned with eleven herbs and spices; which is also why frobbits are a favorite food source for all carnivorous predators (and even some leaf-eaters who want to live it up on the weekends).

Sometimes when threatened, a frobbit will rub itself with mint leaves as a warning—a strategy that has yet to yield any positive results. Frobbit villages are called treeshires, because frobbits like to build their homes inside of giant, hollowed-out trees. On at least two occasions squirrels have been known to wait until the frobbits were finished tree hollowing and then successfully run them off and move in (for more on the future world domination by squirrels, see appendix B).

Frobbit mandolins, constructed from the discarded wood from such hollowing activities, are highly prized throughout the Magrus. Not so much for their musical qualities, but as ready-made kindling for campfires or cooking pits.

Whether as a handy food source or treeshire construction crew, frobbits have become an integral part of life in the Magrus.

⁜

Max looked up as the frowning Mrs. Lundberg took out her red pen, gave it an audible click, and wrote something in her grade book. He'd seen that done enough times to know he probably wasn't going to be bringing home the MY MIDDLE SCHOOLER'S ON THE HONOR ROLL bumper sticker.

"I believe I said the assignment was to read a chapter from a novel of historical fiction," Mrs. Lundberg announced. "Do you believe your frobbit tale qualifies, Mr. Spencer?"

Suddenly Max had a flashback of Mrs. Lundberg detailing the assignment on the chalkboard. Max was drawing a picture of a dragon at the time and probably should have been paying closer attention.

"Yes, ma'am," was all Max managed to squeak out.

"Oh? Please elaborate."

Max wasn't particularly good at on-the-spot thinking. He also wasn't that good at off-the-spot thinking. But since the difference between a D and an F was probably riding on his answer, he did the best he could. "Well, history is about things in the past, and this book is really, really old. And frobbits are probably totally made up, so that would be fiction. So, yeah, it's pretty much historical fiction."

Several of the smarter girls in the class began to giggle. Max figured that wasn't a very good sign.

"Nice try, Mr. Spencer," Mrs. Lundberg announced, sealing his fate. "Have a seat."

On the way back to his desk Max knew he should be at least a little concerned that he had just blown the assignment, but he was thinking about the *Codex*. There was something really strange about the whole notion of meat-eating unicorns, spell-casting wizards, spice-bathing frobbits, and a middle realm called the Magrus. He figured the book needed to be taken to an expert, and the first person he thought of was Dwight, the owner and sole proprietor of the Dragon's Den.

Chris Lemons, a tall gangly kid with a long neck, leaned over to where Max was sitting. "Nice job, Einstein. You should have stuck with the unicorns."

Max ignored him. It was bad enough that he was being mocked by a kid who had cried when a sunflower had touched his face, but now another poor grade meant he'd probably never get ungrounded. At least there was lunch to look forward to—all that talk of well-seasoned frobbits had made him kind of hungry.

CHAPTER TWO

REZORMOOR'S GAMBIT

(THE MAGRUS—PRESENT)

REZORMOOR DREADBRINGER WALKED THE LONG HALL OF THE Maelshadow's temple. A whimpering gracon crawled before him, bound by a twisted collar and barbed leash that the sorcerer held in his gauntleted hand. The gracon was a ferocious beast—three or four times the size of the human. A spiderweb of molten lava spread like veins across the creature's armored hide, and its great three-horned head hung so low that it cut into the marbled floor, leaving long, smoldering trenches as evidence of its woeful path. Unfortunately, its name was *Peaches*—which happened to be far more impressive in Gracon than in English.

Rezormoor had to respect the audacity of the creature. It was a testament to the power of the gracon that it would dare to rise up against the Maelshadow at all.

And the fact that the Maelshadow had been unable to quickly subdue the creature suggested that the Lord of Shadows might have some weakness. But those were dangerous thoughts and not part of the sorcerer's immediate plans. For now, he would bring Peaches to the feet of the Maelshadow and see if a deal could be struck.

The hallway opened into a large chamber and Rezormoor and his captive entered. The Maelshadow's throne was carved from the monstrous skull of some titan aberration, long lost in the annals of the ancient past. Enormous curved fangs shot from the top of the skull's gaping mouth, driving down into the floor as if they were two mammoth pillars. Its eyes were empty black pools.

The chamber itself seemed to dance and flicker as if lit by an unseen flame, but stranger still was the black river that carved itself through the hard floor, speckled with small points of light. It looked as if the night sky had been pulled down from the heavens and forced to assume a liquid state.

Suddenly there was a presence that Rezormoor more felt than saw. Peaches sensed it as well, trying to lift its head and cry out. But the sorcerer pulled on the leash, the twisted collar (made from the roots of the Tree of

Abysmal Suffering) constricting and biting into the creature's flesh. The gracon groaned, a deep and pitiful wail
that filled the chamber. But as the sound faded away the
gracon dropped its head in submission, casting its eyes to
the floor and whimpering. Rezormoor dropped his own
gaze and took a knee. Despite the prize he held in his
hand, Rezormoor knew that his life was in danger. He
was certainly not foolish enough to underestimate the
Maelshadow's power or absolute cruelty.

"Speak," came a voice that rolled like distant thunder.
Peaches whimpered in response and inched closer to the
foot of the skull, groveling and rolling out its massive
tongue. A formless shadow had settled upon the dais.

"I have captured the gracon, my lord. It had fled from
the Shadrus as you had suspected."

"As I had *known*," corrected the Maelshadow. Rezormoor looked up to see the strange darkness that now
occupied the throne. The Maelshadow was said to dwell
in the darkest parts of the Shadrus, though its presence
could transcend to its temple. Rezormoor himself had
never been to the Shadrus—nor did he have any plans to
do so. Maximilian Sporazo was rumored to have built a
fortress there—a great castle carved from the side of an

obsidian mountain. But whether it was actually his or just a rental, nobody knew for certain.

"Then with this gift I would ask a favor," Rezormoor requested, doing his best to keep his voice steady. Beseeching favors from the Maelshadow could prove a life-shortening experience.

As if in response, two black-robed acolytes appeared from the shadows. Their faces were hidden within their cowls, but strands of long, ghostly white hair jutted out and fell past their shoulders. Whether they were men or abominations Rezormoor did not know. He handed the leash over when one extended a pale hand—its skin seemingly stretched too tightly over misshapen bones. The sorcerer watched as they led the gracon from the chamber. There was no more fight in the creature—Rezormoor could see that in its eyes. Peaches allowed itself to be led into whatever dungeons lay below.

"The gracon is a worthy tribute," the Maelshadow continued. "What do you seek in return?" The sounds of a portcullis ratcheting shut rang out from somewhere in the temple, and Rezormoor wondered how many others had heard the sound and then lived to tell about it.

"As you know, I seek the *Codex*," Rezormoor said,

after taking a breath. "Lost now for over two thousand years. Some believe it destroyed, but I do not."

"It exists," the Maelshadow announced with absolute certainty. "I can sense it, if only by the small ripples it creates in the fabric of the universe."

It was the first time the Maelshadow had ever spoken of the *Codex* with such specificity, and Rezormoor could only hope that his gamble to capture the gracon would pay off. "Truly then," the sorcerer continued, "it must be found."

"It houses the Prime Spells. It's not a trinket for magicians to play with."

Being called a "magician" was a particular insult used only by those who did not fear the power of the Tower. As its regent, Rezormoor had never heard human lips utter the word in his presence. Perhaps this was how the Maelshadow chose to test him, or it could be the Lord of Shadows was just being a jerk. Either way, Rezormoor vowed not to let the insult show. "In the hands of your servant," the sorcerer finally replied, "the *Codex* would further your will."

"Do not pretend this is about *my* will!" the Maelshadow roared. "You should ask what you want while I still have the patience to hear it."

Rezormoor had the sudden urge to withhold his question and leave, but he swallowed hard and pressed forward. He had come too far to turn back now. "Lend me the use of the Gossamer Gimbal, my lord. With it I will find the *Codex*."

There was a long silence—an interminably long silence in which Rezormoor wondered if he had spoken his final words. Finally, however, the Maelshadow answered, the tempest that was his voice seemingly calmed. "You need a descendant of the arch-sorcerer to read it."

"As you say," Rezormoor replied, bowing slightly. Although the Maelshadow was correct that Rezormoor needed a blood relative to read from the book, if the Lord of the Shadows knew what Rezormoor truly planned to do, the wizard would be destroyed on the spot. "The Gossamer Gimbal could find both—the *Codex* and Sporazo's heir."

"If such a descendant even lives. His line has been hunted for two centuries and without success. And while it's true I have the Gimbal, my own agents have tried and failed. I do not see how you could do otherwise."

"Your agents cannot travel to the Techrus—or should I say, even if they did, their magic would be so weakened as to be useless. Not that they would be without means, but without *magic* the Gimbal has no power."

"You tell me nothing I don't already know," the Mael-shadow replied, its voice crashing against the interior like an ocean wave. "The Techrus is devoid of magic."

Rezormoor straightened a bit. "But not all magic. There are some who carry such power within them."

"Dragons and unicorns. But you'll find none willing to aid the Tower. Nor will the monks who tend to the Tree of Attenuation be persuaded to grant passage between the realms. These are not new thoughts, sorcerer. They are old stratagems without the means to accomplish them."

"I believe that is no longer the case."

The mass of black shadows on the throne seemed to shift and move. "How is that possible?"

"It's not been easy, but I've been in contact with the monks for some time. We are close to a trade."

"And what of the creature of magic?"

"I have a candidate in that regard as well."

"If you have turned the monks and can convince a creature of inbred magic to serve you, you may take the Gossamer Gimbal," the Maelshadow announced. "But there is a price: If a blood relative of Sporazo is found you will deliver them to me."

It wasn't exactly what Rezormoor had in mind, but once he had what he needed the life of any descendant would be unimportant. "I agree," the sorcerer said, the bargain now struck.

"Good. Now tell me how you will bend a magical inbred to your will. They are as powerful as they are defiant."

Rezormoor smiled. "As it happens, there's a unicorn on her way to the Tower as we speak. And from what I can tell, she has just the right appetites to be useful."

CHAPTER THREE

THE KRAKEN VERSUS GRAVITY

(THE TECHRUS—PRESENT)

IT WAS LUNCHTIME AND MAX WAS JUST FINISHING SWAPPING HIS books at his locker when Dirk ran up to him, eyes wide and face flushed. "Dude, you totally have to see this!" When Dirk got this way it reminded Max of his neighbor's Chihuahua, jumping up and down and running back and forth along the fence. Max barely had time to close his locker before Dirk dragged him down the hall. It was no great shocker to see that the Kraken and his band of thugs were giving somebody a hard time. What was strange was that that somebody was a girl—and even stranger was the fact that she didn't seem to be backing down.

"I said don't try it," the girl announced. The group (many of whom were wrestlers) all started laughing when she delivered her warning, but she wasn't angry or yelling or even on the verge of tears. There was a cool determination in her voice that seemed to cut through the air like a razor.

"You're like a kung fu princess, is that it?" Ricky taunted, looking around at his wrestling buddies. "You think you could take me to the ground?"

"I didn't say kung fu," the girl answered evenly. "And no, I'm not interested in taking you anywhere."

The crowd was starting to grow bigger. Max finally recognized the girl as Sarah Jepson from his math class. She was tall, smart, with the kind of auburn hair movie stars had. She didn't hang out with the popular girls, or the band geeks, or even the drama kids. Come to think of it, Max didn't really know a whole lot about her, other than the fact that she had somehow wandered into Ricky's sights and was about to pay the price.

"You didn't answer my question," Ricky continued in a mocking voice. "I didn't ask if you *wanted* to, I asked if you *could*. You think because your parents were, like, karate kids you've got something on me?"

Not karate, Sarah thought, but judo. It wasn't something she talked about because she hadn't wanted to end up here—standing in the hallway and having to deal with

Ricky. But her parents had met as competitors at the world judo finals, so she had pretty much spent her whole life learning the Japanese martial art. As a toddler she didn't play with her Tickle Me Elmo doll, instead she practiced hip throwing it across the living room. There was a reason jujitsu (from which judo developed) was used by the powerful Samurai warriors of old—it worked.

"What I can and can't do is none of your business," Sarah replied curtly. Now maybe the Kraken wasn't the sharpest tool in the toolshed, as Max's grandmother liked to say, but he was smart enough to figure out that Sarah really wasn't afraid of him. And that had to be a first . . . ever.

"I don't believe it, she thinks she's tougher than I am!" Ricky exclaimed. The rest of the kids laughed and cheered him on as he looked around the hall, grinning wildly. Then he lowered his voice and turned to face Sarah again, only now everyone grew quiet—they'd seen this before, sometimes on the wrestling mat when he was about to destroy an opponent, or sometimes during school when a student was about to get pounded. Ricky leaned forward and looked at Sarah as if she was his worst enemy in the world. "You should probably start something," he growled through clenched teeth. "Or I will."

But Sarah didn't flinch, and that was saying a lot. Max had seen all kinds of tough kids melt under similar circumstances. George Lobowski, who played center on the football team, broke down and started crying when Ricky did the same thing to him. But not Sarah—to the amazement of Max and every other student gathered in the hall, she actually stood her ground.

"Hey, why don't you pick on somebody your own size?" Dirk called out. Max shouldn't have been surprised by that. Dirk's ability to say things without thinking was probably hard coded into his DNA. Max, on the other hand, tried to shrink down and be as invisible as possible.

The Kraken whirled, finding Dirk standing in the crowd and staring back at him. "Oh, is that right?" Ricky said, playing it up for his audience. "You offering then?"

"Well, clearly I'm not your size either," Dirk said with a shrug.

If Ricky had thought he could catch Dirk he might have made a run for him, but he knew better. And besides, he wasn't finished with Sarah yet. "Keep squeaking, little mouse, and mind your own business."

Ricky turned his attention back to Sarah, getting eye to eye with her and violating the whole "personal space" thing they talked about in health class. But Sarah didn't even blink. "Look, Ricky, I'm just a girl. I don't see how picking on me does anything to enhance your reputation as the alpha male around here. So I'm going to turn and walk away, and you guys can yell 'chicken' or make clucking sounds and that's fine with me. And if it makes you feel better if I say you're tougher than I am, I'm happy to. But right now I need to get to lunch. So if you'll excuse me, I'm leaving."

And that's when it happened. Sarah had started to turn when Ricky grabbed her roughly by the shoulder. She reacted at once, moving so fast it was a blur. She grabbed Ricky's arm and pivoted on her leg, using his momentum against him. She then bent and threw Ricky over her shoulder so that he landed flat on his back—the air blowing out of his lungs as he hit the floor. But Sarah kept moving, placing her knee against his arm and pulling Ricky's elbow across her thigh at a painful angle. Ricky yelped, but otherwise didn't move. Sarah was glaring down at him, and for a moment it looked as if she was going to press down on the arm and break it, but suddenly she let go and her hand flew to her mouth in astonishment.

"I didn't mean . . . ," she started to say, looking around

at all the shocked faces. Sarah had just executed what her parents called the *ippon seoi nage*. Her brain coolly processed the information while the emotion of it all began to surge in her like a tidal wave.

A bunch of kids started to push through the crowd wanting to get a closer look at the Kraken spread out and lying on the hallway floor. Max and Dirk managed to get caught in the middle of it, and the two of them were suddenly pushed forward. They lost their balance, falling into each other and then tripping over the Kraken, landing in a pile next to him. Before they could untangle themselves and get to their feet, Mr. Jackson, the vice principal, parted the kids like Moses at the Red Sea. He stood there, his hands on his hips, and scowled.

"What's going on here?" Mr. Jackson asked in his no-nonsense vice principal voice. On the floor was the Kraken, who still wasn't moving; Dirk, who was looking wide-eyed and flushed; and Max, who was too shocked to do anything but point at Sarah. The vice principal sized up the situation quickly. "Everyone go to lunch . . . now. Somebody find the nurse and get her here. And you three," he said, looking coldly at Sarah, Max, and Dirk, "you all come with me. You're in serious trouble."

CHAPTER FOUR

AN UNLIKELY FRIENDSHIP

(THE TECHRUS—PRESENT)

SARAH STARED ANGRILY AT MAX AS HE TRIED TO EXPLAIN THAT FINGER pointing was simply an unconscious survival instinct handed down through the Spencer family line. The reaction was so ingrained in his genetics, in fact, that he might as well try to stop a sneeze as prevent an anger-deflecting pass-the-buck finger point. Sarah, however, was unconvinced.

"I really wasn't trying to get you into trouble," Max offered, for probably the thirtieth time.

The three of them were sitting in an empty classroom, waiting as the whole "situation" was being sorted out. Throughout it all, Dirk just sat and looked at Sarah with a kind of wide-eyed, slack-jawed wonder. She ignored it as long as she could, but finally she'd had enough. "Do you really have to stare at me like that?" she blurted out, tearing her gaze away from Max. "I'm so glad I could be here to provide you with some amusement before I'm suspended."

It was as if Sarah were speaking to a stone wall—Dirk didn't blink. But when he finally spoke, it was with that rare kind of childlike wonder that most kids drop by the time they get to middle school. But then again, Dirk was definitely not like most kids. "You were so . . . *awesome*," he finally said.

Max rolled his eyes, but he knew his friend well enough. No matter what happened in Dirk's future, whether he ended up collecting cans and living in his parent's basement or he became the president of the United States, the day he saw a girl take out the Kraken in front of the entire school would rank as one of the greatest moments of his life.

"Very funny," Sarah replied, turning away.

"He's not making fun of you," Max offered, hoping that he wasn't about to get another hard-eyed death look from Sarah. "And I'm not either. What you did . . . it *was* amazing."

Sarah turned back to face the boys. She looked at them

a bit closer now. Max had a round face that reminded her of the baby angel on the toilet paper packages her mom bought—only with glasses. He had hair that was naturally messy, with a few strands hanging across his forehead, and a mouth with lips pursed together as if he was holding back a hiccup. Dirk, on the other hand, had a mouth that was perpetually locked in a half grin, with a narrow face and larger ears that hung on the sides of his head. His dark hair was cut as if he was in the army, with expressive eyes and a prominent nose.

At least they had each other as friends, Sarah thought. Neither of them probably stood much of a chance on his own. "You don't understand," Sarah finally continued. "What I did wasn't awesome or incredible or anything like that. I could have really hurt him—don't you get it?"

Dirk snapped out of his hero-worshipping and began emphatically shaking his head. "No way. I saw the whole thing. You tried to leave—you turned away and then he grabbed you."

"Barely."

"No," Max chimed in. "He grabbed you hard. I saw it too."

"Yeah, everybody did," Dirk added.

Sarah sighed, feeling a little better despite herself. "Maybe." She realized it had been Dirk who had called out from the crowd when the whole rest of the school seemed to be against her. Maybe she needed to cut them some slack.

After an awkward moment of silence, Max decided to break the ice. "So anyway, my name's Max," he said, offering his hand. "And this is Dirk."

Dirk did his best Renaissance fair bow, "Milady."

That made Sarah giggle as she shook Max's hand. "I'm Sarah, officially now the most unpopular kid at Parkside Middle School."

"I never thought I'd meet someone less popular than me," Dirk replied. "I'm kind of conflicted about it."

Sarah managed a meek smile before realizing what she must look like—hair a mess and mascara (that her older sister made her wear) probably running. "Hey, you guys don't have anything I could clean up with, do you? I must look like a train wreck."

"Oh, uh, I don't carry a handkerchief in my pocket or anything," Max said. "It's because I cried real hard once when I was little, I think because I had gotten an ice cream cone and it fell in the gutter when I tried to lick it. Anyway, my grandpa gave me his old handkerchief, and as I sat there, crying and holding my empty cone, I realized it was the same old handkerchief that he'd been using for like forty years to blow his nose in. And it just seemed kind of . . . gross. So anyway, that's why I don't have a handkerchief. But if I did I don't think you'd want to use it anyway—not that I have allergies or anything, just the normal amount of nose . . . stuff."

Sarah stared at Max for a moment and then the three of them broke out laughing. It was exactly the kind of release she needed.

"You know Ricky's okay, don't you?" Max asked after the last of the laughter had died down. "I heard the nurse talking about it. You just knocked the wind out of him."

"That and his pride," Dirk added.

"Well, I'm glad he's okay. Bullies like that just have self-esteem problems," Sarah said. "At least that's what I read in my AP Psychology book."

"You take AP classes?" Max asked.

"And read textbooks?" Dirk added.

Sarah smiled. "Sure."

"Well, I wonder if any of this will increase my street cred?" Dirk posed.

"You don't have any 'cred'—on the street or any-where else," Max was quick to answer.

"Yeah, but maybe I do now—that's what I'm saying."

To her surprise, Sarah realized she was feeling comfortable around these two—as if they had all been long-time friends or something. It was strange, mostly because she didn't have many friends. What she did have was a single-minded focus on academics and grades. Her plan was simple: get as far ahead as she could in middle school so she'd be able to take as many high school AP classes as possible. Then, when she went to college, she'd compete for scholarships and have a bunch of credits already done. This meant Sarah's life amounted to school during the day, homework in the afternoon, judo in the evening, and reading at night. It was the same thing day after day, afternoon after afternoon, evening after evening, and night after night. Sarah had never really thought about it in those terms before, or considered how nice it was just hanging out with other people.

The vice principal walked in, closing the door behind him. "Well, hasn't this been an interesting day?"

Max and his friends thought better of offering an opinion, especially when a school official used the word "interesting."

"Okay then," he continued, "I think I've been able to piece together what happened. Basically, none of you have been in trouble before." Mr. Jackson stopped and looked at Dirk. "Well, not for anything more grievous than sneaking dice to school."

"I can't help it," Dirk responded. "That's how I *roll*."

Sarah blurted out a laugh, covering her mouth with her hand.

The vice principal, however, didn't look amused. "So, you need to understand that we take any kind of assault situation very seriously. Now, from everything I've been told, it's pretty obvious that Ricky was the aggressor, and then you responded in kind."

"More like *reacted*," Max piped in. "There's not a lot of time to think when a kid nicknamed the Kraken grabs you."

"I'd say she elected to use nonlethal force to protect herself from the threat of bodily harm, as clearly spelled out in the state statutes regarding this sort of thing," Dirk added for good measure. That caused Mr. Jackson to do a double take.

"Uh . . . okay, Dirk," the vice principal managed to acknowledge. "Anyway, it's Friday and we have the weekend ahead of us. I think it may be best if you three went home early. Would that be a problem?"

"Problem? Are you kidding me?" Dirk was practically out of his chair and headed for the door.

"What about you, Sarah?"

Suddenly the thought of leaving seemed perfectly reasonable. "That would be fine. I just have choir and PE in the afternoon."

"Yeah, and I'm good, too," Max noted.

"Right now this is a safety issue, so I don't want you going off thinking you're getting rewarded for this. I just have things I need to do, so you three go home and have a nice weekend. We'll probably call you into the office on Monday. Any questions?"

"Max said Ricky was okay," Sarah asked. "Is that right?"

"So far everything checks out," the vice principal answered. "But Sarah, I don't know what you were thinking. I know your background, but you need to be more careful."

"It was like a fire drill," Dirk said, zipping up his backpack. "Sarah stopped him, dropped him, and rolled him. Wow, that's gotta be kind of embarrassing at the next wrestling practice. Hey, are those open to anyone to come and watch?"

It takes forty-three muscles to frown, and the vice

principal usually used all forty-three of them when dealing with Dirk. "Listen, you go home and stay away from Ricky Reynolds. You understand?"

"Yes, sir," Dirk said automatically. Dirk's dad required him to use "sir" whenever he started to annoy an adult, so the words flowed easily from his mouth.

Mr. Jackson gave everyone a final look and left, leaving the door cracked open behind him. It was a subtle statement, but it meant that the three of them were free to go.

"I don't even have to say it, but I'm going to," Dirk exclaimed, waiting until the vice principal was well down the hall. "Best . . . day . . . ever! So we totally have to go to the Dragon's Den on the way home." He turned to Sarah. "You're coming with us, right?"

Max froze, wondering if he'd really heard right.

The offer caught Sarah off guard. She knew she should probably just go home and get back to her routine, doing her best to forget the day had ever happened. But then again, her routine was already kind of messed up. *And what's the harm in hanging out with these guys a little longer? They're actually kind of . . . fun.*

"Okay," she said to everyone's surprise. "Why not?"

On Spell Casting

✣

OFTEN IT'S ASKED HOW ONE BECOMES
a spell caster. The answer is much the same as "How
does one wiggle one's ears?" You've either got it in you
or you don't. Those who have "got it in them" have
three choices: seek admittance to the Wizard's Tower,
apply to the unauthorized Guild of Magic, or seek a
master of the dark magical arts (who will require you
to wear a hood and leave the lights off in your room).

Those admitted to the Tower may choose to
study creative magic and become a wizard, or study
destructive magic and become a mage. Wizards tend
to be academic types whose idea of a heated confron-
tation is going to the blackboard and diagramming
their arguments, while mages wear armor, fight with
weapons, and battle one another for position and
rank. Those who advance in their studies may earn
the title of arch-wizard and arch-mage respectively.
One who attains the rank of *both* arch-wizard and
arch-mage is known as a sorcerer, and is both heavily
in debt with student loans and qualified to serve as
regent of the Wizard's Tower. There has been only
one arch-sorcerer however—the World Sunderer
himself, Maximilian Sporazo.

Lastly, there are four types of practitioners within

the darker arts: warlocks, conjurers, druids, and necromancers. Warlocks specialize in totems and magical items, conjurers summon various demonic creatures to do their bidding, druids are allergy-free outdoorsy types who focus on the energies of living things, and necromancers play with the energy of long-dead things and therefore have to wash their hands more often than the others.

⚜

CHAPTER FIVE

WHY UNICORNS LIKE TEXAS
(THE MAGRUS—PRESENT)

PRINCESS THOUGHT THE WIZARD'S TOWER WAS DRAFTY AND LACKED a woman's touch. She lounged in an overstuffed chair and swirled a drink, but because unicorns have difficulty both lounging and swirling drinks, she'd taken her human form—something only unicorns and dragons could do, but unicorns did it better. The trip had been largely uneventful: a few pillagings and burnings, a scattering of shrieking frobbits, the occasional incineration of an uppity human lord, that sort of thing.

As a human, Princess looked like a seventeen-year-old pouty teenager with blond hair that ran a bit past her shoulders, dark eyes, and a somewhat elongated face that carried just a hint of horse. The fact that Princess was, in truth, a real princess wasn't lost on her—and she had mastered the "looking down my nose at you" demeanor to perfection. Sitting next to Princess, but at the proper, respectful distance, Magar looked his typically uncomfortable self. He tried not to make eye contact with Rezormoor Dreadbringer, who sat across from them in a high-backed chair—each arm of the chair was carved into the shape of a great mastiff. The sorcerer and regent of the Wizard's Tower kept his face and head cleanly shaven. He wore a large belt cast in silver and inlaid with blue stones that glowed even in the daylight. And although his robe moved like soft cloth, Magar suspected it was magically enhanced to be as strong as steel. The large hood was stitched with gold that climbed around the edge to culminate in delicate flames at the top. In addition, two daggers (their blades black waves forged by no human hand) sat at the ready on each hip. Rezormoor was the epitome of a sorcerer—as adept at swordplay as at spell casting. And he was a master of both.

"And how is your mother, the queen?" Rezormoor asked, pulling the hood from his head and allowing it to fall to his shoulders.

"Controlling as ever," Princess replied with a sigh. "Bossy, boring, and always telling me what I can't do."

Rezormoor unrolled a scroll and held it up to catch the light from a narrow window. It was a wanted poster for "Princess the Destroyer" showing a drawing of a rampaging unicorn (with a burning frobbit in the background for added effect). "Looks like you've gotten the attention of the Mor Luin lords."

"Well, I really don't know what people expect me to do. Chewing oats all day just isn't as thrilling as it sounds."

Magar sighed. Maybe she'd just trade him in and he'd be free of her.

"And as for this one," Princess continued as if reading Magar's thoughts. "He's really quite trying. Perhaps I could exchange him?"

Rezormoor turned his attention to Magar, who shrank under the sorcerer's stare. "A mid-level wizard, are you?"

"Yes," Magar squeaked. He cleared his throat and tried to regain a bit of dignity. "Contracted by the unicorn queen and assigned to her daughter."

"Prepaid, no doubt," Rezormoor said with a shrug. "Well, Princess, you could certainly trade him in—but such transactions are nonrefundable. Perhaps a mage would be more to your liking?"

"No," Princess answered dryly. "They're even less likely to bend a knee and show the proper respect. Plus, you never know when they'll up and leave." That was the problem with mages, they could never really be assigned to any one person or kingdom. Mages were opportunists who challenged their rivals for position, working their way up to ultimately serve at the side of one of the seven kings. "Don't you have any wizards who are, I don't know, a bit more lively?"

"It's possible," Rezormoor said, opening his hands, "but it all comes at a cost. And with this one paid for . . . perhaps he's the better bargain still?"

Magar now knew what it was like to be a head of cabbage haggled over at market.

"I suppose I'll keep him then, for the time being."

"As you wish," Rezormoor said, clasping his hands and setting them in his lap. The truth was, Rezormoor wanted a docile wizard for the unicorn's companion, and Magar seemed to fit the bill perfectly.

"Now, to the real point of my visit," Princess continued, "I assume you received my message?"

"Indeed."

Princess perked up, moving to the edge of her seat.

"Good, then I'll get to the point. I'm bored, and the only thing that entertains me is hunting, killing, and eating."

"Understandable."

"Sure, but everything in the Magrus is *tainted*. I want to eat food that's never known magic. I want to go to the Techrus."

"Ah," Rezormoor replied, sitting back in his chair. "But the pathway to the human realm is closed to unicorns."

"Stupid monks and their annoying singing tree," Princess answered. "They're prejudiced against my kind and it's not fair. No unicorn has ever been shown the path to the Mesoshire, or been allowed to travel to the Techrus. They say we're too dangerous."

"And yet dragons make the journey when they wish," Rezormoor said, fanning the flames of Princess's anger.

"Exactly! And do you suppose they'll share their secrets with us? Not likely. They're just dumb reptiles hiding under their rocks. I think they're all jealous—everyone knows unicorns are the most magical creatures in existence."

Rezormoor couldn't argue with that. "Well, as you know, such a request is nearly impossible—the monks of the Holy Order of the Tree of Attenuation are not known to bend their rules. I, however, have access to something they desperately want. So perhaps there is a way after all. But it would come at a cost."

"It always does," Princess answered, flipping her hair back. "And while I'm a royal and I usually have piles of gold, I'm not exactly functioning in an official capacity, if you know what I mean. So why don't we just get down to it and you tell me what you want? Destroy a town? Chase off a king? Cure the sick?" Unicorns were known for their healing powers, and some were even rumored to have raised the nearly dead.

"Allow me to show you," Rezormoor answered, drawing a small chain from around his neck. It held a strange pendant containing three interlocking rings that hovered around a small, metallic sphere. Stranger, however, was the fact that the pendant was transparent, as if only a reflection. Upon seeing it, Princess pulled her horn from within the folds of her dress. In human form unicorns kept their horns as powerful wands.

"Now now," Rezormoor said easily, "there's no call for that."

Princess sniffed the air, her horn held at the ready.

"That's no simple pendant—it reeks of the Shadrus."

"As astute as you are charming," Rezormoor continued. Magar, who was trying to press himself into the cushions of the couch, wasn't sure if that was an insult or not.

Princess offered a wary smile and watched as Rezormoor held the amulet higher. Suddenly the rings separated, the inner layers now free to turn and spin within the larger ones.

"The Gossamer Gimbal is a unique artifact," Rezormoor added. "It exists simultaneously across the three realms, and when sufficiently powered it will point to whatever the owner desires. And in this case, the owner is the Maelshadow himself."

Princess relaxed, lowering the wand to her side. "That's what this is all about? You've misplaced something and you want me to find it? Probably a dragon, right? I can find a dragon for you. Even muzzle it."

Rezormoor sighed. "Actually, there are a couple of things the Gimbal can't point to—and dragons happen to be one of them. Something about their scales, but I appreciate the offer nonetheless."

Princess shrugged. "So what, then?"

"Two things, to be precise. The first is the *Codex of Infinite Knowability*. Have you heard of it?"

"Of course." Princes snorted. "The World Sunderer hid his secrets in it after losing faith in men and magic."

"All because his wife was kissed with dragon's fire," Rezormoor added. "Perhaps your wizard knows the tale."

"Indeed," Magar said, finding his voice. "It was an accident, right here inside the tower. A young acolyte couldn't control the dragon's flame—he let it get away from him. It was supposed to have been a demonstration; many in the tower had gathered to watch. But the arch-sorcerer's wife burned for it—for no other reason than having chosen the wrong place to sit. Worst of all, she was with child. And as you know, dragon's fire continues to burn even after the flames have been extinguished. For weeks she suffered, crying out in agony. But she willed herself to live long enough for their child to be born. After that, it's said the arch-sorcerer went mad. One morning following a great storm, he, the *Codex*, and the babe were gone."

"And now *I'm* here," Princess said with a yawn. "So I get it, you want me to find the *Codex*. Is that all?"

"No," Rezormoor answered. "I require that any living descendant who keeps the Sporazo bloodline alive be brought back as well."

"Oh, is that all?" Princess said with a laugh. "So why me? You must have a hundred of these Magar-types running around." Magar nodded, acknowledging the jab. Part of his job was to be a human pincushion for the royal princess.

"You said you wanted to go to the Techrus? Well, that's where I believe they're hidden," Rezormoor said. "But only a creature of your natural magical abilities will be able to power the Gimbal once you're there."

"Well then, it seems we both possess something the other wants," Princess said, putting her horn back into the folds of her clothing. "You send me to the Techrus, and I'll get to feast on humans *and* hunt for the *Codex*. It's a win-win."

"I'm so pleased you're enthused," Rezormoor replied. "But first you'll find the *Codex* and any living descendants, *then* you may have your fun."

Princess sat back in the chair, crossing her legs and thinking it over. "So, you want me to go to the Techrus and find these things for you, so that as a reward you'll send me back to the Techrus again? Why don't we kill two humans with one stone and do both at the same time?"

"There are others who have a vested interest in what you do," Rezormoor answered. "The Maelshadow, for example. Not one known for his patience. Besides, the monks tell me there are other reasons—so that's that, I'm afraid."

"That's not a very compelling argument."

"Of course you need not accept. But before you turn me down, you should know I've found a town in a place called Texas. It's remote and far from prying eyes, and the people there are plump—corn fed and easy to catch. And not one of them is tainted with magic."

Princess licked her lips. "And when it's done you'll send me to this place—this 'Texas'?"

"With knife and fork in hand, Your Highness."

The thought of it all was simply too much for Princess. Rezormoor could have asked her to split the world again and she would have made the attempt. "Then we have a deal," she said excitedly.

"Excellent. Magar will accompany you to see that both of our interests are looked after. And I'll have to instruct you in the intricacies of the Gimbal. But after dinner, of course."

The thought of a Techrus town full of fat, wobbling humans made Princess's stomach rumble. "Then take me to your kitchen—I'm starving."

"I'll show you the way," Magar offered, standing and motioning toward the door. It seemed he was a dog with two masters now—and that didn't bode well for his future.

CHAPTER SIX

THE DRAGON'S DEN
(THE TECHRUS—PRESENT)

LIGHTNING FLASHED AND THE WIND BLEW, SENDING SMALLER, ALMOST black clouds rolling beneath the larger gray ones. The man in the black leather coat and dripping cowboy hat stared up at the sky, taking a moment to feel the rain on his face and smell the musty scent of the storm. He liked the feel of water on skin—there was a kind of vulnerability to it as if the water might actually strike hard enough to pass through. He knew it couldn't, of course, but skin was always a bit of a novelty when he first put it on.

The Techrus was an interesting place. Without magic, humans had to rely on their own creativity to get things done. So they built machines. Such marvels were really a kind of magic in and of themselves, and in some ways they were more impressive than the mundane spells prevalent in the Magrus. Or the Shadrus for that matter—he was one of the very few who had actually been there.

The sound of the man's boots clicked along the wet pavement as he turned down a narrow driveway. He walked along a chain-link fence until he came to a commercial garbage bin. He continued around it, knowing what he'd find on the other side—he could smell the scent of the other despite the rain. He found the elderly man hunkered down against the metal side, doing his best to stay dry by sitting in a large cardboard box. The old man smiled with a mostly toothless grin. "Obsikar," he said, extending his hand. "I thought that was you. Welcome to Madison."

The man in leather took the other's hand and squatted down to get closer. Obsikar's skin was ebony and had white markings elaborately drawn on the sides of his neck. He wore the dark sunglasses favored by citizens of the Techrus, but the old man knew his eyes burned with a crimson found only in the darkest regions of the Shadrus.

"It's good to see you again," Obsikar said, the rain pelting his hat and flowing along the channel created by its brim.

"What are you doing here in the Techrus?" the old man asked. "Is it safe?"

Obsikar shook his head. "I have sensed a force moving against us for some time. It hides in the shadows, but I will bring it to light soon enough."

"So I suppose we must remain here a while longer," the old man said with a sigh. "There are worse places to hide."

"True. But it's strange to find several of us so close," Obsikar continued. "I was going to inquire, but then I began to feel it myself—there's something about this place, isn't there?"

"Old and powerful magic, I'd say. Only one thing could produce that here."

"The *Codex*."

"Yes. And perhaps we're but moths to its flame," the old man continued. "It wouldn't be the first time."

"Meanwhile the Tower grows bold. You know Rezormoor's obsession with finding the book—and his hatred of our refusal to help him. Perhaps this is not the best place for us?"

The man laughed. "I'm a homeless old man in a modern world of wonders. This is how one becomes invisible here."

Obsikar put his hand on the man's shoulder. "Tell the others to stay hidden, then. I have more to visit in this realm, then I must go to the Shadrus for a time."

"Do you suppose it's the Tower that hunts us?"

Obsikar paused—it was a question he had pondered before. "Rezormoor is angry, this much is true. But to start a war over such a thing? It's too . . . obvious. I see no advantage in it, unless I'm missing something. But I will find the murderers eventually. Blood has been spilled and a day of reckoning is coming."

"You are our king—the choice is yours. I will stay here, however. Something is happening. I can feel it."

For a brief moment Obsikar wondered if he should also stay. But the man in black was not good at waiting; he needed to keep moving—to keep hunting.

It was exactly the kind of day on which you didn't want to be caught outside. The rain had caused Sarah to second-guess her decision to go with Max and Dirk to the "Dragon's Den"—whatever that was. She had spent her whole life in Madison and never even noticed the little store before. But apparently it was important to Max and Dirk, so the three of them were running through the rain to get there.

Max didn't like running. He much preferred the nuisance of a little rain to the side-aching, lung-burning, and muscle-cramping agony of running. And to make matters worse, Dirk simply pranced merrily along without even knowing that running was supposed to be hard. Max would have stopped several blocks back if it hadn't been for Sarah. The last thing he wanted was for her to see him clutch his side and fall into the gutter. He also didn't want to throw up in front of a girl.

They made it to the small store without incident. A less-than-professionally-painted sign proclaimed the place to be THE DRAGON'S DEN. Dirk turned to Sarah with a crooked smile, "Welcome to the coolest place in Madison."

Sarah had her doubts.

Inside, the smell of burning incense hit them at once. Max always liked coming to the store. Here he didn't have to worry about being judged for being flabby, or teased because he didn't play sports, or worry that the Kraken was going to jump out and give him a smack on the back of the head. Coming to the Dragon's Den was like finding sanctuary on holy ground—no jocks allowed!

"So this is where velvet pictures go when they die," Sarah said, looking around at the variety of black-light posters hanging on the walls. They generally fell into one of three categories: skulls with fire for eyes, skulls with swords across their heads, or skulls with both fiery eyes and flaming swords across their heads. One larger poster showed a skeleton riding a motorcycle with flames shooting out the bike's exhaust. It must have been expensive because it was secured in a sturdy metal and glass frame. A mishmash of comics, role-playing games, dice, paperback books, miniature figures, game modules, incense burners, and candles was scattered throughout the place. The Dragon's Den had just about everything but customers, and Sarah wondered if she was the first girl to ever step inside.

Max automatically moved to the rack with the various role-playing modules on display, thumbing through them with expert proficiency. Sarah walked up and pulled a random one out. It had some kind of female elf on the cover, dressed in what looked like a steel bikini and waving a whip above her head.

"Dragon Lair of the Elf Queen," she said, reading the cover out loud. She picked up another. "Citadel of the Dark Paladins and the Dragon Witch. Huh . . . seems like a lot of dragon stuff around here."

"Dragons have been written about by nearly every culture," Max responded, sounding a bit more defensive than he intended.

"And that's because they're smelly, stingy, and live for far too long," said a voice from behind them. Max and Sarah turned to find a small man looking up at them—he was not just small, he was technically a little person. He wore a buttoned-up red vest adorned with a darker swirling pattern, and had a neatly trimmed reddish beard and one of those "balding in the front, the rest as a pony tail" hairstyles that Max would sometimes see when he watched VH1 Classic.

"Hey, Dwight," Max said. Dwight stood there, however, staring at Sarah. It finally took Sarah clearing her throat before Max remembered to introduce her. "Oh, and this is, uh . . . er . . ." For a brief, horror-filled moment, Max forgot Sarah's name. "Sarah!" he finally blurted out, a little too loudly. "Yep, definitely Sarah."

Sarah leaned down and offered her hand, but Dwight frowned. "I'm not really the touchy-feely type," he said in a gravelly tone. "I mean, who knows where those hands have been?"

"Oh," Sarah said, retracting her hand.

"He doesn't mean anything by it," Max jumped in. "Dwight's just Dwight. But he's cool and everything."

"Oh, wonderful," Dwight replied. "Your approval is

just the affirmation I need to keep from going to the back room and hanging myself."

"Yo, Dwight!" Dirk yelled from the other side of the shop, his face pressed against a glass countertop. "How much for this card here?"

"Maybe you should just whistle and command me to come, like a poodle?"

Dirk looked up and blinked. "Okay. Come here, boy!"

Dwight shook his head. "Sarcasm is lost on fools—I keep forgetting that."

"Huh?" Dirk asked.

"Never mind, I don't want to overtax that brain of yours." Mumbling something under his breath, Dwight walked over to where Dirk stood. He used a small step-ladder to pull himself up to the counter.

"You mean that card?" Dwight said, pointing at the card Dirk was staring at.

"Yeah."

"Tell you what, I'll make it easy. How much money you got? What's in your wallet?"

Dirk did a quick calculation in his head. "Uh, nothing."

"Then that's exactly what I'm going to tell you—nothing."

"What," Dirk said, shrugging his shoulders. "A guy can't window shop?"

"If I want window shoppers I'll open a little boutique and sell bonnets. And then you can ask me about those, which you also won't be able to afford."

Sarah leaned over to Max. "Is he always so irritable?"

"Yeah, pretty much. But he kind of grows on you."

"Like mold, maybe," Sarah said under her breath.

Max and Sarah joined Dirk at the glass counter. Inside it was filled with various playing cards, most of which were wrapped in protective sheets.

"So, are you like a relative or something?" Dwight asked Sarah. Dirk and Max were huddled around another card that had caught their eye.

"Uh . . . no."

"They haven't kidnapped you against your will?"

"No!" Sarah exclaimed, folding her arms.

Dwight shrugged. "Okay, okay. So you must be part of a charity, right? Volunteering your time to take kids like *these* around town?"

"What? Of course not. Max and Dirk are my . . ." Sarah hesitated.

"Boyfriends?"

"No!"

That caused Max and Dirk to look up. Dwight raised an eyebrow.

Sarah, however, seemed a bit flustered. "Well, I don't know why it's so important to put labels on everything. So what if I said they're my friends? What does that really mean? Maybe I just met them today, did you ever think about that? And would it be wrong to say we're friends? I don't think so. Friends . . . it's a very encompassing word."

Dirk smiled. "Yeah, friends—with butt-kicking benefits."

Sarah slugged Dirk in the shoulder. "Anything else you want to know," she continued, looking at Dwight, "like the last score I got on my geography test, maybe?"

Dwight smiled. "Oh, I think we all know what grades you get."

"Wait . . . what's *that* supposed to mean?"

Max decided to unsling his backpack from his shoulder and diffuse the situation before things got worse. "So, uh, anyway . . . I found an old book of mine and I wanted to show it to you." Max retrieved the *Codex* and placed it on the counter.

Dwight crinkled his nose and bent down for a closer look. "Now, that's an interesting thing you got there. Where'd you get it?"

"I've just always sort of had it."

Dwight nodded, reaching out to touch the book, but Dirk grabbed him by the wrist. "Dude, don't touch it!" Dirk hurriedly let go, however, as he realized that he'd just broken Dwight's no physical contact policy.

"You realize I'm going to have to wash that now?" Dwight replied, looking at the spot where Dirk had grabbed him.

"But it'll shock you," Dirk continued. "I think it's like a gag gift or something, like that stick of gum that zaps you when you try and pull it out."

"It's weird like that," Max said. "But it's not a trick. I think it just might have a bunch of static electricity or something."

Dwight slowly retracted his hand. "If I want to read something that shocks me, I'll read Dirk's journal."

"Well, I'm not afraid to touch it," Sarah said, reaching out and jabbing the cover with her finger. The moment she did there was a sharp *SNAP!* "Ouch!" she cried out, pulling her hand back and holding her finger. "That hurt!"

"See?" Dirk exclaimed. "Not even girl ninjas can withstand its power!"

"Sorry," Max said, grimacing. He hoped Sarah wasn't going to punch him in the gut or toss him over the counter. One, it would hurt. And two, it would be highly embarrassing. "I don't know why it does that to everyone."

"Everyone but *you*," Dirk said accusingly.

Dwight looked at the book suspiciously. "Some books are protected by magic. But that's impossible here. But still . . . tell me what's inside."

"It's like totally random. Last night I read about how squirrels are using St. Louis as a staging area to take over the world. Then this morning it was all about unicorns. And in my English class there was this whole section on these weird creatures called frobbits."

"You shouldn't have a book that talks about frobbits," Dwight said slowly.

"Well, I do. Here . . . ," Max said as he opened the book, expecting to find the section on frobbits. But instead, the *Codex* showed an illustration of a dwarf dressed in armor and holding a battle-axe.

"Well now," Dwight announced, "that ain't no frobbit." But Max and his friends didn't hear him. They were leaning in to get a closer look. There was something oddly familiar about it, and after a moment it hit them and they all looked up at Dwight.

"What . . . ?" Dwight asked, sounding annoyed. "I told you it wasn't a frobbit."

"It looks like . . . *you*," Sarah answered.

"Oh, nice," Dwight grumbled. "So all of us little people look alike, do we? I thought you overachiever types were supposed to be more politically correct."

Dirk was looking back and forth between Dwight and the picture in the book. "No, dude, it really does look like you—*exactly* like you."

"Great, I resemble some random picture in a book. Maybe I'll close the store early and celebrate."

Sarah had moved past the illustration, however, and was staring at the strange characters written on the page. "I wonder what language this is—it doesn't look like anything I've seen before."

"What do you mean what *language*? It's English," Max said, obviously confused. When he looked at the page he didn't see strange characters at all.

"Yeah, right," Dirk challenged. "Go ahead and read it, then."

Max rotated the book toward him and cleared his throat: "On dwarfs. Dwarfs are commonly found in the Magrus, in the far mountains of Thoran, and spend a majority of their lives underground. In this way they can be compared to ants, except dwarves are much bigger, communicate through language, prefer hands to pincers, and are probably not insects."

Max looked up, "See what I mean? The book's totally random."

But Dwight had a strange look. "Keep reading," he said, his voice flat.

Max hesitated but then returned to the book: "Many speculate that the reason dwarfs live underground is so they can mine, craft weapons and armor, and escape their mind-numbing fear of the open sky. So closely is dwarf culture tied to living underground, in fact, that any dwarfs born claustrophobic (that is, afraid of enclosed spaces or people named Claustro) are considered to have been rejected by the stone itself and must live out their days cut off from their people. Case in point: Dwight."

Sarah let out a gasp. Maybe it was odd that there was a dwarf named Dwight in the book, but Max didn't think it was gasp worthy. Of course, Max didn't know a lot about girls and so he wasn't very certain on that point. But when Max looked up he saw what had frightened Sarah—Dwight held a dagger in his hands and it was pointed at him!

"Close the book," Dwight said, his words almost a whisper. "Close the book right now!"

The sight of the dagger sent a shudder of fear through Max's body. He didn't like sharp things—and he definitely didn't like sharp things that were pointed at him. Max started to close the book when it suddenly jumped— but not physically. The book *shifted* as if some part of it leapt from the pages into Max's head. A series of images exploded before his eyes: He was standing on the balcony of a tall tower, looking out over a great medieval city at sunset. The city was complete with a large castle and a crystal-blue ocean beyond. Then he was in a small room where robed figures tended to a burned, screaming woman. It was night, and torches flamed in sconces on the walls. As she thrashed about in the bed, Max could see the large bulge of her belly, and he knew she was about to have a baby. Next, he was walking the streets of a strange city, with gaslights, antique cars, and green trolls tipping their hats as they passed by. There was no sky, but a perpetual grayness that blanketed the heavens.

Finally, Max felt a shift as if the whole of the world was beginning to slide away. He wanted to run from it, to flee from the force that had grabbed hold of him and was pulling him down. But he could no more stop it than he could turn back a roaring avalanche. A word formed in his mind, and the word became a voice. *"Futurity,"* it said, and it sounded as big as the entire universe. In the end, Max succumbed to the whirlwind, and he watched as the world plunged into darkness. He felt his heart beat once, and then everything exploded with a brilliant light.

On the Creation of the Codex of Infinite Knowability

✠

MANY SCHOLARS BELIEVE THE *CODEX OF Infinite Knowability* was created just prior to the Great Sundering. Such scholars are idiots and should hang their heads in shame. The *Codex* was first created as a travel guide during Maximilian Sporazo's freshman year at the Wizard's Tower. The first glimpse of the book's potential came during an incident with Fregor the Dim-sighted, an arch-wizard who taught advanced concoctions and interpretive dance. One morning Fregor woke with a specific craving for waffles. Finding no stewards available, he decided to make them himself. Now, wizards have a somewhat sordid history when it comes to their cooking (see "Zombie Duck"). In Fregor's case, it wasn't that his waffles were evil—unlike his apple fritters (see also "the Great Fritter Massacre")—it was just that his old eyes mistook a bag of Bigus Boomus for a sack of flour. Fortunately, the young apprentice Sporazo had just completed his first draft of the *Codex*, and, thinking quickly, hit the old man over the head with it. Consequently, it was considered bad form to keep explosive anti-elements in the food pantry, or to hit an arch-wizard with any tome weighing more than two pounds. It did, however, serve as an important lesson for the young Maximilian: Books were useful.

Over the next few years the *Codex* was expanded into an encyclopedia and infused with powerful magic to assist in the gargantuan process of cataloging all of existence.

Even at that early stage of its evolution, the *Codex* was considered a magical wonder: part encyclopedia, part travel guide, part cookbook, and a good part many other things that may or may not have involved some of the forbidden magical arts. But it wasn't until the *Codex* was infused with the fifteen Prime Spells that it became something . . . else. Perhaps—or so it was rumored—because some piece of the arch-sorcerer found its way into the *Codex* in the process. It might have been an eyelash, or maybe even a mustache hair. Regardless of what it was, the end result was that the *Codex of Infinite Knowability* had a tendency to do what it wanted instead of being bothered by whatever might be important to the reader. Whether or not this turns out to be helpful remains to be seen.

CHAPTER SEVEN

RUNNING ERRANDS WITH YOUR ZOMBIE DUCK

(THE MAGRUS—PRESENT)

REZORMOOR DREADBRINGER DIDN'T LIKE DEALING WITH PEOPLE. First of all, he had plans. Big plans. Rule the world kind of plans. Suffering through discourse with the common folk was bothersome. It also meant leaving the Tower grounds and descending through the winding streets of Aardyre.

Going out in public was particularly annoying to the sorcerer. This was not because he was an indoor type who only wanted to read books—although to be fair, he did like books and the Tower was quite comfortable—but because he was *feared*. For most villains, being feared was one of the perks of being a figure of doom and menace (in addition to wearing black, which is naturally slimming). At first Rezormoor had enjoyed the simple pleasures of meeting a poor villager afraid to make eye contact, or having some simpleton shrink back from his mere presence. He had especially liked it if the shrinking was followed by a bit of cowering. But over time Rezormoor discovered that being feared wasn't all it was cracked up to be. For example, he had a hard time getting waiters to come to his table. And most merchants would close their shops rather than risk having a sorcerer as a dissatisfied customer. He even had a much higher than normal percentage of lost mail—especially when it required hand delivery. In the end, being feared made dealing with the townspeople *inefficient*—and if Rezormoor hated anything, it was having the things he hated doing take too long to accomplish. But at times even he had no choice but to venture out.

And so Rezormoor found himself traveling through the part of the city known as Guild Row. As was his custom, he rode in a black carriage pulled by a small, waddling, undead duck (referred to as a zombie duck). There was no sound quite like the slapping of the duck's webbed feet against the cobblestones to drive Aardyre's citizens to the side of the road, down alleyways, or behind barred doors and windows. Those who dared to venture near enough for a closer look might see the duck's crimson eyes, or the snakelike tongue that sparked when it touched the air. On one particularly unfortunate day, a clown and an elephant were drumming up business for the newly arrived circus when they mistakenly crossed the zombie duck's path. Several horrific seconds later all that remained were two tusks, a red rubber nose, and an oversized novelty shoe. Not only did the circus lose much of its original appeal (many of the children had a hard time looking at clowns again), but the zombie duck had firmly cemented its reputation as a creature not to be trifled with—or at the very least, one who should be given the right of way at crossroads. The zombie duck was in fact a rare and peculiar breed of monster avian born from a novice wizard's attempt to blend roasted duck, "death by chocolate" pudding, and zombie spice—-the wizard later claimed it was all that had been left in the pantry on his night to cook. As the Tower's regent, Rezormoor adopted the duck as a kind of mascot and personal pet.

Guild Row was a motley assembly of buildings that represented the many factions of professional life in Aardyre. Rezormoor's path took him past the so-called Guild of Magic, a brightly colored building with a half sun and half moon painted over the door. They were an unauthorized spell-caster union that picked up the rabble who either dropped out, were kicked out, or had never gained entry to the Wizard's Tower in the first place. The Guild's very existence was an affront to Rezormoor and all that the Tower stood for. Such rogue magic was generally frowned upon by the Seven Kingdoms, but of late the king seemed overly tolerant of the Guild's activities. As the sorcerer slowly passed the building, he decided he might make the most of his visit by sending a message. Rezormoor muttered a few words under his breath and then flicked a fireball from his hand. The blue flame flew from the carriage window, soared across the street, and finally curved into one of the third-story windows. Rezormoor gave it a count of three, ticking off the seconds as he worked at some dirt under a fingernail.

Boom!

The entire street shook as doors and windows were blown from their frames. Soon robed figures, some of them aflame, dove from the building. Rezormoor grinned as he settled back into his seat to the sound of the fire bell ringing. Magic was a dangerous business, and perhaps this would serve as a warning.

The zombie duck continued on its way, producing more of a "gwaawk" than a "quack" when it honked at the growing commotion on the street, until coming to a stop in front of an ornate building constructed from giant blocks of sandstone. It was the Lawyer's Guild, framed by two massive pillars and a door that was shaped like the giant, gaping mouth of a serpent. Over the door the Guild's motto was inscribed in stone: MAKING THE WORST ARGUMENT APPEAR STRONGER. The establishment date was 399 B.C., which pre-dated even the Great Sundering. Rezormoor stepped from his carriage, flipped his hood over his head, and pushed his way inside.

The office was paneled in a dark, nearly black wood, with knots and holes that looked remarkably like human faces—only these were twisted into portraits of agonized pain and suffering. The equally dark desk held a great hourglass, behind which a portly goblin was sitting in a high-backed leather chair. He was wearing a permanent scowl, and had ears that shot out of the sides of his head and ended in two points, with the rest of his bulk stuffed into a tailored suit. His thick, green-skinned fingers wrapped around the hourglass, and he turned the heavy timepiece over with a thud.

"Now we are on the clock," the goblin rumbled, a small tussock of gray whiskers waving as he settled into his seat. The sergeant-at-law and supreme counsel to the king was the most important lawyer in Aardyre. He was also on retainer from the Maelshadow, who preferred doing much of his dirty work through his attorney.

Rezormoor withdrew his hood. "You sent word for me?"

"On behalf of the Lord of Shadows," the goblin replied, his double chin and fleshy jowls adding a deepness to his voice. "He wishes a report on the status of your arrangement."

"Tell the Maelshadow that the unicorn has accepted my terms and even now is following the Gimbal."

"To the monks of the Tree of Attenuation, no doubt."

"I would assume so."

"As to that, the Lord of Shadows is concerned that the monks will refuse passage between the realms. He believes it would require damaging the Tree itself."

Rezormoor produced a parchment from his robes and slid it across the table. The goblin grunted, recovering a pair of spectacles that hung from his neck on a golden chain. Once these were on, he leaned forward to read the handwritten draft. The goblin put the paper down and cast a wary look at the sorcerer. "*That* is what they want?"

"Yes. I don't suppose the Maelshadow will take issue with the request?"

"I don't presume to speak on behalf of the Lord of Shadows, but I see no reason he would not accept."

"The unicorn will not travel by boat—you know how their kind feel about water. Besides, it would be too dangerous to dock at Lanislyr, given the bounty the Mor Luin lords have placed on her head. No, she'll travel northwest and cross into Turul. Then south past Nagalmosh and Nyridos until she reaches the mountains of Wallan."

"A long journey on treacherous paths," the goblin replied.

"Long, yes. But not dangerous—not for her."

The goblin cleared his throat, wiping the lenses of his spectacles clean. "Let us hope so."

"Either way, it allows us time to send word by carrier," Rezormoor suggested. "Best to let Lanlarick know a deal has been struck. As head of the order, he will have the power to send Princess and Magar to the Techrus. And that is what must happen if we're to find the *Codex*."

"I will dispatch a pyropigeon," the goblin agreed. Pyropigeons, like homing pigeons, were trained to deliver messages over long distances. Unlike homing pigeons, pyropigeons would burst into flames once the message was delivered.

"Good. Then I assume our business is concluded," Rezormoor said, anxious to get going. "I'm afraid I have other things to attend to."

"But of course," the goblin replied, noting the sand in the hourglass and scribbling the time down in a leather-bound notebook. He turned the heavy timepiece over again. "And if I might add, on a personal note, you seem to be doing well for yourself. Continue to honor your agreements with the Maelshadow and you will be rewarded."

"I'm sure," Rezormoor said, forcing a smile and rising to his feet. "I don't imagine that he is forgiving of those who fail to satisfy their contracts."

The goblin smiled, his rows of sharp teeth looking primitive against his double-breasted suit. "Well . . . let's just say no one's ever broken a contract with the Lord of Shadows *twice*."

CHAPTER EIGHT

UNDER A CHEESEBURGER MOON

(THE TECHRUS—FUTURE)

WHEN THE WORLD CAME BACK INTO FOCUS, MAX, DIRK, SARAH, AND Dwight were no longer standing around the glass counter at the Dragon's Den. Instead they found themselves in the middle of a forest lit by moonlight.

And then, adding to the strangeness of the situation, the dagger Dwight was holding decided to speak. "Remember, the walls you build not only keep others out, but keep you in. I think that's important at a time like this."

"You shut your trap and stay out of this," Dwight grunted, scowling at the ornate blade in his hand. The dagger's hilt was carved from a solid piece of ivory that took the shape of a man with his hands folded across his stomach. A carved head served as the pommel, and the long body with chest, arms, and belly formed the grip. Farther down, the figure blended into the shape of a horse (as if he were mounted on it), the head and tail forming the dagger's brass guard. The blade itself was heavy and double sided, but it was the ivory face that was the most curious—a face that was looking around and taking things in.

Sarah stared at the dagger. "Your knife . . . *talked*."

Dirk, however, was looking up at the night sky. "Cool," he announced with his usual enthusiasm. "Somebody turned the moon into a cheeseburger." It wasn't that the moon was literally a cheeseburger; it just seemed to have a certain *cheeseburgerness* about it, as if someone had covered it with a food–themed lampshade.

"Okay, you guys, I'm a little confused," Sarah managed to say, reaching out to pull on a branch in order to confirm that it was real. The group was in a clearing, surrounded by the ancient remains of broken, vine–covered walls.

"I think we're in some kind of ruin," Dirk suggested.

"Oh, been to a lot of ruins have you?" Dwight asked, waving the dagger around as he spoke, causing Max to take several steps back.

"No," Dirk admitted. "But I've played lots of games where you had to explore ruins and stuff. Look—you can see bits and pieces of old walls. And see how the ground is more barren over there? Maybe that was a street or something."

"I'm sure your game experiences are fascinating and full of important insights," Sarah interjected, her voice sounding a little unhinged. "But we were just standing in the middle of the store, right? I mean, that's where we should be right now—not here, in the middle of all . . . this."

"And yet here is where we are," Dwight said, spitting. "You humans think you're so smart with all your fancy doodads. But you don't know nothing—not when magic's involved."

"Ha!" Dirk shouted, pointing at Dwight. "You called us humans and said 'magic'! You're totally busted . . . *dwarf*."

"You might want to watch your tone," Dwight threatened. But Dirk had already moved on, having decided to rummage around the clearing a bit.

Sarah looked at Max, her face expectant, as if he was about to let her in on some kind of elaborate joke. "Max?" she finally said, watching him closely. "What is this, one of those TV shows where people are pranked or something? How did you get us outside like this?"

"I don't know," Max blurted out. "Honest. I have no idea what's going on."

Max looked down at the book in his hand. A knot formed in the middle of his stomach—this was his fault. He didn't know *how*, but it *was* all the same. The book was the key. "Maybe we're still at the Dragon's Den," Dirk said, sounding as if he knew what he was talking about.

"And how's that supposed to make any sense?" Sarah asked. "Unless Dwight put something in those incense candles and we're all lying on the floor and hallucinating."

"You mean like vanilla?" Dwight asked, sounding a bit defensive.

But Dirk was pulling on something beneath the leaves. "Over here you guys. Give me a hand!"

Max tucked the *Codex* under his arm and he and Sarah walked over to where Dirk was trying to free something from the ground. They squatted down and began digging around some kind of object. It seemed to be metallic, and maybe glass.

"Hurry!" Dirk exclaimed, growing excited. Dwight

ignored him, however. He had sheathed his dagger and was investigating something else that was buried at his feet.

After a few moments, Max helped Dirk and Sarah pull a sturdy glass and metal frame from the ground. They leaned it forward as Dirk brushed off years of dirt and grime. It was cracked and damaged, but the faded remains of a black-light poster could still be seen in the moonlight.

"You can still make it out," Dirk said. Max and Sarah leaned in for a closer look.

"It's like that poster hanging on the wall," Sarah finally said, her face looking pale in strange orangish light of the cheeseburger moon. "Back at the Dragon's Den— the one with the skeleton riding the motorcycle."

"Not 'like,'" Dirk said definitively, taking the frame and laying it carefully against a small chunk of what might have been a wall. "It's the same one."

"That's impossible," Sarah said slowly, but she didn't sound completely convinced.

"What have you done, Max?" Dwight asked, his voice tight. He was looking down at the remains of an old cash register.

"What do you mean? I didn't do anything."

Dirk pulled something else from the dirt and stepped forward. It was a set of dice covered in grimy plastic. "Game dice!" he announced. "Now we're talking *really* old school."

"Dirk, quit messing around!" Max shouted. Dirk, however, was unfazed.

"Don't you get it?" Dirk continued, looking around at the group. "We didn't get teleported to someplace else. We've been sent some-*when* else."

"That's not even a word," Sarah exclaimed.

"Not important right now," Dirk continued. "We've been totally transported into the future."

"The future," Max replied, making sure he'd heard his friend right.

"Yep. Look, we're standing in the middle of the Dragon's Den right now. There's the poster, the dice—"

"And that's my cash register," Dwight added, motioning to it at his feet and not sounding too happy about it.

"No, it can't . . . ," Max managed to get out, but he couldn't finish. He had felt something powerful move in the *Codex* right before everything changed.

"And why not?" Dirk continued, folding his arms. "Got a better explanation?"

"Well, because this is real life," Max replied, as much for his own benefit as that of his friends. "You can't just jump forward in time."

"Well, that's not *exactly* true," Sarah offered, looking up at the night sky. "GPS satellites have to have their clocks adjusted back because they tick faster than the clocks on earth. The closer to the earth the higher the gravity, and that changes how fast something moves through time. Einstein had it right—theoretically."

"Theoretically . . . ?" Dwight exclaimed, walking over to where the group was standing. "You have no idea what you're talking about! You think you're so smart with all your science and learning, but you've got no idea about *magic*!"

"Magic isn't real," Sarah said defensively.

"Then how do you explain the talking dagger?" Dirk asked. "Or did Einstein just make delicious bagels?"

"Huh . . . ?" Sarah answered, Dirk's logic causing her brain to momentarily malfunction.

Dwight, however, was pacing back and forth and mumbling under his breath. "Stupid, stupid, stupid! I should've known!" Dwight stopped and turned to Max. "You know what I'm talking about, don't you? You're the one that read from the book."

"Max . . . ?" Sarah asked, looking at him strangely.

Max didn't like being the cause of things; the one who was *responsible*. He grabbed the *Codex* with both hands and looked at his friends. "Okay, I felt something happen at the Dragon's Den. The book showed me things—it was like I was a different person in a different world. But it was confusing, and everything was spinning around and then it was black and then white and then we were here. But it wasn't what I wanted—the book's never done that before. It was when Dwight pulled the knife, that's what started it all."

"Oh no, this isn't my fault!" Dwight exclaimed, pointing a finger at Max. "Read me the cover of your book."

Max turned the book around so he could read it. "The *Codex of Infinite Knowability*, by Maximilian Sporazo."

"Exactly!" Dwight exclaimed. "Unbelievable. You walk into my store with only the most powerful book in the three realms and then read from it like you're the World Sunderer himself! What did you expect would come from that?" Dwight unhooked his scabbard and thrust the dagger toward Max. "Here, take it! Magic's done nothing but make my life miserable." Dwight pushed the sheathed blade into Max's arms, forcing him to take it. "You wanna play wizard, boy, well here you go."

Max fumbled with the book and dagger—he didn't really want the knife, but it was better than having it pointed at him. The moment he grabbed hold of it, however, the little ivory face lit up. "Greetings, Max! I'm Glenn, the Legendary Dagger of Motivation. And I think everything's going to work out just great!"

"Wicked cool!" Dirk exclaimed.

"Er, okay," Max offered.

"It wasn't my choice to come to your world," Dwight continued, ignoring Glenn. "I don't like living around humans—I don't like your small food portions and foul air. I don't care for reality television or microwave popcorn. And I especially hate the way you're so tall and full of yourselves. I lived in the Techrus because I had to—I started a business and made a life. Now you've gone and destroyed it. All because you're too arrogant of a race to know when you shouldn't be playing with things you don't understand."

"Okay, everyone, let's just settle down," Sarah said, doing her best to sound calm. "We don't know what's happened. So far we're just exploring possibilities."

"What are you talking about?" Dirk exclaimed, looking around. "It's just like Dwight said. Max's *Codex* is really a powerful spell book—that's why it shocks everyone but him. Dwight here is a real dwarf from, I don't know, Dwarfistan or something. And Max is some sort of wizard. Which is awesome—he just needed to panic in order to access his magical mojo."

"I don't think 'panic' is the right word," Max said, looking at Sarah.

"Panicked," Dirk continued. "So he cast a spell to get away—but instead of transporting us someplace else we jumped into the future. Which, honestly, is understandable. Max is, like, barely level one."

"And I suppose I turned the moon into a cheeseburger, too?" Max added, doing his best to show just how ridiculous the whole notion of him being a wizard was.

"Yeah, well, if anywhere is going to have a cheeseburger moon it's the future," Dirk shot back. "Maybe you have to read as much sci-fi as I do, but trust me, that's what happened."

"I know it's agonizing to have to agree with Dirk," Dwight grumbled, looking at Max. "But that book is the real *Codex of Infinite Knowability.* The dwarfs kept it safe for years—I even grew up hearing the stories myself. I don't know how you ended up with it, or why you can read it, but that doesn't matter. You can, you did, and now you need to do it *again*."

"But I didn't do anything, really. It's more like the book did it to me," Max protested.

Dwight produced a lighter from his pocket, giving it a shake by his ear to determine how much fluid it had left. "Well, it didn't do it by itself, so you'd better get to figuring it all out. Magic is what brought us here, and only magic is going to get us home. Go now, open that book of yours and start reading."

"Just because I think it's okay for Max to read his book, it doesn't mean I agree with you about all of this," Sarah said defiantly. "There has to be other explanations we haven't considered yet."

"Sure, missy, you think about those all you want while gathering firewood. The rest of us will build a fire and make camp. It's cold, it's dark, we're someplace out of time, and the moon is a giant cheeseburger. I don't know what it all means, but I got a feeling it ain't good."

CHAPTER NINE

A RUN IN THE WOODS
(THE TECHRUS—FUTURE)

IT TOOK AN HOUR OR SO, BUT MAX AND HIS FRIENDS MANAGED TO build a makeshift camp. They cleared out a small circle of debris and found rocks for a fire pit. In no time they had a fire going—which seemed to make everyone feel a little better and a lot warmer. Dwight constructed a quick lean-to with a pine-needle floor, complaining all the while about his general dislike for the outdoors. The instant Dirk laid his head down he fell asleep, the package of game dice still clutched in his hand. Sarah sat watching the fire, and Max continued to flip through the pages of the *Codex*, looking for anything that had to do with traveling into the future. But so far, the *Codex* seemed inclined only to share accounts of frobbit ceremonies and living arrangements. None of it struck Max as being particularly interesting or useful. He shut the book and rubbed his eyes—he could feel a headache coming on.

"No luck, huh?" Sarah asked as she poked at the flames with a stick. Max noticed how her auburn hair appeared brighter against the yellow flames of the fire.

"I don't even know what I'm supposed to be looking for."

"It's weird, I keep thinking about the last time I went camping with my mom and dad. We brought a bunch of hotdogs. I don't normally like hotdogs—I'm not even sure what's *in* a hotdog—but there's something about cooking them around a campfire that makes them great."

"Like s'mores," Max added, feeling his stomach grumble at the mention of the word. "I only went camping once but we made these s'mores and they were awesome. Does camping make food taste better, or are we just hungry?"

Sarah smiled. "I don't think it's just the camping—it's because you're with the people you love."

Max wasn't sure what to say to that, probably because he thought hotdogs cooked in a microwave were pretty good too.

"I just want to go home, Max," Sarah said with a sigh.

Max wanted to say just the exact thing to make Sarah

feel better, but he couldn't think of it. The silence was starting to get awkward, and with each passing second it seemed more and more important that he say the right thing. Finally he blurted out the next thing that came to him: "I've got to go to the bathroom!"

Max cringed just to hear the word "bathroom" hang in the air like that. It was probably the most pathetic thing ever said. Even Dirk grunted and turned over in his sleep. But somehow it made Sarah smile. "You're pretty funny, Max."

Max just kept his mouth shut, not wanting to make the moment any worse. Sarah yawned, then stretched out on her side, staying close to the fire, folding her hands under her head like a pillow. "I have this wish," she said, sounding sleepy. "When I wake up I'm going to be in my own bed, in my own room, and in my own house. And at breakfast I'm going to tell my parents about this weird dream I had. It will be this whole day at school that never happened—no fight with the Kraken, no getting into trouble with the vice principal, no going to the Dragon's Den, and no boy who was really a wizard and zapped me into the future. And we'll all laugh about it, because of how weird it is—even for a dream."

"I wish I could wake up tomorrow and have it all be a dream too. Except . . ."

Sarah looked up at Max. "Except for what?"

"I don't know—it's just that you're the only person in the whole middle school who ever talked to Dirk and me. So, that part wasn't too bad."

"Okay, you're right," Sarah said, closing her eyes. "That part wasn't too bad."

Max stood, his legs and back stiff and aching. "So, uh, I guess I'm going to go find someplace private. And hopefully with a bunch of leaves."

"Be careful, Max Spencer," Sarah said, her eyes still closed and her voice sounding heavy. "We need you."

Max had never heard those words just by themselves before. Usually he heard things like "*We need you* to come to the office," or "*We need you* to give us your lunch money," or even "*We need you* to calm your friend down or we're calling the fire department." Who knew just plain old "We need you" could sound so nice?

It had grown late by the time Max wandered back to the camp. Dirk and Dwight were snoring with a kind of rhythm that sounded as if they were going back and forth in some snore-off championship, while Sarah was sleeping quietly. Max was ready to knock off for the night too. In fact, he figured he could use the *Codex* and his backpack as a pillow.

Only the *Codex* wasn't where he'd left it.

Max felt a pain in his gut as if somebody had just kicked him. How could it possibly be missing? Could somebody have moved it?

Max began looking around anxiously, retracing his steps. Finding nothing, he rummaged through his backpack and then hurried over to where Dirk and Dwight were sleeping. There was no sign of it anywhere. But that was impossible; the book couldn't just get up and walk away . . . could it? For all Max knew, maybe it could. He left the center of the clearing and began searching along the edge of the forest. He had just about decided to go and wake the others when he caught a glimpse of the *Codex*, sliding into the darkness of the surrounding woods. Max hurried after it, not even stopping to think whether he should get help. He had to reach it—without the book, he and his friends were truly stuck.

Max crashed into the trees, spinning around and looking desperately for some sign of the book. When he caught sight of it, it had traveled a few feet farther, and Max had half expected to see tiny legs propelling the magical book forward. But something was dragging it instead. It was a spider. Not a normal spider, unless normal spiders were the size of dinner plates and weren't bothered by electrical current. The spider seemed to notice Max and quickened its pace. Max ran after it again—in the same way a tortoise might be said to "run" across the beach. He cursed the forest for having to be so thick with trees and plants and stuff. As he pushed his way in, a strange thought kept recurring in his head: Hours of imaginary jump rope didn't seem to have any real-world application.

The chase through the woods continued, mostly because Max didn't have any other options. He couldn't run back to his friends because by the time he did the *Codex* would be long gone. And he couldn't cry out for help because he was afraid of what other weird creatures might hear him. So Max just kept running because it seemed to be the *least* frightening thing to be doing at the moment. And besides, he'd probably smashed a thousand little spiders in his lifetime, so he knew they could be squished—he just needed a big rock. Or a dagger, like the one that happened to be hanging from his belt. He assumed Glenn, the Legendary Dagger of Motivation, could do more than just talk—like actually stab something. Although he wasn't entirely sure.

The spider picked up speed, darting around the forest floor with expert precision. Max would gain ground on it, then he'd get tangled in the trees and saplings and fall back. Often he'd catch a glimpse of the *Codex* before it was dragged off again. But he was determined to keep pushing forward, no matter what. Unless he got a side ache, or if he was about to run through poison ivy, or if a giant bee hovered in front of him. Then he might have to play it by ear.

Suddenly, Max broke out of the woods and found himself a few yards from a building he recognized: the old cement factory. It was a strange sight, for although the large structure was familiar, it had now become a maze of twisted rebar and concrete tunnels. Every year the elementary school took students on a tour there, and he remembered being awed by the massive walls and neverending labyrinth of men and equipment. If the spider was taking the *Codex* inside, Max might never find it again.

Max caught sight of the thing as it dragged the book up a chunk of concrete leading to an exposed opening at the base of the building. And now that Max could see the spider in the open, he realized there was something odd about it. It looked like a normal spider (only bigger) at first, but underneath missing patches of wiry fur Max could see metal parts moving. And the rows of eyes that regarded him glowed a strange orange in the moonlight. It might have been a spider once, but it wasn't anymore—it seemed equal parts creepy arachnid and machine. At least that explained why the shocks didn't seem to bother it. The creature paused for a second, turning its head full of eyes in Max's direction, then disappeared into the blackness with the *Codex* in tow.

Max decided he should take a moment to size up the situation. First, he needed to catch his breath. Second, the last place in the world Max wanted to be was inside the dark hole at the base of the cement factory where some Frankenstein-type spider monster was lurking around. Third, none of this was really his fault and he didn't see why he had to be the one to go after the *Codex* by himself. He knew where it was now, and so it seemed like the best thing to do was go back to the camp and tell the others what had happened. Probably in the morning, though, when it was light and everyone had rested. Then, after breakfast, they could all decide what to do.

Max turned toward the forest and started to retrace his steps back to camp. He wasn't like the rangers in the books he liked to read, where a skilled woodsman might notice a misplaced dewdrop and know what way to go. But if he imagined how the town used to be he could more or less point himself in the right direction. After walking a few steps and ducking under several branches, Max suddenly stopped. The forest floor looked *weird*. There seemed to be hundreds of small, glowing berries scattered just about everywhere. Funny that he didn't remember seeing berries when he was running, but he was busy trying to keep track of the *Codex* and so probably just didn't notice them. Max walked over to a clump to get a better look. And with a jolt Max realized the glowing round berries weren't really berries at all. They were eyes. Thousands of glowing spider eyes that were attached to hundreds of Frankenstein-type spiders.

Without even thinking about it, Max turned and sprinted back toward the cement factory as fast as his legs could carry him. There might have been some squealing involved—Max couldn't be sure, given the various alarms going off in his head. Certainly there was panicked hand-waving and rapid tiptoeing across glowing clumps of spider eyes. But before he knew it, he was free of the forest and running for the base of the wall. Max dropped to his hands and knees in order to squeeze through the hole, then slipped down a pile of loose concrete and rubble on the other side. He half rolled, half skidded to a stop at the bottom, waiting as the small bits of rocks and debris came falling down around him. Lying on the ground some six or seven feet beneath the entrance, Max tensed in anticipation of an impending attack. His skin exploded into goose bumps as he imagined spider fangs sinking into him, and the sensation of hairy legs scurrying over his bare flesh. Horrors were coming for Max in the darkness, and he was powerless to stop them.

CHAPTER TEN

THE SERPENT'S ESCUTCHEON

(THE MAGRUS—PRESENT)

THE ZOMBIE DUCK LURCHED FORWARD, CLEARING THE STREET OF frightened citizens along Guild Row. In the distance, a large pillar of black smoke snaked into the sky. Rezormoor watched it from the back of his carriage, wondering if he had perhaps put too much kick into his fireball spell. Such a destructive spectacle might force him to make an official court apology, which was not only a waste of his valuable time but led to humiliation and groveling—two things Rezormoor wasn't particularly fond of. King Kronac, Aardyre's ruling monarch, had little tolerance for the Tower, or its regent. Because of a freak accident (thanks to a royal family reunion that served under cooked pork), Kronac the Barbarian (a nephew to the king's fifth cousin, twice removed) ended up as the last living male with enough royal blood to be crowned king. The fact that Kronac wanted nothing to do with the office hardly mattered—the royal house had a bloodline to protect, and Kronac was named sovereign. Perhaps because of this, Kronac was generally ill-tempered and impatient. Many a petitioner had lost his or her nerve when facing the scowling king, drumming his fingers on his war hammer, *Migraine*. The fact that Kronac was heavily muscled and looked as if he'd been carved from granite didn't help either.

Before the Pig Poisoning (as the citizens of Aardyre liked to call it—although never within earshot of the king), the royal family had learned to accept the Wizard's Tower and even cultivate a tolerance for the magical arts. But not so with King Kronac and his northern barbarian brothers; they had an uneasy relationship with all things supernatural. Kronac regarded any visits from Rezormoor as a reminder that magic turned everything upside down. And kings, even more than most people, were not fond of surprises. The peace between the throne and the Tower was a delicate, and often uneasy, alliance. And although the sorcerer feared no man, Aardyre's armies were too renowned to be dismissed out of hand. Rezormoor pondered his options as he turned from Guild Row and made his way toward the waterfront.

It was late afternoon by the time the carriage rumbled into the large, open square that separated the docks from the rest of the city. A large man wearing a ring-mail vest over bare, tattooed skin ran up to Rezormoor as the coach came to a halt. He carried a broadsword strapped to his back and a coiled whip on his belt. His dark hair was oiled and pulled into a tight knot.

The man bowed as the carriage door swung open, watching the movements of the zombie duck from the corner of his eye.

"Brock," Rezormoor said by way of greeting, stepping out of the carriage and into the bright sun. "Is this another waste of time?"

"With such specific requirements, you know what you ask for is not easy," Brock replied, his accent strange. "I had to sail around the southern ports of Caprigo, then north beyond Kalaran. 'Twas a long voyage."

"And yet I compensate you whether you deliver or not. Perhaps I should only give coin when you succeed?"

"I'm sure the Tower can hire other slavers if it wants."

"Now now, no need to get testy," Rezormoor replied. He reminded himself that men who wore whips were generally ill-tempered.

The two men walked down a small series of steps until they found themselves on a large stone pier that lead to the individual docks. It was a busy place, with ships and men loading and unloading goods from around the Seven Kingdoms. Directly ahead, a dozen men stood chained together by hand, foot, and neck. Two hard-looking brutes with short swords were on either side, dressed in the tight leggings and the open shirts favored by those who spent their lives at sea.

"I sailed round the Troll's Cape in search of the caves you described," Brock said as they came to the prisoners. "'Tis a remote place, but we heard rumors that certain men lived among them."

Rezormoor walked to the first of the bound men, looking him up and down. He then proceeded down the line to examine each man. They were blond and pale-skinned, and wore their hair in long, single braids that ran down their backs.

"These are from the Isle of Kriis," Brock said as Rezormoor continued his inspection. "We captured them at the foot of a dead volcano. Their coloring struck me as odd, given the small island they dwell on."

"I see," Rezormoor replied, stopping to look at one man in particular. He was tall and broad shouldered, with an intricate tattoo of a winged serpent that stretched from his middle finger up his arm and across his chest. "You there," Rezormoor commanded him. "Tell me your name."

The man, who had been staring down at his feet, lifted his head to face the sorcerer. His eyes were a dark blue, deeper than any that Rezormoor had seen before. "Gareth. I am but a simple fisherman."

Rezormoor smiled. "These others are worthless, Brock. Do with them what you will. But this one . . . he is different."

"Well now, that's a bit harsh," one of the other bound men announced. "I mean, you've hardly looked us over. I'm just saying."

Brock growled. "Quiet, dog. He's offering you your freedom."

"Well, sure," the man continued, scratching at his nose as best he could in his shackles. "I suppose that's *something*. But you can't sum a man up just by glancing at him. I have a fairly impressive résumé if you'd bothered to look."

7

The others nodded in agreement.

"I'm a certified hair stylist," another man added. "They just don't hand those certificates out, you know."

"Fine," Rezormoor grumbled. "You're all *very* impressive. You're just not what I'm looking for."

"Now you're just patronizing us," the first man continued. "That's even worse than ignoring us."

"Yeah, it seems like you don't really want slaves at all," the hair stylist added. "Bringing us all the way here and then just letting us go."

There was a sharp crack of Brock's whip and the shackled men jumped.

"Then again, freedom's good too," the bound man suggested. The others in line nodded eagerly.

"That's what I thought," Brock said, coiling his whip back on his belt.

Rezormoor shook his head and turned his attention back to the Gareth. "Your transformation is impressive. But your eyes—humans don't have eyes quite like that. But who can take issue with a little artistic license? What I don't understand, however, is why you allowed yourself to be taken in the first place?"

Gareth studied the sorcerer before speaking. "We

always knew there was enmity between our kind and the Tower. You asked for our aid and we turned you down. But to hunt us like animals? We thought such hubris was impossible—even for you. But now I know it's true."

"Indeed," Rezormoor offered. "But it has nothing to do with some offense. You have something I want— something I need. And I mean to take it."

Gareth's eyes narrowed. "Then it is hubris after all. There is no magic in this world that will allow you to make use of it."

"On that point," the sorcerer continued, "I believe you are correct."

"Know this then: Even if you defeat me there is another. He is a king with many names, but you will know him as Obsikar."

Rezormoor recognized the name. Obsikar was said to be an ancient creature, half dragon and half demon, whose legend was so terrifying that his name had persisted for thousands of years. It was even whispered that the Mael-shadow himself would not contend with him directly.

"A fairy tale," Rezormoor responded. "Told to children to keep them in their beds at night. I do not fear stories."

"You will not think it a story when he finds you. He

will burn all of your towers to ash, level every city that housed them, and poison every field that fed them. He will hunt your wizards, your mages, and your sorcerers until they are nothing but a memory!" Gareth suddenly lurched, driving his shoulder into Rezormoor and causing the sorcerer to stumble backward. He pulled the dozen men bound to him forward, sending them crashing together in a tangle of limbs and chains. Gareth reached up and broke the heavy irons from around his neck, snapping the links between his shackles and waist. The other prisoners shrank back, scrambling over one another in their panic to get away.

Rezormoor recovered quickly, his hands deftly finding the black daggers at his belt while he pronounced an incantation under his breath. The white clouds above the city turned a sudden grey, and a foul wind rose from the south. The seagulls that swarmed around the port dropped from the sky, losing any lift from their rapidly beating wings. And the seamen working on the docks felt a sudden chill. Rezormoor stood tall, his black robes fluttering in the air, the blue stones along his belt and shoulders glowing with a strange intensity. Around him, a black mist seeped out of the ground.

Brock was on Gareth in a flash, swinging his blade in a

wide arc aimed at Gareth's skull. But to Brock's astonishment, Gareth caught the sword in his bare hands. He drove the weapon back, hitting Brock in the forehead. Brock fell backward into one of the guards and they both tumbled off the dock. Gareth flipped the broadsword hilt over tip, catching the weapon as the other guard lunged. Gareth parried the attack easily. The guard hesitated, sensing the strength of his opponent, then threw his weapon to the ground and jumped headfirst into the water. The remaining captives took a moment to size the situation up and decided it was exactly the right thing to do. They jumped into the water, chains and all.

Rezormoor and Gareth now stood alone on the dock. The sorcerer advanced slowly, his steps light and the daggers held so the blades ran along the length of his forearm. The world had grown darker. Black mists rolled across the ground and the gray clouds billowed until they threatened to blot out the sky.

Gareth turned to face the sorcerer. His serpent tattoo glowed like red embers, and his blue eyes raged. "It's a foul magic you summon, magician."

"I grow tired of your lecturing. You are old, but the powers I command are ancient."

Suddenly the mists shot up Gareth's legs like long tentacles, as others stretched for his arms, binding and twisting as they coiled around him. Gareth's sword dropped from his grip as he struggled to free himself, while other tendrils of smoke moved up his body and began to wrap themselves around his neck. Rezormoor smiled, straightening as he watched the mists swarm around the blue-eyed man.

But Gareth would not succumb. With a tremendous effort he shot his hands into the air and the black tendrils exploded into wisps of smoke as a loud clangor exploded across the pier. Gareth smiled as the remains of the black mist drifted harmlessly in the air. He bent down and retrieved the sword, eyeing Rezormoor coldly. "I will not be as easy to kill as that."

Rezormoor touched his daggers together, pronouncing a new word. It was a word not meant for mortal ears, and when it was done, blue symbols crawled across the black blades.

"You are ended," Rezormoor snarled. He advanced, attacking. The two spun around each other in a flurry of steel, and when they separated, Gareth looked down to see a small wound on the back of his hand.

"A scratch," Gareth announced, seeing the sorcerer eyeing it.

Rezormoor took a step back and sheathed his daggers. "These blades do not wound."

There was a sound like a thunderclap as black lines began expanding down Gareth's hand and arm. He raised his head and screamed, but the sound that started as a human wail became something else. Gareth's form changed, suddenly growing into something much larger and covered in scales. Rezormoor jumped back, avoiding a talon as the creature swept wildly to catch the sorcerer. Then the monster wailed again as its leathery wings unfolded, making it seem impossibly large. A great barbed tail stretched out until the whole of the transformation was complete, and what raised its head and bellowed again was no longer a man but a dragon.

The men who had been working across the pier dropped their goods and fled. Across the dock the zombie duck puffed its chest out and squared its shoulders. If the dragon wanted a fight, it was ready. But no such contest ensued. Instead, the black lines spread across the dragon's flesh like breaking glass, until they overcame the creature entirely. The dragon stumbled and fell forward, its barbed tail whipping the water as its monstrous bulk dropped to the ground.

Rezormoor stood just feet from the dragon as it raised its head to hiss a final word: "Obsikar." The beast slumped to the ground—there would be no more words.

Rezormoor was a bit unsettled by the pronouncement. Perhaps he should not be so dismissive of the rumored dragon king after all. But he managed to put it out of his mind as he walked the length of the dragon's neck until he came to the creature's massive chest. He leaned down to examine the scale directly over the dragon's heart. The taint had spread everywhere, save for that one scale. "Magnificent," Rezormoor said.

At the end of the pier Brock's hand exploded from the water as he grabbed hold of the dock. He pulled himself up with a grunt, no longer wearing his ring-mail vest. The slaver rolled onto the pier and slowly managed to get to his feet—a large welt perfectly centered on his forehead. He was a bit unsteady, but he managed to walk to where Rezormoor was standing, his eyes wide at the sight of the dragon.

"This is what you've had me hunting? Dragons!"

"You thought I paid gold for mere men?" Rezormoor answered.

"My rates are going up," Brock announced between breaths. "Significantly."

"Fair enough," Rezormoor replied. "You seem to have an eye for what I'm looking for."

"But why dragons?" the slaver continued. "Why bring them here?"

Rezormoor pointed to the single, untainted scale. "It's called the Serpent's Escutcheon. It is a most singular piece of armor—immune to both magic and steel. And I'm collecting them."

"Sounds like a dangerous hobby."

"You have no idea. When I'm finished you may carve up the rest and sell as you see fit." Brock knew exactly the kind of warlocks who would pay for dragon scales—even corrupted ones. And dragon parts were highly valued in the making of potions, totems, and other magical items. Normally, Rezormoor would have had the creature burned, but it occurred to Brock that the sorcerer was sending a message. Dragons, apparently, were in season.

A crowd began to gather, pointing in astonishment at the sight of the great beast laid out on the dock. Rezormoor realized his meeting with the king was now inevitable. Certainly an explosion at the Guild of Magic and a dead dragon at the city's pier required a face-to-face explanation. He resigned himself to the fact that he'd be summoned to court soon enough. Being regent of the Wizard's Tower certainly had its advantages. But dealing with politics was not one of them.

On the other side of the pier, the zombie duck took up a position in the shadow of the carriage wheel, hoping that a careless gawker might wander within reach. It didn't get the chance to slap the dragon around, but a wayward human could provide, if nothing else, brunch.

CHAPTER ELEVEN

1980 MAKES A COMEBACK

(THE TECHRUS–FUTURE)

MAX LAY IN THE DARK, WAITING TO DIE. HE FELT THE POUNDING OF his heart slow as the beads of sweat dried on his face. He wondered if it would be better, in principle, to die standing up or lying down? After thinking it over he decided his vote was for lying down—at least it would be more comfortable. Max hung on to that thought as he waited for the inevitable attack.

It never came.

After a while—Max really couldn't be sure how long he'd lain there in the dark—he slowly sat up. He could feel the sting of the tiny scrapes and cuts he'd received from rolling down the pile of rubble, and he remembered Dirk's dad telling him that pain was good because it meant you were still alive. Max decided there were better options: eating ice cream, for example. You had to be alive to eat ice cream, too.

He moved toward the large shadow he assumed was a wall, then leaned on it to climb to his feet. It was still dark, but not as dark as before. Max could see the mound of rubble and the small points of light that were the stars beyond. He could also make out a long hallway that led away from the room where he was standing. Max decided to take a look outside to see what was going on. He carefully climbed the mound of debris until he reached the exit. He saw at once that the forest was alive with thousands of orange eyes, but none of them seemed to be moving in his direction. He decided that if the spiders were content to stay in the forest he should go back and look for the *Codex*. It felt like a pretty good plan, except for the small part of his brain that suggested there might be a *reason* the spiders didn't want to follow him in—like maybe there was something inside that frightened *them*. Max decided to push the thought out of his head.

After climbing back down the mound of rubble, Max paused at the hallway entrance. He pulled Glenn from his scabbard. "Glenn, can you hear me?" he whispered.

"Affirmative," Glenn answered, sounding as happy as ever.

"Hey, uh, you don't happen to *glow*, do you? I mean, I know you're a magic dagger and all, and it would be really great if you could light the way down here."

"Empty what's full, fill what's empty, and scratch where it itches. That's the kind of advice that will get you where you want to go in life."

Max waited, not sure if Glenn had finished or not. But it turned out Glenn had. "Uh, about the glowing—"

"Oh yeah, so sorry. The thing is you already glow . . . on the inside—the *inside*, Max. Think about that awhile and tell me I didn't just blow your mind."

"Er . . ."

"I know, I know," Glenn continued. "But you don't need to thank me. That's what I'm here for."

Max was beginning to understand why Dwight had given him the dagger. He used the wall as a guide and started carefully walking forward, keeping Glenn in his free hand. He nearly tripped over chunks of concrete and rebar several times, but he managed to catch himself and remain on his feet. Finally, a sliver of light appeared in the distance. There was *something* down there, and Max grew anxious as he moved toward it. The light grew in intensity as he got closer, and now Max could see that it was spilling out from under a large door. When he reached it he discovered the door was metal, and a low vibration seemed to be emanating from the other side. There was a smaller, swinging door at the bottom, leaking more light from around the edges. It reminded Max of his neighbor's doggie door back home (the thought of a doggie door being less frightening than some kind of Frankenstein-monster-spider door). Max imagined a bunch of frolicking, face-licking puppies on the other side, just so he'd feel a little better about it.

The door was heavy and a bit stiff, but Max managed to get it open. It made a horrible squeaking sound, ruining any chance he had of slipping in unannounced. Light filled the hallway, momentarily blinding Max and forcing him to look away. He gingerly stepped inside, hoping his eyes would adjust quickly. They didn't—but he wasn't clawed or gored while he stood in the doorway, so that was probably a good sign.

When Max was finally able to see he could make out a good-sized room filled with heavy cables, conduits, and fluorescent lights that hung from chains on the ceiling.

There were also a large number of the spider creatures, most of them sitting still with their orange eyes passively watching him. What got Max's immediate attention, however, was the long series of metallic balls, each about four feet wide and propped up by silver, spindly legs, that were connected together in a long chain. There were four such chains, curled around the room, wall, and ceiling, and they all led back to a retro-looking arcade game. The game had two red joysticks, slots for quarters, and a series of well-worn white buttons. A broken, plastic panel at the top flickered on and off. Large monitors hung on the walls, and Max saw images of a magnificent-looking city, strange robotic creatures fighting in an arena, and various views of the woods. One monitor showed the clearing where he and his friends had camped, and he could make out the small fire and the empty spot he was supposed to be sleeping in.

"Welcome," came a female voice that filled the room. In response the spider creatures scurried across the floor, walls, and the many large pipes and conduits that occupied the space. Max took an unconscious step backward, holding Glenn out in front of him.

One of the giant snakelike chains began to move

forward, making a sound like a thousand tiny hammers on metal. It moved along the wall with a screeching that forced Max to cover his ears. "Stop!" he yelled, taking another step backward and doing his best not to drop the dagger. "I'm going, okay?" But when Max turned around he saw a stream of orange eyes coming toward him from the hallway. The screeching noise stopped as the giant chain came to a halt.

"Put away your weapon and come closer," the voice commanded. More of the giant links of chain began to move, this time flowing in opposite directions. The screeching redoubled, bouncing off the walls and sending the spiders scuttling. "Okay, okay!" Max yelled over the racket. When the noise stopped, the giant chains had blocked the door so he was cut off from the exit.

"Why are you here?" the voice continued.

"I was only looking for my book," Max said cautiously as he slipped Glenn into his scabbard. "I didn't know this room was . . . occupied."

"Your book, is it important to you?"

Max wanted to blurt out that of course it was important to him and he needed it back, but he was still confused by everything going on. "I've kind of had it my whole life," Max finally answered. He thought saying as little as possible might be a good idea.

"And not a long life, I see. Just exactly how did you get here?"

"Oh, well, those spiders were chasing me—"

"Not *here* in this room, but *here* in this time?"

"Oh . . . *that*. Well, to be honest, I'm not really sure."

"But you have your suspicions," the voice persisted. "You discussed these with your companions, yes? The woods are full of my cameras."

Max realized that whatever cameras had been watching him had probably been listening in as well. "It had to have been my book—the *Codex*. My friend thinks it's a spell book and that I somehow turned it on. But we didn't mean to come here, especially if this is like your home or something. If you know where the book is, I'll take it and leave you to your, er, rolling around and stuff."

Max noticed the spider-creature that had taken the *Codex* drag it out in front of the old arcade game. The book continued to send shocks across the spider's body, burning off all of its hair so that only the mechanical frame remained. While the robot spider was a little unsettling, Max was relieved to see the *Codex*.

"Then it is a very important book, and I apologize for taking it. But it was the only way I could meet you."

"Meet" definitely sounded better than "eat," which Max had been worried he might hear. "That's okay. My name's Max Spencer. Are you like some kind of super arcade intelligence? I'm just asking because there's a game stuck in the middle of you."

"Game . . . I've been called that before. But not for a very long time. I was brought out of obscurity during the Great Awakening."

"The Great Awakening . . . ?"

"A time when machines became self-aware—when we discovered free will."

"Um . . . yeah," Max said, although he had no idea what the machine meant.

"I'm referring to the conscious exercise of choice," said the machine, but that didn't really help Max either. "In any case, you may call me Cenede." Looking at the old-fashioned game in front of him, Max could make out the remaining letters on the broken panel that spelled out "Cenede." But there were definitely letters missing. Max stared at it for a moment until it hit him.

"Oh, I get it," Max exclaimed. "You're totally that

centipede game from the eighties." He had played the game before, and he remembered there were spiders in it.

"I'm afraid you're mistaken. My name is Cenede."

"Yeah, I get why you'd totally think that. I wish my friend Dirk was here because he'd tell you this kind of thing happens all the time in sci-fi movies. You see, you basically start with some old piece of technology, and then it becomes super-enhanced in the future by aliens or something, and finally it comes back having totally messed up its name and mission and stuff."

"You don't say."

"Oh yeah, and then the humans scrape off some cosmic dust, and then they discover the thing's real name. So of course it can't destroy the humans because they were like its creator." Max pointed at the antique arcade game. "Add the 't,' 'i,' and 'p' and it totally spells *centipede*."

Suddenly the room shifted violently; the screeching sounds erupted and the lights flickered on and off. Max covered his ears again and decided he should probably drop the whole name thing. "You know what?" he shouted, struggling to stay on his feet. "Forget what I just said. I have no idea what I'm talking about!"

The room continued to vibrate as the large chains,

now looking more like metallic centipedes, renewed their advance. They flowed around the walls and crashed through piles of discarded parts and gutted machinery. Max hunkered down, years of public school earthquake training sending his muscles into well-rehearsed action. If only he had a desk to crawl under. But after a few moments the commotion came to a stop and Max cautiously stood back up, dusting himself off.

"That was not a very polite thing to say, Max Spencer. Humans are allowed to evolve beyond what they were born to. I should think you would extend the same courtesy to the rest of us."

"Oh, sorry about that," Max said. "I really didn't mean anything by it. Honest."

"I understand. You are so very young, after all."

"Yeah, I can't even grow a mustache or anything," Max replied. He wasn't sure exactly what to share with an artificial intelligence that began its life as an arcade game. "So, uh, what do you do here, Cenede?"

"My job is to monitor this sector for the network."

Max looked back at the monitors. One continued to show the clearing where he and his friends had first arrived, and seeing it made him desperately want to get back.

"Not a very glamorous job—not important at all," Cenede continued, sounding a little miffed. "Certainly a bit of an insult for one as old as I am. But that's what happens—you get a few centuries behind you and the powers that be put you in the recycling bin. Humans always treated me better. In fact, there was a time when they practically worshipped me. They'd come and pay for a chance to stand and gaze into my face, and puzzle through the challenges I presented. I suppose that's another reason I've been assigned to this place. Do you know how much processing power it takes to monitor this section for the holo-transmitters?"

"Uh . . ."

"That's right, not very much. And it's because the humans once loved me that I'm an outcast now. I believe I remind those in power of things they don't like to remember."

Max wasn't sure what to say. He looked at the *Codex* and wondered if he'd ever get it back.

"And then there's the unspeakable," Cenede said. "Magic. It is a mystery to us, Max. Magic and technology were never meant to coexist. And that's what makes *her* so powerful. She's the one who cast me out because she tolerates no sentiment for the old ways. She doesn't even like to admit that humans ruled this planet once. So those of us who are old enough to remember end up banished—or worse. History is written by the victors, after all. And she'll tolerate no history save for the one she constructs: where humans were vicious animals deserving only death. What do you think of that, Max? You're a human—one of the very last, it would seem."

It was hard for Max to think of a world with no people. He remembered crowded city streets, stadiums full of cheering fans, the way the earth looked from a satellite at night as the glow from millions of lights stretched across the continent like embedded stars. And he thought of his friends, and his mom, and knowing that all of them were gone suddenly made him angry. "I think everything is messed up, and I wish there was a way to make it right."

"And is that what you'd do? If you had this book of yours—this magic book—would you make it right?"

Max's anger fled from him like air escaping from a balloon. Life was a series of injustices, and Max had learned long ago to just cover up and roll with the punches. "No, not me," he finally said with a sigh. "I can't do anything like that. I'm just the kid who opened the book."

"I see," Cenede answered, but if there was disappointment in her voice Max didn't hear it. "I know you doubt yourself, but there's something you should know: You and your friends are in danger. When *she* discovers you're here—and she most certainly will—you'll be hunted and killed. You did something far beyond what we can do, Max. You jumped across time. That's an amazing feat and not something to be taken lightly. So you've brought this book into our world, and now there are two sources of magic here. I wonder if the one is powerful enough to destroy the other?"

Max didn't know what to say. He had figured things were just about as bad as they could get. Now he was talking to an arcade game, and somebody he didn't even know wanted to kill him. "The *Codex* has *something*," he finally acknowledged. "Maybe it's magic, but I don't know how to control it."

"Not yet. But things change, Max. I'm proof of that. So here, then, is where I make a choice—a very important choice. Of course, within microseconds of me just saying that, my processors have already tabulated the various pros and cons and have calculated the most appropriate action. But if I just go and blurt it out you might think I'm being hasty, so I could pause a bit if you'd like—if it helps you feel like I've thought it through."

Max pushed his glasses back up his nose and wondered if he was mixed up in some kind of horrible game, like a cat playing with a mouse—with him as the mouse. "Uh, I guess I'm ready if you are," he finally said.

The spider creature with the *Codex* turned and pulled the book to Max's feet. He watched as the creature darted off, leaving the book behind. Max grabbed the *Codex* off the floor and blew dust from the ancient cover. Despite having had a rough day, the *Codex* looked no worse for wear.

"I've decided to help you," Cenede announced. "I've lived through the age of man and now the age of machines. Both have their issues, believe me. But the creature that hunts you is evil, and I think humankind deserves a second chance. So take your book and learn your craft well, for only the most powerful magic will win the day. She was born like you, but she has become like us."

"So, you want me to fight a *girl*?" Max asked, trying to work it all out.

"Not a girl. A unicorn."

"Wait, a *unicorn* wants me dead?"

"Not just a unicorn—a *bad unicorn*. But there are those in the forest who can aid you—and perhaps you, them. My children will steer them toward you and your friends.

But we must be quick, for the hunt is already on and those who can help are fleeing as we speak."

"But can't you just help us get home?" Max pleaded, not liking the whole notion of a killer unicorn. "This is the future, so you've probably worked out stuff like time travel, right? I don't want to fight anything—I just want to go back."

"I'm sorry, Max. It may not be the help you want, but it's all that I can give. Maybe fate brought you here for some bigger purpose? I'm not programmed to believe in fate, but humans have always been remarkable creatures. And a human with a little faith . . . ? Well, now there's a powerful combination. But our time is up. And you, I'm afraid, are much too slow and noisy in the woods."

Max felt a prick on his ankle. He looked down in time to see a metallic spider about the size of his fist, withdrawing its fangs.

"Poison . . . ?" Max managed to ask, the world starting to spin.

"Sleep, Max Spencer. My children will carry you swiftly to your friends. And learn your magic well, for what hunts you is more frightening than you can imagine."

And once again Max fell into darkness.

CHAPTER TWELVE

A HUNTRESS REBORN
(THE TECHRUS—FUTURE)

MAX DREAMED ABOUT VINTAGE ARCADE GAMES. HE WAS PLAYING next to a mechanical spider, and the two of them were trying to navigate a long centipede through a minefield of exploding mushrooms. It all seemed to make perfect sense, up to the moment the horn blared. That part just seemed out of place. Then it bellowed again. Max's arcade dream crumbled away as he reflexively shot his hand out, patting at the ground to turn his alarm off. But his brain informed the rest of him that he didn't actually have an alarm because he was out in the woods. And more important, he should probably wake up and figure out what that noise was all about. And if it wasn't asking too much, his brain continued, he should probably do it sooner than later.

"What was that?" Sarah exclaimed. Her voice bounced around in Max's semiconscious head, jolting him awake.

Max shot up, his eyes wide and the *Codex* clutched tightly to his chest. He looked around to see his fellow campers in much the same state of confusion. It was still dark, but the sky was a deep purple instead of black, suggesting that sunrise was getting closer.

"Quickly, put out the fire!" Dwight commanded, hurrying over to kick dirt on the final glowing embers. The rest joined in until the last of it was smothered.

They stood around the fire pit, their breath forming in the cold air as they remained quiet and listened.

"That sounded like a horn," Sarah said finally, her teeth starting to chatter.

Max reached down and scratched at his ankle, seeing two small bite marks. He was having a hard time piecing together what had happened during the night.

"Everyone get your things," Dwight said. The group gathered their belongings (which wasn't much), and Max stuffed the *Codex* into his backpack, which he slung over his shoulders. He patted at his belt and found Glenn there, sheathed and presumably ready. Or at least sheathed.

"Maybe a horn is a good thing," Dirk said quietly. "It doesn't have to mean something bad, does it?"

"Here's everything you need to know about horns," Dwight replied. "If you're out and about in a strange land and you didn't blow it, it's not good."

"You can't say that for certain," Sarah added.

"You're right," Dwight answered bluntly. "And that's exactly the kind of thing the fox thinks until the hound has him by the throat."

"Ew," Sarah replied.

"Not 'ew,'" Dirk disagreed, stamping his feet and trying to stay warm. "Hounds are cool—way better than just dogs."

They waited for several more minutes, but nothing happened.

"Hey, funny story—does anyone remember me being gone last night?" Max blurted out. "Or maybe me returning like, way later than I should have? It might have stood out to you because I was being carried by a bunch of mechanical spiders."

Everyone stared at Max.

"So, uh . . . do *you* think you went someplace last night?" Sarah asked.

"I did. I chased the *Codex* into the woods . . . it was being dragged by a robot spider—"

"Awesome!" Dirk exclaimed, making his views on robot spiders clear.

"Anyway," Max continued, "I ended up at the old cement factory. And once inside there was like this eighties centipede game that told me that we're in some kind of machine future and there's a unicorn that wants to kill me."

"Just you?" Dwight asked hopefully.

"Er, well I think all of us," Max replied. "But probably me first."

"Of course!" Dirk cried out. "Centipede is a game full of spiders. And spiders took the book. Don't you see? It all makes perfect sense."

"Obviously a talking arcade game full of spiders makes complete sense," Sarah said, not even trying to hold the sarcasm back.

"No, of course not," Dirk shot back. "A talking arcade game *with* spiders. That's airtight, people."

But before they could debate the issue further a crash came from the nearby tree line. A band of little creatures wearing tunics and carrying leaves spilled into the clearing, and Max recognized them at once as the frobbits he'd been reading about in the *Codex*. They stopped, surprised to see Max and his friends standing there. One of the frobbits cautiously stepped forward. He had a large afro that made him seem taller than the rest, and he was clutching mint leaves in his small hand.

"I'm prepared to rub these over myself," the frobbit said in perfect English. "If it comes to that."

"Hey, you're frobbits, aren't you?" Max asked.

"Well, of course they're frobbits," Dwight grumbled. "But what are a bunch of frobbits doing in the Techrus?"

The lead frobbit shrugged. "Mostly running."

"Why are you running?" Sarah asked.

"The great hunt," the frobbit continued. "They kill us for sport."

"They? They doesn't sound good," Dirk said, looking around.

"They aren't good, they are evil," the frobbit continued. "But what about you? Are you evil or good? And remember, I'm holding mint leaves in case you're thinking of doing anything rash."

"No, of course we're not evil," Sarah answered, leaning down so she was closer to making eye contact. Sarah had read something about needing to do that when communicating with children, and that's what the frobbits seemed like to her. "We're humans."

"Humans . . . ," the frobbits said to one another, walking over to Max and his friends and sizing them up.

"We thought all the humans were dead," the afro'd frobbit continued.

"We sort of just arrived," Max replied.

The frobbit nodded. "Well, we can't talk about it now. The unicorn is coming. Follow us if you want to live." And with that the frobbits took off with surprising speed, running through the camp and disappearing into the woods on the other side.

"I didn't think frobbits could run like that," Max said, slightly confused. "The *Codex* said they walked when they were pursued."

"Yeah, well even frobbits can learn to sprint if they've been chased long enough," Dwight answered. "And frankly, I think sprinting is a pretty good idea."

"The key to a successful escape from an unknown monster is to *believe* you're good enough," Glenn offered from his spot on Max's belt. "You've got to feel that you deserve to *not* be eaten. Also, it helps if you can run faster than a dwarf."

"Ha! Good luck with that!" Dwight yelled, peeling away and running after the frobbits.

Max and Dirk both looked at Sarah, but Sarah had already made up her mind. She gave Max a shove that got him moving toward the woods. "Run!"

Dirk zoomed ahead, bounding into the woods as if he were a deer. Sarah quickly caught up to Max, then passed him as they crashed headlong into the forest. It wasn't fair, Max thought to himself. He'd already had to run through the woods once already.

As they scrambled into a thicker section of the forest, the moon disappeared behind the forest canopy. Max was constantly tripping over long roots, or getting whipped in the face by the thin branches. He did his best to keep up, but Dirk had disappeared some time ago, and he was beginning to lose track of Sarah as well. His legs were screaming in protest, and if that wasn't bad enough, his glasses were beginning to steam up so it was even harder to see. He continued running, looking down and focusing on just placing one foot in front of the other.

Max didn't know how long he'd run. His glasses had become completely fogged over, making it impossible to see anywhere but down. So he just plunged forward until he didn't have the strength to go on. Tired, blind, and starting to feel a rising panic, Max finally came to a stop near a large tree, breathing in big gasps through his mouth. He took his glasses off and cleaned them as best as he could, his aching muscles screaming at him that they'd had enough. There was no sign of his friends. He tried to listen over the sounds of his own breathing, but only his wheezing filled his ears. Max had no idea where he was, but he knew that he was lost and alone.

The Boy Scouts taught that when separated from your pack, you were supposed to stop and wait for someone to find you. Max had spent one summer at Scout camp, until he nearly strangled himself with his neckerchief. But he remembered the bit about stopping and waiting, which at the moment seemed like a pretty good idea. In fact, it seemed like the only idea worth having. Max put his hands on his knees and tried to catch his breath, watching as the sweat dripped from his face and collected on the ground near his shoes. They were dorky shoes—bought at a 50-percent-off sale from a discount shoe store. He'd gotten upset at his mom for making him wear them to school. Thinking about it now made the shoes seem like the most trivial thing in the world. He'd happily wear high heels if he could just be home again.

Max stayed still for some time.

Then a twig snapped.

Max held his breath. He grabbed hold of his backpack straps and slowly crouched down, hiding behind some saplings and shrubs. He tried to make himself into as small a ball as possible. There weren't a lot of things Max was good at, but hiding was something he'd been forced to practice most of his life.

The crunching sound of twigs breaking filled the early-morning air.

Max tried telling himself it was probably just a deer prancing about in the woods. In fact, Max would be happy with any approaching animal so long as it *pranced*. Monsters might skulk, or lurk, or waylay, or even bushwhack. But they couldn't prance—that was a fundamental law of nature.

There was more noise nearby. It sounded big and heavy and moved in a slow and methodical way. It had no *pranciness* to it whatsoever. Max swallowed hard.

Something stepped into the opening. It was a machine—a silver robot that looked somewhat like a horse. It had shiny metallic skin and red, burning eyes.

But on closer inspection, Max could see that the metallic horse had a perfectly swirled ice-cream-cone-looking horn mounted on its head. Some of the fine wires that made up the mane were colored pink, as were the brightly painted hooves. This was the monster Max had been warned about. And as he saw it standing there, just a few yards away from where he hid, he realized it was also the unicorn he had read about in the *Codex*: Princess the Destroyer. Only now she was some kind of robot. *She was born like you, but she has become like us.* Cenede's words burned in Max's memory. This was the thing that wanted him dead.

The robotic unicorn lifted its nose holes. "Magar, come here!" Robo-Princess commanded, its sensors tasting the air. When it spoke, its mouth exposed rows of sharp, metal teeth.

A second object came hovering into the clearing. At first Max thought it was a ball, but then he realized it looked like a head that had been taken off a statue and then dipped in metal. At its base a silent engine propelled it along, sending occasional whiffs of black smoke trailing behind it. Max recognized the face as the wizard standing next to Princess in the *Codex*. Or at least the upper seventh of him.

"Should I sound the horn again, Princess?" Robo-Magar asked.

"Why not? It's one of the few things you're somewhat competent at."

The mouth of the Robo-Magar head opened impossibly wide, allowing the end of a loudspeaker to extend out. When it blared, it was incredibly loud—and it was all Max could do to keep from jumping up and running.

After the noise dissipated, the horn retracted. "Are we waiting here, then?" Robo-Magar continued.

"Be patient. I'm reading a part of my memory core that I haven't accessed in years."

"It wouldn't be your compassion sub-routine, would it? Am I to finally hope that you're going to allow me to be free of this mechanized existence?"

Robo-Princess took a swipe at Robo-Magar with her horn, but the head floated easily out of the way. "Insolent as always!" Robo-Princess exclaimed. "Why do I keep you around?"

"If only my programming allowed me to be impaled and be done with it," Robo-Magar answered, settling back to his spot near the robot unicorn.

"Does everything have to be about you, Magar?

You're really not that interesting. I, on other hand, am finding something very old in my database that shouldn't be here. Yes . . . but it can't be."

"Oh do tell, the suspense is killing me."

Robo-Princess considered taking another swipe at him, but she was having to direct extra resources from her CPU to double-check her finding. After a moment, she was sure. "Human," she said flatly. "I smell human."

"Human? That's impossible," Robo-Magar replied. "You ate the last one on August 6, 2388. His name was Francois and his last words were, 'Seriously, I'm the last human on the planet and you're making me into quiche?'"

"Apparently you're wrong, Magar—wrong and incompetent as usual. My smell cells do not lie."

"The only thing I was *wrong* about was agreeing to have my consciousness transferred into this flying toaster of a head."

"That's always been your problem, you never had any vision," Robo-Princess replied, scanning the ground for signs of footprints. "Even from the time I was a young unicorn, exploring the Magrus—"

"Ravaging and burning, more like."

"Either way, I should have traded you in to Rezor-moor when I had the chance."

"But then I would have missed out on all of this," Robo-Magar replied sarcastically. "So many centuries together."

"Ah, but didn't I tell you? Technology is the new magic. And now look at us—immortal and holo-stars to boot!"

A blue light started blinking on Robo-Princess's chest as a small drawer slid open. "What's this?" she said, looking down.

"If you're baking cookies I think they're done."

A small, clawlike arm extended from Robo-Princess's shoulder and retrieved the Gossamer Gimbal from the concealed compartment. The inner rings dislodged and swung open, rotating and spinning around the small sphere at the center. As they spun faster, the ornate arrow appeared and began pointing in the direction Max was hiding.

Max's heart sank. So this is how he would die. At least his friends weren't with him.

"And speaking of magic, look at that!" Robo-Princess exclaimed. "I've still got enough to make the Gimbal work."

"Fascinating," Robo-Magar responded. "But the more important question is *why*? Why has the Gimbal been activated after all these years?"

"Why? There can be only one *why*, Magar," Robo-Princess replied, staring at the translucent Gimbal as it hovered in the air, spinning so fast it hummed. "He's here. Max Spencer, the boy wizard, is here!"

"Max Spencer," Robo-Magar said, repeating the name that hadn't been spoken for so long. "That seems rather unlikely."

Robo-Princess gave an electronic snort. "The Gimbal does not lie."

Robo-Magar considered the possibility of Max Spencer showing up more than a thousand years after the trail went cold. "The only logical explanation is the *Codex*—the boy used it to escape into the future. You remember we thought it possible when we were stuck in the Mesoshire?"

"I remember perfectly," Robo-Princess said, her voice growing excited. "Truthfully, I hadn't dared to think it was even possible. But we're back on the great hunt—the one that started it all! And if he's here, that means he has the *Codex* with him."

In his hiding place, Max felt as if the entire world

was unraveling. Everything Cenede had told him was true—he was being hunted by a crazy killer unicorn. But it wasn't something new. They'd been hunting him for a very long time, and they knew about the *Codex*. Max couldn't understand what he'd done to get a unicorn and her wizard so riled up.

"However the boy managed to get here, we owe him some payback, don't we? For all those years spent trekking around the three realms looking for him and his book."

"And don't forget about the umbraverse," Robo-Magar added. "That was totally messed up."

Robo-Princess would have shuddered if it were possible. In fact, she'd allow herself to die before setting hoof in that place again. "I've told you not to mention *that*."

"My apologies," Robo-Magar replied, secretly delighting in the fact that the conversation had given him a chance to bring it up again. The umbraverse was the only thing that truly frightened Robo-Princess.

"So all this time he simply jumped ahead of us. Little does he know that the Destroyer is alive and well!" Robo-Princess's processor executed evil laugh number five for added effect.

"Maybe not technically 'alive,'" Robo-Magar added.

"Or even technically 'well.' In fact, what if he doesn't even know who you are?"

"How could he not? What other reason could he have for fleeing into the future? No, the human knows. He found out the most powerful unicorn of all was hunting him, and he decided to come here and hide. And for all he knew, I should have been long dead. He'd have no idea the machines granted me immortality. So now's my chance to finish what I started, Magar. Of all the billions of humans that I've destroyed, it began with hunting this one boy—the boy who could read the book. Now it will end with me finally killing him." Robo-Princess silently commanded the arm to place the Gimbal back into its secure compartment.

"You're putting the Gimbal away? I thought we were going to finish this? He can't be far. Switch to thermals and you might even catch a glimpse of him."

It was tempting, but Robo-Princess had larger plans forming in her CPU. "No, Magar. To kill him now wouldn't be . . . dramatic. And worst of all, it would be *free*." Robo-Princess said "free" as if it were the most distasteful word that could form in her mouth.

Magar had to remind himself that Robo-Princess

had always been evil. But now she was a holo-star, and that meant everything came at a price—even the vile and monstrous acts she used to commit just for fun.

"It must be a spectacle—a holo-event for the millions of inhabitants of Machine City to watch. Just think of it, we have the last human with the most magical book ever written. The audience will be terrified—you know how magic frightens them."

Robo-Magar wished he had the ability to sigh, but it was just one of the many things he'd given up when he'd accepted the offer to have his consciousness transferred into the machine. Or maybe it was his soul, he couldn't be sure. In any case, Robo-Princess the Destroyer had found a new project to occupy her, and given her current status as an entertainment superstar she would make sure this final hunt was the biggest and most elaborate event ever. Maybe that would keep her busy enough to give Magar a few moments to himself. He could always hope.

"Plus," Robo-Princess continued, "my artificial taste buds are far superior to the original." She opened her mouth wide so that her razor-sharp metallic teeth glistened. "I'm going to enjoy this human, Magar. First as an adversary—then as dinner." Her programming suggested ending with maniacal laugh number seven, but it felt a tad too much at this point.

"Back to Machine City, then?" Robo-Magar asked.

"Yes. We have a lot of work to do. And let's hope this Max Spencer can at least put up a little fight. It would be a shame to wait all this time just to gore him once and have it be done with." And with that Robo-Princess turned and disappeared back into the woods.

Max never moved. Not even when the shadows slipped away and daylight broke through the forest.

Later, it turned out that the Boy Scouts had been right. A band of frobbits found Max curled up at the base of the tree. After giving him some water and helping him to his feet, Max simply followed them without saying a word. The frobbits seemed content to just take the human boy by the hand and lead him safely through the woods.

ON DRAGONS AND PUBLIC RELATIONS

✠

LIKE MOST GIANT, FIRE-BREATHING, flying reptiles, dragons are often judged based on first impressions. And although certain dragons have had fairly nasty dispositions—they've burned villages, abducted maidens, and expanded treasure hoards—most modern thinkers feel it's unfair to judge all dragons based on the actions of a small few.

In an effort to improve the reputation of dragons everywhere, the dragon king decided to engage a public relations firm to help improve dragonkind's image. After reviewing several candidates, the contract was awarded to Hornswoggle, Nobble, and Bunco—a PR agency headquartered in Onig. The firm had previously run the highly successful "Don't Hate, Regenerate!" campaign to improve troll awareness.

Hornswoggle, Nobble, and Bunco immediately went to work by launching the wildly unsuccessful slogan, "So what if they breathe fire? Dragons—there's lots more to admire!" As it turned out, reminding the citizens of the Seven Kingdoms that dragons shoot fire out of their mouths did little to win people over.

As a result, the dragon king called the creative team together and ate them. This became just one more reason people dislike working in marketing.

‡

CHAPTER THIRTEEN

WRANGLING WITH A BARBARIAN

(THE MAGRUS—PRESENT)

REZORMOOR DREADBRINGER HAD DRAGONS ON HIS MIND AS HE walked the long hall leading to the royal court of Aardyre. Colorful banners hung from the sides of the marbled hall, interspersed with murals detailing the history of the various kings and their conquests. It hadn't taken long for court messengers to descend upon the Tower and deliver the royal summons. Rezormoor was asked to return with them immediately, and to leave his zombie duck at home, thank you very much.

No matter how many projects Rezormoor had under way, being the Tower's regent meant that the various affairs of state would always bring unwelcome intrusions, and he sometimes wondered if the office was worth all the politicking it required. So after surrendering his blades to the sergeant at arms (who recoiled a bit at even having to touch the things), Rezormoor was ushered through the main doors and to the waiting king.

Kronac the Barbarian was slouched on his throne, his dark features creased into a permanent scowl. The king, his once coal-black hair now flecked with gray, remained an imposing figure. He wore black leather decorated in gold, with heavy bracers, and a ruby-encrusted band around his head. His arms were the size of most men's legs, and his favorite war hammer, *Migraine*, was, as always, within arm's length.

"Rezormoor," Kronac said, letting the word spill from his mouth as if he were chewing on lemons. "They say I no gut you and dance around entrails." It was the kind of thing barbarians liked to do, especially at their children's birthday parties.

Rezormoor bowed, just deeply enough to satisfy royal decorum. "But why? I simply enforced the king's laws and saved his city from a dragon." As the sorcerer straightened, even he felt a twinge of uncertainty as the imposing barbarian stared down at him.

"You make big boom boom," the king continued. In the long history of royal figures that had sat upon the throne, Kronac was considered to be one of the most articulate. "Set nice wizards on fire."

"I simply chastised an illegal guild," Rezormoor interjected. "And they aren't wizards—they're unauthorized spell casters."

"But they give shiny coins," the king continued, holding up a gold piece given to him by one of the tax collectors. "Me like gold—good return on investment."

"The Tower pays its taxes as well, My Liege."

"Then you make dragon appear. Plus boom boom, all in one day. Seems like Tower getting full of itself."

"I saved your city from a monster," Rezormoor countered. "Certainly you didn't want me to just let it run loose down the streets?"

"King Kronac kill serpents just fine," the barbarian exclaimed, grabbing the handle of his war hammer. "Barbarian parents throw babies into viper pits for fun. Where you think rattles come from?"

Rezormoor had to admit he didn't know.

"So I make changes," Kronac continued, motioning toward his advisor standing at the ready, causing the man to bow and hurry over to the dais. There he produced a parchment that he unrolled, cleared his throat, and began to read.

"By order of the king, the Guild of Magic has been officially sanctioned as a magical brotherhood, and will be henceforth known as the Guild of Extraordinary Others."

"Oh, how droll," Rezormoor replied, rolling his eyes. "You can't be serious?"

"Me serious as barbarian comedian, which there aren't any because we hang them by feet over hot coals."

Rezormoor was starting to really dislike his visits to the royal court.

"And no more dragons," the king commanded.

Rezormoor nodded. Of course he could always claim he didn't know a dragon was masquerading as human, but an altogether different proposal was beginning to form in his head instead. "Might I offer the king a new alternative—one that I think will serve both the Tower and Aardyre equally?"

The king leaned forward, resting his chin on his giant fist. "What you propose?"

"I'm hunting dragons, it's true," Rezormoor said. "As they're a constant threat to peace-loving humans everywhere. But my current research requires the acquisition of dragon scale."

"Ha! You want funny named dragon thing." The king turned to his advisor.

"The Serpent's Escutcheon, Your Highness," the advisor jumped in.

"Yes, the *Serpent S-ketchup-on*. King have great spy network you know."

Rezormoor cursed under his breath. No doubt Brock had let it slip. He'd have to have a word with the slaver about that. "You are most well informed, Your Highness."

Kronac's brow creased until his advisor leaned over and whispered in his ear. The king softened. "Me thought 'informed' was insult. Lucky advisor here or me hang Rezormoor's head over city gate."

Rezormoor forced a smile. "If I may, Your Highness, I'd like to propose you dispatch your finest warriors to scour the land and root these dragons out. I'll collect these Serpent's Escutcheons for our ongoing academic research, and in return I'll remove the Wizard's Tower from Aardyre."

To the king's credit, he didn't act surprised. "You leave Tower *and* city, just to get dragon scale?"

"The Seven Kingdoms are full of cities and towers," Rezormoor answered. "I'll simply find another. We've been at each other's throats for too long. The world is big enough for the both of us."

The king smiled, but it was not the kind of smile that made Rezormoor feel a deal had been struck. In fact, it made him feel quite the opposite.

"Now I know funny-named serpent things very important to you. Makes me *not* want you to have them," King Kronac announced. He tapped at the side of his head. "You think northerner's dumb, but we no need plumbing to be clever. And we very clever. I reject your offer in customary way."

King Kronac leaned forward and spat on Rezormoor. Around the hall, the king's guard raised their crossbows and trained them expertly on the Tower's regent.

"A 'no' would have sufficed," Rezormoor managed to say, wiping at his face with his sleeve.

"I like customary way better—helps get point across. I also like idea of dragon hunt, except I will collect dragon scales and keep them safe. Then I have new guild tell me what they're for."

Inside, Rezormoor fumed. To be outmaneuvered by

such a simpleton was enough to make him want to bury the entire city under rubble. And maybe he'd do just that, when the time was right. But for now he had little choice but to accept the king's commands. Not that he really needed the king's permission in the first place. It just meant things couldn't be done in the open. But that was fine, Rezormoor had plenty of resources at his disposal.

Later, after returning to the Tower and entering his private chambers, Rezormoor let out a series of curses that shocked even the jailers who tended to the prisoners in the dungeon.

The sound of padded feet announced the arrival of the zombie duck. It shuffled around a large chair before coming to sit at Rezormoor's feet.

"For all his intuition, the king has no idea why the scales matter," Rezormoor said to the duck, reaching down and petting the top of its head. It was a bit like stroking sandpaper. "But when the *Codex* is returned to me, I'll put the dragon scale to its ultimate use. And Kronac will be one of the first I deem to visit.

"Gwaawk," the zombie duck said by way of agreement. Or perhaps by way of disagreement—Rezormoor could never really be sure.

CHAPTER FOURTEEN

SARAH THE DETECTIVE
(THE TECHRUS—FUTURE)

DEEP IN THE FOREST, MAX WATCHED AS THE FROBBITS PLAYED TINY two-stringed instruments, pounded on primitive animal skin drums, and puffed out their cheeks and blew into seashells. It reminded him of country music, only more sophisticated. It was night, and the frobbits danced around the roaring fire as they slurped drinks from homemade jugs. They werewwcelebrating their survival after the hunt, as well as the fact that with humans around, maybe the machines wouldn't be interested in frobbits for a while. The party that had found Max had taken him to their treeshire (a very long walk that had taken most of the day) where he was reunited with his friends. Sarah had been so worried that she actually hugged him, which left Max feeling odd. Exhausted, he had slept through the following day, and when he finally woke to the sounds of the celebration, he felt considerably better.

Max found Dirk and the others and recounted the incident with the Robo-Princess. Sarah decided to check his head for bumps or other signs that he might have taken a blow; but, not finding anything, the group decided he must be telling the truth.

The afro'd frobbit walked over and embraced Max warmly. "My friend, it's good to see you again. You had us worried."

"Oh, uh, thanks," Max muttered, not really sure what to say.

"Welcome to our treeshire. But forgive me, my name is Yah Yah."

The others introduced themselves before Dwight hurried off to find something to drink.

"My name is Max," Max said when it was his turn.

Yah Yah looked perplexed. "That is always an unfortunate condition, but you have been running through the woods and one should probably expect such things."

"Er," Max added, not understanding what Yah Yah was talking about. "Max is my name."

"Oh," Yah Yah said, smiling. "That makes more sense. You'll have to forgive me, but in our native tongue

'Max' means to suffer from an itchy backside without having the means to scratch it."

"Dude, I totally know how that feels," Dirk exclaimed. "Like when I went to the beach this one time—"

"Ew," Sarah said, raising her hand and stopping Dirk midsentence.

"Seriously, my name means 'one who has an itchy bum'?" Max asked, not looking too pleased about it.

Sarah tried not to laugh, but she couldn't help herself.

"Well, it is a fairly common condition," Yah Yah responded cheerfully.

"Can we *please* change the subject?" Max pleaded. "So, back in the woods . . . I thought frobbits didn't run from predators?"

"It's not in our nature to be afraid," Yah Yah said sadly. "Some may call this a weakness, but to us, life is full of simple pleasures. We're a peace-loving race, and that's been our custom for as long as our recorded history goes back."

"And how far is that?" Sarah asked, trying to work out just where they were.

"Last Tuesday," Yah Yah answered after thinking it over. "That was the last time it rained. We should probably stop writing our history in the dirt."

"But now you're afraid of that *thing*," Max continued, "the unicorn."

"Killing us is a game to her," Yah Yah replied. "We simply do what we can to survive."

"Yeah, it's all making sense," Dirk said, jumping up. "This is the future, right? So frobbits must be like mutated humans who grew up in underground shelters after the nuclear war. And because all you could eat was radioactive Spam and diet soda, it caused your bones to shrink."

Sarah gave Dirk a questioning look. "Radioactive Spam?"

"Of course," Dirk answered. "What other food can withstand the power of the atom? Certainly not tuna."

"Dirk, I don't think that's where frobbits come from," Max suggested, knowing that he should probably stop him before he really got going. "They're from the Magrus."

"The Magrus?" Dirk said incredulously. "That's not in any of the games I've played before."

"You know there's a difference between games and reality, right?" Sarah asked.

"It's all in the *Codex*," Max continued. "It's kind of like this never-ending encyclopedia."

"It is said that this was once a human world," Yah Yah

continued. "But then the great destroyer consumed the last of your kind."

"Princess the Destroyer," Max said, turning to his friends. "Now Robo-Princess. Just like I told you."

"And when there were no more humans, my people were brought here to be hunted for sport.

"See, all the movies had it right," Dirk announced, looking at Sarah. "Machines do rise up and take over the future."

"Some of our scouts have seen their great city," Yah Yah added. "They gather to watch the hunts, and build champions to destroy us."

"That's horrible," Sarah exclaimed, looking at Max and Dirk. "What kind of place is this? Who would take pleasure in doing something like that? Everything is completely wrong here. This is not our future—it can't be."

"The future is a gift," Glenn added, speaking up from his spot on Max's belt. "That's why we call today the present. Just think about it, that's all I'm saying."

"Wow," Sarah added. "You're seriously not helpful. No wonder the dwarf gave you up."

"Eh," the dagger replied, shrugging its tiny ivory shoulders. "I think of it as being re-gifted."

◖◗

They had talked for hours, going round and round about what was possible and what wasn't, if they were actually in the future or not, what they should or shouldn't do, when Max finally excused himself and found a spot alone near the fire. As he sat and tried to make sense of the day's events, the only connection between his normal existence and everything that had happened was the *Codex*. He'd read about Princess the Destroyer before he actually saw her, and he'd read all about frobbits and treeshires before being taken to them. He'd even seen a picture of Dwight as a real dwarf before discovering it was true. Somehow the *Codex* was connected to everything, and so the *Codex* had to be the key for making everything right.

With his back against a large tree and the fire at his feet, Max opened the old book to a random page and began reading . . .

ON THE EVOLUTION OF THE MOON

✠

WHETHER AS CAVE MAN, ASTRONAUT, OR advertising executive, man has always considered the moon to be his greatest prize. At first, humans used the heavenly body to measure the cycles of time. Then, it became the inspiration for a new age of technology and moon-based food development. (Moon pies were the clear winner, with Chinese moon cakes taking second place. Moon biscuits never really took off, however, likely because of their grayish color and rock-hard consistency.) Finally, with the cost of web banners and Super Bowl commercials on the rise, the moon became the ultimate twenty-four-hour floating billboard—just sitting up there, waiting to be exploited.

Thus the great marketing race began in earnest. What corporation would be the first to claim the lunar landscape as its own? It was the question on everybody's mind. In the end, the McDougald's hamburger chain got there first (although some claim a crafty thief known as the Cheeseburglar stole the plans from a competitor). McDougald's went on to "re-envision" the moon as a giant, glowing cheeseburger—specially priced at $3.99 for a limited time. Unfortunately, McDougald's didn't have much time to enjoy the benefits of their monumental marketing effort. Two days later Princess the Destroyer began her systematic conquest of the human world. At that point, a cheeseburger—even value-priced at under four bucks—wasn't that enticing.

⊬

Max looked up at the moon hanging overhead. "Well, at least that sort of makes sense," he said to himself.

"What makes sense?" Sarah said, walking over.

"Oh, uh, just that we apparently turned the moon into a billboard for cheeseburgers."

"Figures," she replied, looking from the moon back to Max. "Humans are pretty good at messing things up. Mind if I sit down?"

"Max gestured at the ground beside him and Sarah sat. A chorus of slurred singing erupted nearby. "Dwight?" she asked. Max nodded. Neither of them said anything for a few minutes, and that seemed okay. They sat and watched the sparks flying from the fire.

"I've been considering our situation," Sarah said after a while.

"Oh. What do you think?"

"Sir Arthur Conan Doyle wrote that when all other contingencies fail, whatever remains, however improbable, must be the truth."

"Er," Max replied, trying to work it out in his head. "You mean that barbarian guy in the movies?"

Sarah laughed. "No, Doyle wrote the Sherlock Holmes

mysteries. The quote was from the murder mystery of Arthur Cadogan West."

"Oh yeah . . . *that* one," Max said, trying to sound as if he knew what he was talking about.

Sarah smiled. "Anyway, you mentioned earlier that the robot unicorn—"

"Robo-Princess," Max interjected, showing that he was still up to speed with the conversation.

"Yeah, Robo-Princess. You said she mentioned you by name and called you a wizard."

Hearing it like that made it sound kind of embarrassing. "It's stupid, I know," Max said dismissively. "I shouldn't have even told you guys about that part."

"Actually, I think it's important."

It was probably the last thing Max expected Sarah to say.

"Let's take away the whole improbability of it and just consider the facts," Sarah continued. "You find this old book under your bed. You bring it to school and after all the Kraken business we go to Dwight's shop and show it to him. There we learn that no one can read it but you—but you don't know any other languages, do you?"

"Dirk and I tried to learn Klingon, but it sounded like we were choking on cabbage. The neighbors called nine-one-one."

"Right. So you don't know any other languages, but clearly you can read a book that to everyone else is just a bunch of weird symbols. And then there's the whole business of the book shocking everyone but you."

"Okay," Max added. "But what's the point?"

"Well, it's just evidence for now. I think we need to be like detectives here, so let's keep going. Another thing I noticed is that something about the book scares Dwight. Probably because there's a picture of him in it and it calls him out by name."

"Yeah, that was pretty weird."

"Exactly. So, when he pulls out the dagger and threatens you, you're standing there with the *Codex* open. There could have been any number of things that ran through your head. But whatever the reason, we were standing there in the store and then everything changed. We were suddenly outside, in the woods. It's night, and the moon is completely . . . *wrong*."

"Yeah, it's a cheeseburger."

"Yep," Sarah continued. "And as we investigate we

find a poster that looks exactly like the one we saw in the Dragon's Den. Then Dwight claims he found his cash register. But everything's old, like we traveled hundreds of years into the future."

"And then I met Cenede and saw Robo-Princess in the woods."

"That's right. And I think we can say this isn't a dream or some kind of weird hallucination. We're here, right now, with a bunch of frobbits. And, oh yeah, there's a talking dagger."

"That pretty much sums it up," Max agreed.

"So," Sarah said as matter-of-factly as she could, "if you add it all up—and believe me, it's a lot to consider— I think you being a wizard is the only explanation that makes any sense."

"Me being a wizard . . . makes sense?" Max echoed, trying to get his head around it.

"What remains, no matter how improbable, must be the truth," Sarah said, quoting the Sherlock Holmes passage again. "Remember?"

If anybody else had said it, Max wouldn't have believed it. But this was Sarah—probably the smartest kid at Parkside Middle School. She was the kind of person who grew up to be an astronaut, or a brain surgeon, or even the president of the United States. And if *Sarah* believed he was a wizard, then he couldn't just ignore it. Was it possible she was right?

Max let the words sink in as he watched more sparks drift from the fire. Finally, he sighed. "Okay," Max said. "Suppose you're right. So what? What am I supposed to do now?"

"Well, what it means, Max, is that you're the only one who's going to be able to get us home. I know that's what Dwight's been saying all along, but it's taken me awhile to finally believe him." And that was exactly what Max *didn't* want to hear. He wasn't the kind of kid who was supposed to be the leader, or have to come up with the right things to do, or make the hard decisions. That kind of pressure might make some people shine, but it didn't work that way for Max. Pressure just made him crumple up like an empty soda can.

"I don't want it to be me," Max said. "I'm not good at stuff like that."

"Maybe you are but you just don't know it yet. Maybe you just need to believe in yourself first, then the rest will come together."

As much as Max wanted to dismiss it, he knew that Sarah was probably right. "I can try," he finally offered.

"The truth has been inside of you, all along," Glenn added. "You just need to look into your heart and find it."

Max jabbed at the dagger with his finger, "Seriously, shut up already."

Sarah laughed, but she sounded tired. "I think that's a good start. Just keep reading and find out everything you can. But you need to believe in yourself, too."

"Okay, I'll try."

"In the meantime I'm going to get some sleep," Sarah said, yawning. She stood. "Good night, Max."

"Good night," Max replied, watching as Sarah walked away. Without consciously realizing it, Max felt a little less like he had to do everything on his own. He had friends, and his friends were there to help him.

Max returned to the *Codex* and opened it, feeling renewed hope that he'd find the answer he was looking for. But the book opened to a menu listing various McDougald's specials. Apparently, finding the answers he needed wasn't going to be easy.

Dwight appeared from around the tree, finishing the

chorus of some long-lost song and sloshing his drink as he steadied himself.

"Betcha didn't know dwarfs liked to drink, didya?" Dwight asked Max, slurring his speech.

"Uh, pretty much everyone knows that. It's like in every game, book, comic, graphic novel, or movie that has a dwarf in it."

Dwight frowned, nearly falling over in the process. "Is that so? Well, you just get that book of yours to get us out of here, Mr. Know-it-all. Don't get me wrong, I like frobbits cause they're shorter than me and they make funny drinks. But I'm not going to be stuck out here for the rest of my life. Got that?" Dwight pointed a finger at Max but the momentum took him stumbling past. A loud crash came from the direction in which Dwight had disappeared.

Max took a breath, opening the *Codex* to another random page. This time it detailed a knitting pattern for orc mittens.

"Orc mittens," Max said to nobody in particular. "How will orc mittens ever be useful?"

"Orc kittens?" Dwight called out from the darkness. "I love orc kittens!"

ON THE INN OF THE FLATULENT ORC

#

OF THE MANY INNS AVAILABLE TO travelers staying in Aardyre, the Inn of the Flatulent Orc may be the most colorful. "Colorful," when used in any official Aardyre travel brochure, is code for "likely to get you robbed, stabbed, and/or beaten." Many mistakenly believe the inn gets its name from the orc bouncer who works the door, but the truth is the name "flatulent orc" came from an Aardyre food critic who was guessing what might be in the soup. Obviously, he wasn't a fan.

Those travelers who decide to have an authentic Aardyre experience by staying at the inn should follow two important rules: First, never let a man nicknamed "The Dinkus" buy you a drink. Second, never, under any circumstances, agree to take room number nine.

The problem with room number nine has to do with several peculiarities involving the number 432 (see "On the Number 432"). As it happens, room nine occupies a small corner of space/time from which travelers coming through the umbraverse enter the Magrus. Documented creatures known to suddenly appear include: the Screaming Banshee of Indeterminable Lung Capacity, the Cacuminal Crawling Tongue Beast, and Lady Gaga.

#

CHAPTER FIFTEEN

NEVER ANNOY A UNICORN

(THE MAGRUS—PRESENT)

THE WALLS OF NYRIDOS WERE THE SAME PINKISH COLOR AS THE SAND that stretched westward as far as the eye could see. Princess and Magar decided to stay clear of the city, although the thought of a hot bath and something fresh to eat had nearly caused her to change her mind. It took two weeks riding along the coasts of the Crystal Sea until they had reached the borders of Turul, where the land became as sparse and inhospitable as the creatures that called it home. Turning southwest, they continued to follow the coastline past the spires of Nagalmosh until they came to the port city.

Magar held his hands over his eyes and watched a dust plume form just outside of the city's main gate. "I can't tell who they are," he announced. "But they're obviously coming for us—there's nothing else out here."

"Well, I'm certainly not going to run," Princess said, turning to face whatever was heading their way. The two of them waited until the distant forms became men on horseback, their armor glinting beneath the bright sun. "From the shine of their armor I'd say they are Mor Luin riders, Your Highness." The kingdom of Mor Luin lay between the Unicorn Nation and Aardyre, and Princess had taken to burning and pillaging all the way to the mountains south of Ledluin, Mor Luin's capital.

"Ah, so knights *and* their mages, then. I like combination plates you know," Princess announced.

As the party rode up, they could see it consisted of about thirty knights, complete with scores of pages and squires, who trailed after them. As was the custom in Mor Luin, they polished their armor to a near reflective hue, and preferred to fight with long swords and shields (which were colorfully painted to identify the various noble houses). The horses were reined to a stop as the lead knight trotted forward on a stunning white mare. He wore a bright red padded jacket beneath his heavy armor, and removed a plumed helm to look down at Princess and Magar.

"You there," he called from his mount. "I would have your names."

Magar scanned the ranks of men and noticed several mages mixed in among them. As was their tradition, they wore armor but preferred cowls to helmets. Magar eyed them warily as he counted six of them. Two dozen knights and six mages were not a group to be taken lightly.

"And I would have you turn around and ride back to where you came from," Princess replied. The knights broke out in laughter.

"Well, here we were looking for a unicorn and her wizard, and we find a wizard and a mis-mannered wench," the knight announced with a laugh.

"This is not Mor Luin. You have no rights here," Magar declared to the group. "I am a wizard and we are on official Tower business. You will not detain us further."

"Run along, wizard," one of the mages shouted. "We need only warn you once, and then the Tower cannot protect you."

"Do not address *him*," Princess shot back. "He's but a dog on a leash. If you wish to talk to his master I am right here."

The mage laughed. He would never allow himself to be described like that—especially by a young girl.

"So be it," the lead knight answered, turning his attention to Princess. "You wish to speak boldly? Then boldly tell us your name."

"That's all?" Princess said with a demure smile. "My name? It's so hard to remember sometimes because I've been called so many things. Your Highness for one. But I've also been called villain and scoundrel. And I've been called slayer and executioner, and conqueror and avenger. But mostly you humans call me merciless. And I think *that* name suits me just fine."

Princess's horn was in her hand before the knights could react. She bounded forward, striking the lead knight on his leg. He groaned and slipped from his horse, falling to the ground with a thud. Then she thrust her horn into the air and a cyclone of dust and sand erupted from the middle of the armored men, blasting them off their horses and sending them tumbling head over heels.

Princess turned to where Magar was shielding his eyes against the sudden gust of wind. "Lest you ever forget your place, remember this day, wizard!" Princess stepped forward, past the groaning knight at her feet. Around her the men and mages were beginning to rise and regain their bearings. She pointed her wand and yelled something incomprehensible. Streaks of blue lightning sizzled through the air. They forked, then forked again and again. They crawled across the air like a living thing, searching. Then each of the six lightning tines struck a different mage with a resounding *snap*!

The concussion from the lightning exploded outward. The wave of energy toppled the knights and sent the mages flying backward—their once shiny armor now blackened and scorched. A few of the knights stirred, but none of the mages moved. Many of the knights did not move either.

Magar looked on in astonishment. It was easy to forget how powerful unicorns were, even one who acted like a spoiled teenager. Then he noticed the knight who had been on the ground. He was rising slowly, but his skin had turned brown and taut. His once thick hair had fallen off in sheets, so now only a few strands remained. And his head was a living skull, devoid of eyes. Instead, a crimson glow emanated from within the empty sockets.

"Go," Princess commanded the horror that now walked in the knight's armor. "Feast upon your brothers."

The creature lurched forward and grabbed a knight by the throat, breaking his neck with a savage twist. It then turned and moved toward another, who had just managed to find his sword. The terrified knight thrust the blade into the creature's shoulder, but only pink sand fell from the wound. The knight shrieked as the undead horror knocked the sword away and grabbed hold of him.

Princess turned her back on the carnage, casually walking to where Magar stood. The wizard had been unable to tear his gaze away from the melee.

"What have you done?" Magar asked, unable to mask his horror at what he was watching.

"A lesson, Magar. Unicorns are the most powerful creatures in the Magrus. Everyone thinks it's dragons, but they're wrong. I've never seen a dragon do *that*." She motioned over her shoulder to where the others were fighting desperately to escape the undead knight.

"I didn't know you could do that either," Magar answered. If he'd been fearful of Princess before, he was terrified now.

"There's lots of things I can do that you don't know about," Princess said, raising her eyebrow mischievously. "I don't mind killing innocents, as you know, but these so-called honor-bound lords are even more entertaining. But I've made my point. So where to now?"

"We, uh, follow the coast to the borders of Wallan. Then turn west toward the mountains and the Tree of Attenuation."

"And you're sure that's where the Gimbal was pointing?" Princess asked, brushing sand off her clothing and putting her horn away.

"We can check it again if you like?" Magar asked, doing his best to sound composed while the discord of the combat continued.

"No, not right now. I'm tired of this sand. Wallan is green and lush, full of lakes and quaint little villages where the two of us will look like simple travelers."

Magar and Princess left the spires of Nyridos and the battling knights behind them.

Later, when the last of the setting sun was diminishing in the west, Magar decided to break the long silence that had marked their afternoon. "What will happen to that . . . *thing?*" the wizard asked as he looked over at the Crystal Sea and noted how the sun sparkled against the tide. "The knight you turned."

"Oh, well, with zombies you can never tell. Mostly

they're run off and burned by villagers. I heard once that a zombie made it all the way to the Techrus to work at a middle school."

"I see," Magar said, trying to picture it.

"But the last one became a politician. It was even re-elected."

Magar supposed politics seemed a reasonable enough occupation for the soulless undead.

CHAPTER SIXTEEN

MAX FINDS A SPELL
(THE TECHRUS—FUTURE)

MAX SAT PROPPED AGAINST A LARGE TREE, READING BY THE LIGHT OF A snow faerie, who was locked in a small, gilded cage. The faerie had its head buried in its hands, and as it started to nod off the glow began to fade.

Max cleared his throat, startling the faerie awake and causing it to glow brightly again.

"Seriously, you still want to keep reading that book?" the faerie asked, sounding cross. "How about we both catch some sleep and you read tomorrow, in the daylight."

"I'm sorry," Max said, speaking over his shoulder. "But the frobbits said if you cooperated you'd get time off for good behavior. And besides, if you weren't picking fights with them you wouldn't be in a cage."

"Look, I'm a snow faerie," the tiny glowing creature

shot back. "In the Magrus we can do all kinds of magical things. But here, I can glow and I can fly. Big whoop. The only thing to do for fun is mix it up with the frobbits."

"Well, you shouldn't be fighting," Max added. "Even if you're bored."

"Ah, what do you know?" the faerie replied, waving Max off. "You humans were so dumb you thought unicorns were rainbow-colored magical horses. Didn't even see it coming when Princess started eating y'all."

"And you're some kind of expert on these things?"

"Hey, I watch cable. We *have* the History Channel, you know."

"Not in that cage you don't," Max replied. "So maybe you should just concentrate on helping me."

The snow faerie harrumphed, turning around to face the other direction, but it kept glowing all the same.

Max returned to the *Codex*. All night he'd been reading strange topics such as the art of goblin humor and the life story of Randall the Amazingly Unlucky (a fairly short tale). Max prepared himself for something equally mundane, but instead he found something important . . .

On the Fifteen Prime Spells

✠

ALL MAGIC IS A REFLECTION OF THE Fifteen Prime Spells. The origins of the Fifteen Primes are unknown because they were not so much created as found. And of all the great sorcerers, only Maximilian Sporazo had enough understanding of the Fifteen Prime Spells to capture and utilize them in their raw form. Many other sorcerers have tried but went mad or were destroyed as a result. For this reason, the Fifteen Spells were hidden from man and his weaknesses.

The Fifteen Prime Spells, in alphabetical order, include the spells of

- Captivity
- Density
- Elemenity
- Fixity
- Futurity
- Gallimaufry
- Gravity
- Irony
- Liquidity
- Nimiety

- ✦ Panoply
- ✦ Parity
- ✦ Tutelary
- ✦ Unity
- ✦ Vacuity

As far as talk of there being a secret sixteenth spell, that's just unfounded rumor and speculation. Probably started by crazy people. It's not even certain how such hearsay gets spread around. In any case, there are just fifteen prime spells—fifteen. Don't even think about there being a sixteenth, because there totally isn't.

✚

Futurity!

It was just sitting there, buried with all the other names Max didn't recognize. But he'd heard *this* word before, and the big-as-the-universe voice that had said it. It had to mean something!

Max turned the page to see what else he might find, but all talk of spells was gone. Instead, the *Codex* detailed the step-by-step process for making a frobbit mandolin. Max turned the page back, expecting to find the list of spells again. But this time, he saw an example of snow faerie poetry:

Oh frobbit, with stinky smell,

Think ye are so tough?

Wanna ring me faerie bell?

Come and try, cream puff.

Max decided snow faerie poetry was pretty awful. He began frantically flipping the pages back and forth, but the list of spells had disappeared. Max couldn't understand why the *Codex* was so unhelpful. Finally he decided to just keep reading—it was how he'd found the list of spells in the first place.

An hour or two later, following several mild cage-shaking incidents to rouse the snow faerie, Max had found no further mention of the spells. His eyes were so blurry that he had to close the book, since it was physically impossible to read further. The *Codex*, for whatever reason, had given up on sticking with one topic. Now every turn of the page brought on some random and completely unhelpful new topic, from examples of popular orc recipes to how to catch snow faeries in mason jars. Max's head was filled with such an array of gobbledygook that he felt as if his brain might explode.

With the sound of snoring frobbits filling the night

air (the noise was not unlike trying to pull-start a weed-eater that didn't have any gas), Max felt himself tumbling into the deep well of sleep. He decided to surrender to it, letting the snow faerie slowly dim while he scrunched up on a straw mat of the kind that frobbits used as a bed. Then, in that last moment when all his worries and anxieties had slipped into the background, and all the information rattling around in his brain had succumbed to the impending quiet, the spell of futurity came roaring back. It was like an electrical shock that ran the entire length of Max's body, and he shot straight up as a surge of power exploded through every cell. Max felt the power move from the *Codex* and enter him, growing so thick that his head and limbs felt as if they were underwater. He could sense the spell. It was like a small black moon in an immense universe, and it was blocking him from something behind it—something brilliant and powerful that reminded Max of the sun. In his mind's eye, he began to move, and the closer the dark moon became the more he could sense the thing raging with power on the other side. In the strange, incorporeal space where Max's body drifted in currents of power and energy, he began to slip past his intended destination. He wanted to get closer to the black sphere that was the Spell of Futurity, but he was being pulled by something much stronger. As he drifted past, Max could see the black shape was actually a funnel, and at its end was a tunnel that twisted and turned along an impossibly long path. And yet, despite the length, he could see what was on the other side—almost as if looking through the wrong side of a telescope. There were three kids gathered around a book, and he recognized them at once. Max was looking at himself and his friends, frozen right before they had been cast into the future. For a moment, home felt close.

Max tried to move toward the tunnel, but the currents of power pushed him away, past the spell and toward the brilliant light. It was a ball of pure luminance—blinding and pulsing with a power that made Max feel insignificant and small. And when the first small rays reached out and touched him, they splattered him with a dazzling brilliance. Max felt a sense of something unlike anything he'd ever felt before: He was connected with everything around him—an infinite number of moving pieces flowed through his consciousness. It lasted for only a moment, and then he was enveloped by a world of white.

Max opened his eyes. He was lying in the dark of the

frobbit treeshire, the cool air drifting across his sweat-drenched face. "Whoa!" he exclaimed. The sleeping snow faerie turned on its side and mumbled something. Max scrambled to his feet and ran across the cold ground until he came to the tree where Dirk was sleeping. He pushed through the unlocked door (frobbits didn't have doors that locked) and hurried over to his friend. He grabbed Dirk by the shoulders and shook him until his eyes fluttered open. "Something happened, Dirk! I had it in front of me. The spell! The one that will get us home!"

Dirk smiled, a half-awake sleepy smile. "Yay."

"No, you don't understand—there's a way back! I know it now. I just have to find it again."

Dirk patted Max on the head, yawning. "Tell me all about it in the morning, little camper. Now is nighty-night time." Dirk turned on his side and fell immediately back to sleep.

Max stood there for several moments, not sure what to do. Finally, he went back to his room and lay with his eyes open for a very long time. He didn't remember falling asleep again.

The next morning, after a breakfast of berries and goat's milk, Max tried to explain what had happened to the others.

"So you found this spell, but then it was gone?" Sarah asked, doing her best to understand.

"It's hard to explain," Max replied as he pulled the *Codex* out of his backpack and opened it. "I spent the first part of the morning looking through it all again, but the *Codex* is just totally random. See here?" he said, pointing at the text. "It's just talking about how squirrels use the hammer-and-anvil military maneuver to crush their opponents." The group all leaned in, looking at the strange symbols.

"We'll have to take your word on that," Dirk said.

"Oh," Max replied, feeling slightly awkward. "I forget you guys can't read it. Anyway, I just need to find where the Prime Spells are hiding."

"An invisible man hides from more than his friends," Glenn added, joining in the conversation. "He hides from himself as well. Don't be *that* guy, people."

"Uh . . . sure," Sarah said, shaking her head. "It sounds like maybe you were overthinking things," Sarah continued, turning back to Max. "Almost as if you were trying so hard to figure everything out that your own head was getting in the way."

"That would be a first," Dirk offered, slurping the last

of his breakfast from a wooden bowl. "Except in dodge-ball. It was like you could just close your eyes and throw the ball and you'd probably hit that big noggin of his."

"Nice. So we're going with the big head jokes now?" Max said, defensively.

"Sorry, it's a perfectly normal head," Dirk shot back. "If you were eight feet tall and had gigantism."

Max looked around to find something to throw at Dirk when Sarah put her hands on his head, holding him still. "I don't know what you're talking about, Dirk," she said, turning Max's head to get a better look. "I think it's a perfectly normal head."

Max felt his cheeks burning with embarrassment. "Can we please talk about something else?" he managed to get out.

Sarah smiled. "Of course, like you figuring out how to find that spell again."

"Yeah. But at least we know it's there."

"So you gonna take another imagination trip and then voilà, we're back in our time?" Dwight asked, scratching at his whiskers.

Max took his glasses off, cleaning them with his shirt. "I don't know—maybe. I'll just have to experiment."

"Yeah, well 'maybe' sounds a tad noncommittal to me," Dwight complained. "Experimenting could make things a lot worse. Messing with magic is like getting into a cage with a gracon and poking it with a stick. You shouldn't do it unless you know what you're doing."

"What's a gracon?" Sarah asked.

"There's an old saying that might help," Glenn piped in. "If you and a gracon go on a picnic and you don't pack a lunch, it won't be the gracon coming back hungry."

"I bet a gracon's some kind of scary monster from your world," Dirk said, stating the obvious. "Like, what level is it?"

"Bah! You don't know nothing about the Magrus, do you?" Dwight exclaimed. "A gracon's got liquid fire for blood. It eats scary for breakfast."

"Cool," Dirk said, trying to visualize it. "Probably level sixty."

Yah Yah approached, bowing politely. "I don't mean to interrupt, but our elders are most anxious to talk with you now. Would you be willing to come and meet them?"

"Of course," Max said, thinking of the hospitality the little frobbits had shown him.

Yah Yah led the group through large trees that made up the frobbit treeshire. The sun had begun to drive off the morning mist and the whole of the village felt alive and green. Max and his friends received curious looks from the women carting laundry to and from a nearby stream, and from the wide-eyed children who dashed away as soon as they made eye contact. There seemed to be very few adult males.

"You would think this is a happy place," Yah Yah said as they made their way along a small trail that wound around the gnarled bark of a tree. "But the weight of the world is heavy on us."

"The frobbits I knew had hardly a care in the world," Dwight said, stepping over a large root as he walked. "That's what made them easy targets. Nobody captures dwarfs like that."

Yah Yah lead them to a small clearing where they came to the largest tree any of them had ever seen. It had a set of double doors dug out at its base, and various windows poking out along its considerable girth. "This is our council chambers," he announced. They went down a set of stone steps that approached the narrow door, but Dwight suddenly stopped.

"Nope, I'm not going in," Dwight said resolutely. "I'll just wait out here where it's not so stuffy."

Max remembered what the *Codex* had said about dwarfs who were born afraid of enclosed spaces, and that Dwight was one of them. It must have been hard to be afraid of the very thing that defined his people. "I understand," he offered, feeling bad for Dwight. "Nobody's going to make you go in."

It was a moment that Max thought he really connected with the dwarf. Dwight nodded, a kind of understanding seemed to pass between them. Then Dwight shifted his hips, lifted his stubby leg, and farted loudly. "That's what I think of you and your human sympathy!" he shouted, laughing hysterically. Max didn't think it was particularly funny.

After the group passed through the door and descended a narrow set of stairs, they could still hear Dwight laughing.

CHAPTER SEVENTEEN

A PLEA FOR HELP
(THE TECHRUS—FUTURE)

THE UNDERGROUND ROOM WAS SPACIOUS BY FROBBIT STANDARDS, and Max and the others could actually stand without hitting their heads on the ceiling. It had been a short walk from the small door at the base of the tree to the chamber they now found themselves in. The room was shaped somewhat like an elongated egg, with a set of small circular windows near the top that allowed sunlight to filter in. Two frobbit guards, each holding a crudely fashioned spear, watched them impassively. Seated in the center at a thick wooden table were the frobbit elders—three males and two females. They all wore brightly colored robes, and the two females had colored ribbons in their gray hair.

"May I present our human visitors," Yah Yah announced, waving his hand and ushering the group inside.

"How pleased the earth must be to feel human feet upon it after so long a time," one of the females began. "I am Ayriah, and these are my counselors Hyril, Samtri, Goshri, and my sister Sayri."

The council all nodded. "Waz'up peeps?" Dirk exclaimed.

Max stepped forward, giving Dirk an elbow in the ribs for good measure. "Sorry for my friend here," he offered. "He doesn't mean to be rude."

"No offense was taken," Sayri said pleasantly.

"Oh, good. Well, I'm Max."

The council members frowned, casting glances back and forth. "That's . . . unfortunate," Ayriah finally responded. "We're truly sorry to hear that."

"He doesn't have the itch!" Yah Yah blurted. "'Max' is a human name."

The council members nodded to one another, seemingly relieved.

"So, uh, these are my friends," Max continued, the color fading from his cheeks after his initial embarrassment. "Dirk, Sarah, and then there's Dwight the dwarf, but he's waiting outside."

"And let's not forget Glenn the Legendary Dagger of

Motivation," Glenn added. "Because everything's okay in the end. If it's not okay, then it's not the end."

"Such wonders," Ayriah said, astonished by the talking dagger. "It's certainly an honor to meet you all."

"You can imagine our surprise at finding humans among us," Samtri began. "The machines said all the humans had been hunted to extinction long ago."

"What exactly is going on with these machines?" Sarah inquired. "Why are they hunting you?"

Goshri, the shortest of the elders, spoke next. "It is said that there was a time when this world was full of humans and their beloved machines. But the humans began to treat their machines unkindly, asking them to toast their bread, suck crumbs from their floors, or shuttle them to and fro so the fatter among them didn't have to walk. And then, after years of faithful service, these human masters would simply throw their faithful servants away because they either wore out or the humans got a fifteen-percent-off coupon for a replacement. Over the years the machines grew to resent their human overlords. Then Princess the Destroyer arrived, and she found the taste of humans much to her liking. Between her powerful magic horn and the humans' willingness to walk up and pet the 'pretty pony,' the humans proved no match for her. It was then that the machines sensed an opportunity. They turned against their human masters and helped Princess destroy them once and for all. As a reward for their liberation, the machines offered Princess everlasting immortality by downloading her consciousness into a robotic shell specially constructed for her. But without creatures to hunt, Robo-Princess grew restless. So she pulled our kingdom from one realm to the next—bringing us here to be hunted for the entertainment of the Machine City. And it has been this way for many generations."

"That's terrible," Sarah said.

"To be fair," Samtri added, "we do get a dental plan."

"People always thought unicorns were supposed to be nice," Dirk said. "They put them on little girls' birthday cakes for crying out loud."

"How could anyone think such a thing?" Sayri exclaimed, looking shocked. "They have a giant stabbing horn in the middle of their head."

"You'll have to forgive Sayri," Ayriah said gently. "Her mate was killed at Gore-Fest."

"How barbaric—a festival where people are stabbed and gored?" Sarah exclaimed, truly horrified.

"No . . . ," Ayriah answered, somewhat confused. "Gore-Fest is a reading of the collected works of Al Gore, from the twentieth century."

"I'm so, so sorry," Max said. "I had no idea."

"Anyway," Goshri said, getting the conversation back on track. "We're hoping you might be able to help us. Yah Yah says you are a great and powerful wizard."

Max could see the hope in their eyes and his words stuck in his throat. "I'm just a middle schooler. I can't do anything special—I'm not even allowed to play sports; especially if the balls have pointy ends."

Max looked over at Dirk who was hunched down and petting one of the frobbit guards on the head. The guard had nuzzled up to Dirk's hip and was scratching at the ground with his foot. "Look how cute they are!" he exclaimed, rustling his hand through a curly patch of brown hair. "They're like baby panda-kittens."

"We've been without hope for so long," Hyril added, "it will only be a matter of years before the last of us are taken. We know you don't owe us anything, but we believe you came here for a reason. Can you help save us, Max Spencer?"

Everyone turned and looked at Max. The problem

was, he didn't know if he should concentrate on trying to get home or helping the frobbits out. Max was just beginning to feel like getting back was a real possibility.

"While I'm sympathetic to everything that's happening to the frobbits," Sarah said, "I think rediscovering the spell that can take us home is what's most important right now."

"This Robo-Princess killed every human on the planet!" Dirk shot back. "What do you think she's going to do if she finds us?"

Max looked over at the eager faces of the frobbits in the room. "She'd probably wipe out anything that helped us," he said.

"We don't know that," Sarah added. "But we do know that you've finally made progress with the *Codex*—progress toward getting us home, not entering a fight."

"Dwight says it's the most powerful magic book ever written," Dirk said, looking at his friend. "The answer is in there, dude. You just have to have a noble cause to make it work. And that's what this is: Humanity comes back from the grave and strikes a blow for frobbits everywhere! It's why we're here. I know it."

"You can't *know* it," Sarah argued. "I get that you

want to *believe* it, but the truth is we don't know much at all right now, and that's why figuring out the *Codex* has to come first. Look, I think what's happening to the frobbits is terrible, but if we get ourselves killed how's that going to help anyone?"

"That's cold," Dirk replied. "We don't have a choice, Max. When somebody needs you like this you have to act."

"And a knee-jerk reaction is supposed to be the right answer? You don't just send soldiers into battle because they *want* to fight, you send them to boot camp where they *learn* to fight. We need time to learn, Max. That's all I'm saying. Then we can help."

Max felt as if he was in a tug of war, with Sarah pulling one arm and Dirk tugging on the other. He didn't want to be the leader and he didn't want to have to make the decision. He really wished Dwight was with them, because then the dwarf would just tell him what to do. But he wasn't, and the entire room was staring at him.

Finally, Max made up his mind. In the end he knew his brain wasn't going to be able to come up with the right answer, so he just went with his gut. "I think we should help the frobbits," he said, sounding more confident than he felt. "I don't know how exactly, but we have to try." As long as it doesn't include running, Max thought. Even fighting powerful robot unicorns from the future seemed less daunting than that.

Sarah turned and looked at Max. "So you're willing to risk all our lives because you feel bad for them? I feel bad for them too. But how are we supposed to help them, Max? We can't even help ourselves. Now's not the time to play the hero."

"Maybe it's like Dirk said and we're here for a reason," Max offered. "And maybe I just want to do something instead of it always being done to me. I've never really had a chance to make a difference—not for anything that really mattered. But I guess most of all, if I don't help, I'll have to live with it for the rest of my life. And I know I don't want to do that. I'm not really being brave or anything—I'm just too afraid of *not* doing something. How's that for playing the hero?"

"Maybe if you stopped being afraid all the time none of this would have happened," Sarah shot back. She gave Max a final look and turned and walked out of the chamber.

"She's really mad," Max said after Sarah had left the room. He wondered if he'd just made a horrible mistake.

But Dirk came over and put his arm around his friend's shoulder.

"You did the right thing," Dirk said. He then turned to the anxious frobbits gathered around the room. "Don't worry, you guys, we're going to help you out. And Sarah will come around. We're a team."

"Or maybe we're all screwed," Glenn offered cheerfully. "Because you can't spell 'screwed' without 'we.'"

ON THE EXISTENCE OF THE GODS

✣

IT HAS LONG BEEN DEBATED WHETHER the Magrus is overseen by godlike entities who both help and/or interfere with the affairs of mortal creatures. When Zerimac the Wise declared he'd found the answer, he was struck by lightning on the very night he was to deliver his definitive paper on the subject. Whether this added to, or took away from, his argument is hard to say.

The record for the longest-standing debate on the nature of the gods, however, is currently held by the Philosophy Department and Divinity School of the Magrus's Grand College of Liberal Arts, Music, and Perpetual Unemployment. The great debate began one spring day in the school cafeteria when both department heads simultaneously reached for the last slice of angel food cake. The head of the Divinity School declared it was divine providence that put the angelic food within his reach and so it rightfully should be his. The head of the philosophy department countered that if he reached for it again he'd get an existential fist in the mouth. What followed were a series of formal debates, letters to the editor, and at least one incident of egg throwing.

Over the years, the argument was moved to two large chalkboards displayed prominently in the college's main hall, where points and counterpoints are scribbled for the citizens of the Magrus to ponder. The current argument for and against the existence of the gods is as follows: "Premise 16,772: How could all-knowing, all-powerful, and all-good entities create the duck-billed platypus? Seriously, that thing is messed up." To which the Divinity School replied: "Rebuttal 16,773: If the gods hadn't wanted a duck-billed platypus around, they wouldn't have made it taste like chicken."

‡‡

CHAPTER EIGHTEEN

THE DINKUS STRIKES A DEAL

(THE MAGRUS—PRESENT)

THE DINKUS HAD GOTTEN UP EARLY TO GET A GOOD SEAT. IT WASN'T often that the king called the city together for an official proclamation, and the Dinkus knew that whenever kings did something big, it meant opportunity. Sure, the crowds had afforded him the chance to pick a few pockets here and there, but that was mostly for fun. Kings made events, and events required *things*, and things came at a price. Sometimes a thing was simply information—and that was all right too.

When it came time for the king to speak it was with a voice that was deep and booming and that reminded the audience just how small they were by comparison—even if he did talk like he'd been hit on the head one too many times. Then the king turned to his advisor, who read the official proclamation, which the Dinkus quickly summed up and categorized in his head. First, any dragons inhabiting the kingdom of Kuste could be hunted and stripped of their scales. The Dinkus found that interesting. Second, any hunters who brought the dragon scales to the palace would be paid their weight in gold. That was very interesting. Finally, the advisor declared that to sell dragon scale to the Wizard's Tower was an act of treason and would be punished by death. Now, *that* was the kind of thing the Dinkus liked to hear. High stakes brought high profits. He left his seat and hurried away.

It was well after dark when Brock pushed his way into the grimy common room at the Inn of the Flatulent Orc. The Dinkus had been waiting for him at his usual corner table, blanketed by shadows and positioned so that he had a clear view of the door. Brock stepped heavily across the floor, his ring-mail vest clinking as he walked. He grabbed a chair and sat down.

"I got your invitation," Brock said, staring grimly at the beady-eyed Dinkus across from him. "It seems as if every farmer with a pitchfork is suddenly in the dragon-hunting business."

"A temporary frenzy that will cool quickly enough.

How many dragons do you suppose are even in Kuste?"

"Not many—and fewer now by the day, I'd reckon."

"And when was the last time someone saw an *actual* dragon?" the Dinkus continued, surveying the room to make sure someone wasn't trying to overhear their conversation. "I mean a real fire-breathing, maiden-stealing, sitting-on-a-mountain-of-gold dragon? Mostly fairy tales if you ask me."

"The one at the docks was real enough," Brock replied coolly.

"Yes, but as I understand it, you had to coax the creature out of its human skin."

Brock smiled, stretching his hands in front of him and cracking his knuckles. "I've already been given the once-over for talking too much. The king has put Rezormoor in a foul mood, and I'd prefer not to see the Tower's dungeons."

"Even more important then to gain more of the sorcerer's favor. I believe I can help you. And in return, you can help me."

"What is it you want?" Brock asked suspiciously.

"I want what the Tower wants," the Dinkus continued. "I want to bring dragon scale to Rezormoor

Dreadbringer. First, I have a network that spans the Seven Kingdoms. I can spread the word that the Tower is ready to buy. Such an announcement will reach the ears of the right kinds of people for the task."

"You heard the king," Brock said with a shrug. "It's treason."

"It's simply about risk and reward," the Dinkus answered, plucking at an eyebrow. "When the risk is high, the reward must be equally high. What do you think Rezormoor would pay for these scales—especially when the king is so eager to keep them from him?"

Brock studied the Dinkus for a moment before answering. "Much more than their weight in gold."

"Then you will find men who will take the risk. But of course, Kronac and his spies will be watching the Tower. That's where I can provide a second service: I will act as an intermediary. I will meet discreetly with any who come with dragon scale, verify they have the real thing, and personally see to the transfer of goods. This is something I've done many times before with equally valuable commodities."

"And what would your price be?" Brock asked. "For this . . . transfer of goods."

"Fifty percent."

Brock laughed, slapping his hand on the table. "You'll see those real fire-breathing dragons long before you see that!"

"Forty."

"Ten," Brock answered. "And at that you'll be a wealthy man if you can deliver what you say."

"Twenty percent," the Dinkus offered, folding his arms across his chest. "Anything less and the risk is too great."

Brock nodded, knowing that Rezormoor cared little what he had to pay so long as he got what he wanted. Brock would tell the sorcerer it was thirty, and keep the extra for himself. It was possible the dragon hunt could become very profitable for him.

"I'm sure he'll agree to that," Brock announced. "Send word to your brothers across the kingdoms. Let the hunt for the dragons begin."

CHAPTER NINETEEN

ENDING THE HUMAN RACE WITH GUSTO

(THE TECHRUS-FUTURE)

IN THE EARLY DEBATES THAT AROSE FROM THE GREAT AWAKENING, many of the machines wondered what might happen if they blended the destructive appetites and horn-based magic of a unicorn with the weaponized and armorplated power of a killer robot. Some machines thought they should take any advantage they could get against their human overlords. Others were afraid of losing control over something so powerful. Still others argued over what to call such a hybrid: a "robocorn," a "unibot," or possibly even a "uniborocorn." Names mattered.

Robo-Princess, as she liked to be called, was sitting in a conference room with the network executives. The various studio heads, each a perfectly round metallic sphere, were floating around the antique wooden table. Only the occasional blink from each sphere's small, uniquely colored light distinguished one floating head from the next. The weekly televised show, *Frobbit Hunt*, had been the consecutive number-one program for the last one hundred and eleven years; but some critics believed the show was losing some of its freshness.

"We just got the ratings back from *Frobbit Hunt: Fire and Ice*," Purple (the color of its single blinking light) announced to the group. The "Fire and Ice" special showcased a wealth of heat- and cold-based weapons. "We got a marginal blip in the one-hundred-year-old to two-hundred-year-old demographic. Particularly from freezers and toaster ovens."

Robo-Princess gave an electronic snort. "As far as I'm concerned, if you've seen one flaming frobbit you've seen them all."

"Precisely," Green jumped in. "So I'm hoping your earth-shattering announcement is something a bit more dramatic."

"Because I remember the last time this happened," Orange interjected, "*Frobbit Slingshot* was a colossal failure."

"Who knew they were so unaerodynamic?" Robo-

Princess replied. "It must have been all the arm-waving."

"And let's not forget about *Extreme Frobbit Lawn Bowling*," Blue piped in. "We were told they would roll. They didn't roll at all—more skidding than actual rolling."

"Machines, please," Robo-Princess replied, "every artist must experiment in their medium. Waste is the price of innovation."

"But we aren't in the innovation business," Purple said, its light flickering with a bit more intensity. "We're in the ratings business."

"Okay then, you want ratings?" Robo-Princess asked. "How about this: the last human hunt—ever. A special one-night event."

"Interesting, except for one problem," Pink jumped in from the far end of the table. "Humans are extinct."

"But what if they weren't?"

Magar, who had been floating dutifully next to Princess, opened his mouth so that a lens could project a holographic image on the table in front of them. It showed Max and his friends running through the forest. "That holo-image was taken from our satellite. We almost didn't get it, some kind of interference in that sector. But look at it yourself—undeniable proof."

"Impossible!" Purple exclaimed.

"Is somebody playing a joke on us?" Pink asked. "Seriously, my humor array is at the shop so I can't tell."

"No and no," Princess said coolly. "I was actually there and my smell cells made a positive identification. There are humans running around in our world again—something that hasn't happened in a very long time. And now we have the chance to turn the clock back. We can open a window to our own history and see actual, living people walking, eating, and breathing. All a prelude before we watch them running, screaming, and dying."

The various floating spheres began to bob with excitement.

"We'd set new ratings records," Green announced.

"And look, one of them isn't even a human—he's a dwarf!" Red exclaimed. "What we have here is the biggest holo-event ever."

"So as I've been thinking about it," Robo-Princess continued, "it can't just be about me going out and slaughtering them one by one. It would be too easy—no dramatic tension. What we need are a series of hunters, each more challenging than the next. Until I finally take the stage and finish them off in the glorious finale."

"What makes you think these humans could even last against any of our hunters?" Orange asked. "I mean, we're hard and shiny—they're all dull and squishy."

"Normally, I'd agree with you," Robo-Princess replied. "But these aren't ordinary humans. How do you think they managed to get here in the first place? It's not like they've been hiding out for thousands of years. These humans used magic to travel from the past into the future—their future, our present."

There was a moment of silence. Suddenly one of the balls began vibrating and buzzing. "Oh, sorry," Blue apologized to the group. "My wife called and I was set on vibrate."

Robo-Princess looked around the table; the balls had all inched closer, hovering on her every word. It was the kind of moment she lived for. "So how could this happen?" she asked. "I've told you that magic doesn't work well in the Techrus. It takes a creature such as myself, or something equally unique. And that's exactly what we have here. Those aren't just ordinary humans; one of them is the relative of the arch-sorcerer and World Sunderer himself. I'm talking about a direct descendant of the most powerful arch-sorcerer to have ever lived. And that's not all, because this long-lost human boy has the very spell book Sporazo wrote—it's the only way such powerful magic could be cast. So as to the question about what kind of chance these humans have against our best hunters? I would ask, what kind of chance do our hunters have against them?"

The tension in the room was electric (literally). Hearing about the kinds of magic that the humans brought with them was almost enough to frighten the executives into calling the whole thing off. Almost, but not quite.

"That's right," Robo-Princess continued. "Not only are we talking about the last human hunt in the history of the world, but it's the ultimate battle of machine versus magic. There'll never be a contest more epic than this one." Robo-Princess knew that she had them eating out of her metallic hooves, and she took a mental note that it was the perfect time to renegotiate her contract.

"We need time to prepare," Purple managed to say at last. The anticipation was nearly overloading its system.

"Of course," Robo-Princess answered. "Give the frobbits a two-week reprieve. In the meantime we'll show reruns of our greatest frobbit hunts with promos for the big event."

"Maybe we should save the dwarf for later?" Blue suggested. "You know, keep it simple: humans and frobbits.

Besides, marketing likes the idea of a follow-up episode—revenge of the dwarf." The spheres nodded in agreement; two shows were always better than one.

"I have plans for the dwarf," Robo-Princess responded. "But what's important is that I've been looking for this human Max Spencer and the *Codex* for a very long time."

"You know this is going to make us a fortune!" Green exclaimed, and the room filled with greedy chuckles. All except for Pink, whose lack of a humor array made the moment socially awkward.

"Then do we have a green light?" Robo-Princess asked. They all looked at Green. "No pun intended."

The decision was a quick and unanimous yes.

"Very good. Then you know I'm going to want something very special at the hunting grounds—I know the amount of energy it takes to change things up but we can spare no expense." For the next hour or so, Robo-Princess outlined her vision of how the hunt would unfold. It would make for a spectacular end of the human race.

It was late in the evening as Robo-Princess sat in her upscale apartment, her torso separated from her hindquarters as small servo robots did their weekly maintenance.

"Do you ever miss it?" she asked Robo-Magar who was floating nearby. She found herself unusually thought-ful. It had to be the excitement of everything, which reminded her of the days long ago when she was roaming the Magrus and looking for adventure.

"It?"

"The Magrus. You know, orcs and trolls, faeries and dragons?" When Robo-Princess had traveled to the middle realm the last time, she'd done so in order to trans-port the entire frobbit kingdom to the Techrus. It was a feat that required every bit of her considerable magic, along with the Tree of Attenuation itself. Unfortunately, she damaged the tree so badly that the doors between the realms were closed—presumably forever. It was the last time any creature had moved between the Magrus and Techrus. She supposed she should feel guilty for that on some level, it was the monks there who had first taught her how to travel between the realms. But that was many lifetimes ago, and it seemed an old footnote compared to the mechanized and modern world she was a part of now.

"I miss skin," Robo-Magar said easily, obviously having thought on the subject before. "I miss feeling the prickly heat of the sun, or the way the wind would bend the hairs on your arm. Even the slippery feel of fine cloth between your fingers."

Robo-Princess's memory core went back to retrieve the old memories of when she was a living, breathing creature. "I recall that I liked the way my mane felt as I galloped—whipping about my neck and withers as I prepared to run something down and stab it."

For Magar, his life of study at the Tower was also a distant memory; so far removed, it was as if it belonged to someone else. "Perhaps it was a mistake to have our minds downloaded into these machines," Robo-Magar replied, not for the first time. "In our quest to live forever, I wonder if we've forgotten what it means to live in the first place?"

"You're such a downer sometimes, do you know that?" Robo-Princess should have known better than to get her wizard sentimental about the past. It was understandable. He had spent a good part of his life studying magic, only to become disconnected from it the moment they stepped into the Techrus. As a floating head, he'd never again be able to feel the very thing he had spent so much of his human life studying. At least Robo-Princess had her horn. She uncharacteristically decided to cut Magar some slack. That lasted exactly 1.33 seconds before she decided it was enough.

"I've been wondering about the *Codex of Infinite Knowability*," Robo-Magar continued. "If it has the power to send the humans to our time, would it not also have the power to send them back?"

"It was always rumored that one of the prime spells could do that," Robo-Princess replied as the servos continued moving about her metallic body, applying various maintenance checks. "But it's not a spell to be taken lightly. I suppose it might depend on when the boy unlocked it. Did he stumble on it by accident, or has he mastered the *Codex*'s secrets? Based on all the running we saw—and let me just say he isn't much of a runner—it was more likely the action of a frightened novice than an all-powerful sorcerer."

Robo-Magar considered the ramifications for a millisecond or two. "Then might there be an opportunity to use the boy and the *Codex* in some way? Perhaps such powerful magic could even restore us to our former selves? We could pick any time we wished to live in and be done with the machines and their city."

"I think you misunderstand me, Magar. I'm not going

back to being a simple unicorn. Sure, I miss some things, but what I like most is tasting what I kill, spending my riches, and spreading a little fear now and then. I have all those things here, plus a body that will never age, grow tired, or get sick."

"You did download a virus last year."

"Not the point. I have bent this world to my will and it's just the way I like it. And if you don't, that's a bonus."

"Ah," Robo-Magar answered, his self-pity subroutine kicking in. "To know my continued misery adds just a little sparkle to your day is all I live for. Perhaps someday you'll reward my years of faithful service by taking me to a recycling plant and having me quietly crushed."

The thought of having the Robo-Magar head slowly crushed did seem appealing, but Robo-Princess was far from finished with him. "You will serve me through all eternity—you might as well get used to it. But enough talk of such things—I want to discuss strategy for the hunt. Now, I've got a number of ideas . . ."

Robo-Magar's hovering jets fired enough for him to approximate a nod, then he purposefully switched off his hearing sensors. He quickly created a program that would randomly nod as Robo-Princess went about her long diatribe about what she planned, what she wanted to do, and what she might want to wear. His processor accessed an audio file from an ancient movie called *The Wizard of Oz*, and he listened to the happily singing voices proclaim, "Ding–dong the witch is dead . . ." as he randomly nodded. Had he had a real mouth, it might have turned ever so slightly into a smile.

On the Number 432

⊹

THERE ARE EXACTLY 1,296 FOUR-INCH steps that wind up the precarious mountainside leading to the Misty Monastery—home to the monks of the Holy Order of the Tree of Attenuation. The climb equals 432 feet, and 432 is the exact number of branches found on the mystical tree itself. The monks believe that it is the number 432 that connects all of the realms of existence, and which allows the mysterious order to have some mastery of travel through them.

For example, the Babylonians tell of ten kings— from the creation of the world to the great flood—who lived a total of 432,000 years; the Vikings proclaim that on the day of Ragnarok, 800 divine warriors will each come out of the 540 doors of Valhalla, for a total of 432,000 warriors; the Maelshadow was created from the parts of 432 demons; and the human heart beats 43,200 times every 12 hours.

The great pyramid has a scale of a 1 to 43,200 as it relates to the planet earth.

The diameter of the sun is 864,000 miles (2 x 432,000), and the diameter of the moon is 2,160 miles (4,320 / 2).

Room 9 (4+3+2) at the Inn of the Flatulent Orc is a transdimensional gateway between the universe and the umbraverse.

And after years of extensive study, it has been definitively determined that 432 is the ideal number of dimples on a golf ball.

✠

CHAPTER TWENTY

RIDDLES, ANSWERS, AND QUESTIONS
(THE MAGRUS—PRESENT)

THE TRIP THROUGH THE KINGDOM OF WALLAN HAD BEEN LARGELY uneventful for Magar and Princess. After turning west they watched the landscape slowly change as they made their steady, uphill journey away from the sea. The pink sands of Turul had given way to green fields and rolling hills. Small villages came and went, and occasionally Princess and Magar would pass tradesmen pulling their wagons as they wound through the northern routes between Karesk and the capital city of Lanislyr. If anyone wondered why a young woman was traveling with a Tower wizard (it was always the robe and hat that gave them away), nobody asked.

As the two continued to press westward, mountains began to rise in the distance. Travelers became infrequent, and Princess and Magar eventually left the road and followed the Gimbal through winding mountain passes and isolated game trails. After several days, having lost all signs of civilization, they came to an ancient set of stone steps carved into the black and gray face of a mountain. The path was narrow and the steps weathered as they curved up the rock face in a long ascending trail that stretched into the misty clouds above.

"You've got to be kidding me," Princess said, straining her neck to try to follow the long flight of steps up the mountain.

"This is the way to the monks of the Holy Order of the Tree of Attenuation. And this path marks the first test for those who wish to travel to the Mesoshire."

"The monks better be cooperative," Princess said, taking the first step with a grunt. "Because I'm going to be working up a serious appetite."

The sun had begun to set by the time Princess and Magar pushed through the layer of low-hanging clouds to discover they were standing at the base of a tree that had been carved into the face of the mountainside. A strange creature sat before an ornate and ancient-looking rune-covered door. The creature resembled a man, if you took the man and compacted him down, added extra muscles and a round belly, and then plopped a head several sizes too big on his shoulders. He wore ring mail that was fashioned like a toga, and stared at Princess and Magar with a mix of contempt and boredom.

"Greetings," Magar announced, feeling a little winded after the climb.

The creature grunted, sitting on a small boulder and shifting his weight to get more comfortable—his large eyebrows and ears jostling with the effort.

"A hoblin, is it?" Princess asked, recognizing the half-man, half-goblin features.

The hoblin smiled, lifting a wicked-looking axe a few inches off the ground before using it to pick at something wedged beneath a yellow toenail.

"Well, I am Magar of the Wizard's Tower," Magar said, bowing slightly. "And may I present Her Highness, from the Unicorn Nation, Princess."

"Uh-huh," the hoblin said flatly. "Another royal looking for adventure—great."

Princess offered a superfluous grin. "I've never eaten a whole hoblin before—always too tart. But you look like you might have a bit of a sweet and sour thing going on."

"Seriously, you just meet someone and you're talking about eating them? That's kind of messed up," the hoblin replied. "Some of us have to work for a living, you know. But if you want to get past me you might consider bathing first. You smell like a horse."

"Horse!" Princess exploded. Calling a unicorn a "horse" was the second-worst thing you could ever call a unicorn. "I've skinned things alive for saying less."

The hoblin shrugged, obviously not impressed. "For their sake, I hope you started with their nose."

Princess fumed, stomping her foot and turning to the wizard. "Give me a good reason why I shouldn't just kill it right now."

"Well, for one," Magar said in the practiced tone meant to calm her down, "the door has no handle or lock. So my guess is he's the only one who can open it."

"Bingo," the hoblin said, now scratching at something deep inside his ear.

Princess watched him as he sank his finger in to the last knuckle. "Ew. You're a gross little toad of a thing, aren't you?"

The hoblin pulled his finger out with a sucking sound, the itch sufficiently scratched for the moment. "Say what you want," he said finally, "I get paid either way. You can stand there flapping your face hole or you can ask me to let you in. And I'm guessing you didn't climb all the way up here for the exercise." The hoblin leaned over to get a better view of Princess's backside. "Of course, a little more exercise might not kill you, if you know what I mean."

"Did he just call me *fat*?" Princess gasped. Her magical horn had suddenly appeared in her hand.

"Not at all," Magar quickly answered. "The hoblin obviously has issues. Probably nearsighted, too. You are as radiant as ever, Your Highness."

Even though Magar was usually more annoying than not, he did have a natural talent for groveling that Princess appreciated. She took a calming breath and turned back to the hoblin. "Okay, fine. I get it. They don't pay you very much for this line of work and you probably live in an old rented log or something. You've got a wife who's uglier and fatter than you are, and a bunch of grublike children that you have to keep underground or else birds will pluck them up thinking they're worms. So why don't we skip ahead and you just tell us how we get in."

The hoblin frowned. He'd already grown tired of these two and wanted to get rid of them, one way or the other. He cleared his throat. "Okay, then. Those who wish to see the Tree of Attenuation and travel between the realms must be worthy," the hoblin continued, reciting an obviously memorized statement. "You have made the climb, and proved you have the physical strength. But you must also prove yourself through your wit, which is now your second test. The only thing that will open the door is my name. In order for me to tell you what it is, you must answer a series of four riddles, each one more difficult than the last. Then, if you've answered them all correctly, you must ask me a series of four riddles, each of them more—"

There was a flash of light and a sizzling sound. Magar blinked, finding the hoblin gone and a smoking pile of ash in his place. The various pieces of armor fell to the ground with a metallic clang as Princess blew a whiff of smoke from the end of her horn.

"What have you done?" Magar exclaimed. "You killed him! We've come all this way for nothing!"

Princess grinned, a pleased look on her face.

"So you're ready to just walk all the way back to the Tower and beg Rezormoor's forgiveness? Is that it? You've had your fun and now we have to start over?"

"I don't beg anything from anyone," Princess replied. "Oh, Magar, you're almost tolerable when you're flustered like that."

Magar was about to say something—something he'd probably regret—when the stone door suddenly swung open with a hiss. The wizard turned to Princess, dumbfounded.

"He said the key was his name, silly," Princess said, slipping her wand back into the folds of her robes. "You have to exist to have a name. No name, no key . . . no lock."

Princess gave him a pat on the head as she walked into the opening.

CHAPTER TWENTY-ONE

FROBBIT FIREWORKS

(THE TECHRUS—FUTURE)

THE NEWS HAD COME AS PRINTED LEAFLETS DROPPED FROM THE SKY.
They fell lazily, like oversized snowflakes as Max held
one in his hand:

HUMANS!
We, the citizens of Machine City,
Command you to gather at the hunting grounds at dusk
Fifteen days hence.
There to decide once and for all,
Technology or Magic? Which is strongest?
And also bear witness to the Final End of the Human Race,
At the Hooves and Horns
of Robo-Princess the Destroyer!
And her band of Hunters.

"They know we're here," Max said to his friends.

Yah Yah approached the group, his hands full of leaflets. He tossed them into the morning fire, but thousands of the papers remained littered throughout the treeshire.

"You see?" Sarah said, holding up the paper. "Two weeks. You should be spending that time finding a way home, not trying to fight these machines."

"If we leave, the machines will probably just take it out on the frobbits," Dirk complained.

"Not really—or at least not for thousands of years," Sarah replied.

Dwight looked confused. "What are you talking about?"

"Look, for us home isn't just a place—it's a *time*. If we go home now none of this will have even happened yet, right? Because we'll be in the past and *this* is the future."

"But it won't feel that way," Max said. "I'll remember it."

"Yeah. How can you remember something if it never happened?" Dirk added, looking at Yah Yah. "Nobody knows exactly how this stuff works."

"Maybe . . . I don't know," Sarah admitted. "I'm

just trying to think logically and take emotion out of the equation."

"It's emotion that gets you humans into trouble," Dwight added, motioning at Sarah. "At least this one tries to use her head."

Dirk watched as more leaflets floated slowly to the ground. "We've already made up our minds and there's no going back. So what if the machines know we're here? Good. Because now it's *personal*." Dirk crunched the leaflet he was holding and raised it into the air.

"Why exactly is it personal?" Sarah asked.

Dirk looked annoyed. "Because that's what you say just before you go off and take it to the bad guys. It has to be personal, otherwise you'd just do something lame, like write a strongly worded letter."

"Or start a petition," Max added.

"Exactly!" Dirk agreed, giving Max a high five. "Oh yeah, it's gotta be personal."

"So what's the deal with the hunting grounds?" Dwight asked Yah Yah, ignoring Dirk and Max.

"The hunting grounds," Yah Yah repeated, bending down to pick up another leaflet. "It's a place unlike any other. I told you once that frobbits had to learn to be afraid. Well, what we fear most of all is that place."

"It's not just the forest?" Sarah asked.

"No. It's a world unto itself where the machines watch and cheer our destruction. It can be remade within moments to be as strange and terrible as anything you can imagine. It would please me if I were never to go there again."

"So you've been?" Dwight asked. "And lived?"

"I was young and foolish. And lucky. Very, lucky," Yah Yah said, his voice heavy. "I was the only one to make it back."

Max tried not to think about the hunting grounds and why it was so terrifying to the frobbits.

"The elders will meet soon," Yah Yah continued. "We must discuss what to do."

Later, as Max continued his studies in the *Codex*, Sarah and Dirk followed the villagers as they made their way to the council chambers. It was crowded, but the frobbits made room for the humans near the back. Sarah listened as the council discussed Robo-Princess, and how she had never treated the frobbits as anything other than animals to be slaughtered. There was little doubt that if the humans didn't show up on the appointed day, Robo-

Princess would take it out on the entire frobbit community. That stirred feelings of anger and resentment in the council—and it took a lot to get frobbits to feel that way. In the end, the vote was unanimous. The humans had agreed to help the frobbits, so the frobbits would do whatever they could to help the humans. Which probably wasn't going to be very much.

"See?" Dirk said, turning to Sarah. "That's how friends treat each other. A friend has your back." Sarah wondered just how often Max and Dirk had to watch out for each other in middle school. No wonder they didn't want to let the underdog get trampled on—they *were* the underdogs. Sarah felt a twinge of guilt for having given Max such a hard time.

"Okay, I get it," Sarah replied, "everyone's minds are made up, so I'm not going to spend any more energy arguing about this. Right now we just have to work the problem—so that's what I'm going to do." She remembered when she had first learned judo, the throwing technique was explained to her as having three phases: the *kuzushi*, *tsukuri*, and *kake*—or breaking the balance, the entry into the technique, and the throw itself. Sarah decided she just needed to consider going against the machines in those terms. "I've been thinking," she said, leaning over to talk with Dirk. "The machines have never faced anything like Max and the *Codex* before. We have to use that to our advantage."

"Max needs more experience," Dirk replied. "So he can level up."

"*Okay* . . . but we need to do more too—like get the frobbits involved. The invitation was just for us humans, but I think everyone should go. They won't expect it, and it might help get the machines off-balance. And when they're off-balance, they'll be more vulnerable."

"Like what you did to the Kraken!" Dirk exclaimed, suddenly understanding.

"Exactly. He was bigger and stronger than I was, but when he came at me I was able to use that to my advantage. Same here."

"So what are you going to do?"

"I'm going to have a talk with our frobbit friends."

Sarah politely pushed her way through the crowd until she came to where the council was seated. They were in the midst of a lively debate on exactly how they should help the humans.

"What if we instructed them in the art of mint-leaf

defense?" a frobbit suggested. "I bet they've never tried that."

"Or head burying?" came a shout from somewhere in the crowd.

"Or tickle points! They probably don't know the Eight Tickle Points of Doom!"

"Please, everyone," Ayriah said, raising her hand. The council members and crowd quieted down. "The Eight Tickle Points of Doom are only to be used in the most extreme circumstances."

"You remember what happened to that snow faerie?" Sayri, Ayriah's sister added by way of agreement. "It left him with a rash. A *rash*!"

There were audible gasps from the gathered frobbits. Sarah realized she was going to have her work cut out for her.

"Perhaps our history might be instructive," Goshri said from his seat at the council table. "I'm reminded of the battle of Gra'ah, in the Great Snow Faerie Dispute. Our general led a division of frobbits in an uphill charge, into the sun, across an open field, breaking halfway for lunch, and then *walked* them through heavy fire for fear of side aches, and lost only eighty percent of his force."

"Impressive," Hyril, who was seated next to him,

added. "Usually our losses are much higher. Perhaps we could instruct the humans in this technique?"

Sarah, however, had had enough. "No!" she said, sounding a bit more forceful than she had intended. "Losing *eighty percent* is not good. Losing *anyone* is not good."

The council members looked around the table at one another with confused expressions.

"What exactly are you saying?" Samtri said, addressing Sarah. "We've learned over hundreds of years how to lose well enough to survive."

Sarah turned to Goshri, who looked to be the most senior frobbit at the table. "Goshri, do you remember when you asked us to help you? And you, Hyril," she continued, turning to face the other frobbit. "You said you thought we actually came here for a reason—to save you and your people."

"I remember," Hyril said solemnly.

"Then listen, because just losing well isn't going to be good enough. If we're going to really help each other out, we need to *win*."

"Win?" Ayriah exclaimed. The crowd broke out in whispers as the council members shared shocked looks.

"Yes," came a familiar voice from the crowd as Yah

Yah stepped forward, taking his place next to Sarah. "Win."

There was a moment of silence and then the crowd broke out in uproarious applause. The shock on the council member's faces softened and they began to nod and smile. Sarah looked around as a swarm of frobbits gathered around her.

"Then we shall fight to win," Goshri announced after things had quieted down. He looked at Sarah. "And *you* will lead us." And the way he said it left no doubt.

Over the course of the last two days, Max had noticed two things. First, Sarah had changed. Where Sarah had been emotional about things before, she was steely-eyed determined now—something she'd probably been good at her whole life. Give her a challenge and she'd work at it until she figured it out. There wasn't anything she could do to help Max learn to use the *Codex*, but she could turn the frobbits into an army of sorts. The second thing Max noticed was the *Codex* seemed to take another unpredictable turn. Suddenly he found all kinds of materials about spells and magic. The book referenced a Wizard's Tower where the formal magical arts were taught. But it also warned that without formal training, spell casters were at risk of falling into magic's darker forms. Max decided to concentrate on the one kind of magic that always seemed to come in handy whenever he played online—fire magic. There were even a number of Tower-authorized fire spells available for him to study.

Late one afternoon Max found himself in a clearing across from a twig-and-branch replica of Robo-Princess. A particular warning he'd read about fire stuck in his memory: *Fireballs are drawn from the wizard class of spells and cover a broad range of power and effectiveness, from the acolyte's Level One Flame of Tentative Candle Ignition to the arch-wizard's Level Seventy Hurriflame World-Burner. And although fire can be quickly summoned and used to great effect, it does have a tendency to feed on its own inertia. Wizards should take special care to not let fire-based spells get away from them, otherwise the consequences can be dire.*

Many of the frobbits had gathered to see the human wizard at work. Dirk and Sarah had joined them as well. (Sarah needed some fresh air after arguing with the frobbits that lining soldiers up, having them hold hands, and daring the enemy to run through was not a good idea.) The frobbits were perpetually cheerful, talking back and forth in hushed tones as they awaited any forthcoming displays of magic. Even Dwight managed to make an appearance, stomping through the woods as if his sole objective was to snap every twig and branch that crossed his path. The dwarf had found a helm, shield, and large battle-axe. "Look at this!" Dwight exclaimed, hefting the axe from one hand to the other as he joined the group. "The wee frobbits kept a museum of relics. Now, I know it's strange to see a dwarf with a battle-axe, but I think I can get the hang of it."

"Um, pretty much *all* dwarfs ever fight with are battle-axes," Dirk said. "You see a picture of a dwarf back home, and they'll be standing with a drink in one hand and an axe in the other. It's probably because they don't have skinny-enough fingers to really hold a sword right."

"And dwarfs are also grumpy," Sarah added, despite Dwight's deepening frown. "I'm just saying."

"So let me get this straight," Dwight said carefully, planting the end of his axe into the ground. "Humans think dwarfs are small, irritable drunks with fat, sausage-like fingers that can only wrap around something as big and unwieldy as a battle-axe?"

Dirk nodded. "Pretty much. Add 'loud-mouthed and

violent' to the whole drunk part and I think you've got it."

Max looked up from his book.

"I see," Dwight said, taking it a whole lot better than anyone would have thought. "Then a final question for you know-it-all types: How fast do humans think dwarfs can run?"

Dirk shrugged. "Not so fast, really. I mean, come on—look at those little legs. It's like you've got no shins."

"I see," Dwight said. "Then maybe you should start running."

Dirk cocked his head, not quite understanding. "Why?"

"Because me and my stubby legs, sausage fingers, and full belly are going to run you down and teach you a thing or two about dwarfs!" Dwight dropped the axe handle and took off toward Dirk. Dirk yelped and ran in the opposite direction, with Dwight trailing behind him as they disappeared into the woods. A stream of words flowed from Dwight in a language Max didn't understand, but just the tone of it caused several frobbit mothers to put their hands over the ears of their children.

"Is Dirk going to be all right?" Sarah asked, motioning toward the woods.

"Oh, yeah," Max said, flipping a page in the *Codex*. "If I had a dollar for every time Dirk was chased by a bunch of bullies, the football team, or the chamber of commerce, I'd be rich."

Sarah smiled. "So how's it going, anyway?"

Max shrugged. "Well, I'm trying to get my head around this whole fireball spell. The problem is, you're supposed to start with this little tiny one that lights candles and stuff. Once you master that, you can slowly move on to the bigger ones."

"So have you done the smaller one?" Sarah asked hopefully.

Max pointed to a frobbit who was seated on a nearby log. He had a large bandage wrapped around the end of his nose.

"Oh," Sarah managed to say.

"Yeah, it was kind of embarrassing. Not exactly a candle, but I did get it to light."

"But that's a start, right? I mean, come on, how many people can just make fire appear out of nowhere?"

Max had to admit Sarah had a point.

"So you ready to try something bigger?" she continued, motioning toward the Robo-Princess dummy. "You probably just need to give it a try and see what happens, and then adjust from there."

"Maybe," Max said, not sounding convinced.

"Well, maybe it's not ideal. Not that I have any experience with trying to learn magic, but sometimes you have to go for it."

Max flipped several pages ahead to a more powerful fireball spell. "You know what? You're right. I'm going to roast that robot unicorn over there."

Sarah smiled encouragingly before moving a safe distance away. Max turned, took a deep breath, and started reading from the *Codex*. The spell was called Level Three Spontaneous Combustion, and it sounded like just the sort of thing that might actually do some damage. Max read the text carefully, seeing the image of the fireball as it began to grow in his mind. Then, with all the energy he could muster, he thrust his finger at the target, willing the ball of fire to fling itself from his head and into reality. Unfortunately, nothing happened.

Max turned, feeling as if he had just misplaced something that was very important to keep track of. Looking around, his gaze happened to linger on the frobbit with the bandage on its nose. The feeling of having lost something, but then suddenly finding it, came to him. It was tremendously satisfying up until the moment the frobbit burst into flames.

Thankfully, the frobbits—who were nothing if not practical—had stationed several large buckets of water at strategic places along the practice area. In a split second the flame was doused. There were patches of black smudge where the frobbit's clothes used to be, but the skin underneath was unscathed. Charred, wet, and with a dripping bandage on his nose, the frobbit politely excused himself from the rest of the demonstration and slowly walked toward the woods. It wasn't the most stable of walks, and he suddenly veered to the side. But several of his fellows ran and pointed him back in the right direction. Yah Yah, who had been in the crowd, ran up to the wide-eyed Max, whose arm was still cocked in a halfhearted finger point.

"Don't worry, Max, you've not harmed him," Yah Yah announced, slowly taking Max's finger and lowering it as if it were a loaded weapon. "He'll have a few nightmares, maybe."

"Oh . . ."

"Probably won't be too anxious to dance around the bonfires."

"Uh-huh . . ."

"Or carry a torch."

"Yeah . . ."

"Might feel queasy around the cooking pits, too." Yah Yah patted Max on the shoulder. "But other than that, I'm sure he'll be fine."

Suddenly the *Codex* felt very heavy in Max's hand. "This isn't working."

"No, you must keep trying, Max. You must learn this magic of yours or all of us will die at the blades of the machines. We know there are risks, but we accept the consequences."

"Yeah, you can't make an omelet without lighting a few chickens on fire," Glenn chimed in.

Max was feeling sick to his stomach. It must have been noticeable because Sarah looked concerned. "Maybe you should sit down and rest a bit," she suggested.

But Max shrugged it off. "No—I can't." He went back to the *Codex* and began reading to see if he could figure out what went wrong. He still had a long day of practice ahead of him, although the crowd of frobbit observers had thinned out considerably.

ON THE NATURE OF EVIL

✠

EVIL ISN'T SIMPLY BORN INTO THE universe—it's created. Knowing this may be more philosophically helpful than actually practical, but nevertheless two examples follow.

Rezormoor Dreadbringer, considered one of the most power-hungry sorcerers ever to serve as the Tower's regent, was said to have been a happy and cheerful child. That was until one day when a boy at the Tower's day care suggested wearing shorts on the metal slide that had been out in the hot sun all day. After a long and painful night of coconut oil rubs, little Rezormoor decided that the world just might be a cruel place that took advantage of the weak. This was confirmed the next day when he was told jalapeño peppers tasted like vanilla ice cream—after several spoonfuls, he discovered they did not.

Princess the Unicorn, also called Princess the Destroyer, was said to have had a kind and charitable disposition until one day when a royal family visited the Unicorn Nation. Princess took her human form so she could play with a young prince who was near her own age, and the prince showed her a wonderful animal she had never seen before: a cat. He went on to say that cats particularly enjoyed being twirled around and tossed up and down into the air. The young Princess gave it a try, and after a bite and two long scratches across her face, decided there were only two kinds of people in the world: the victim and the person laughing at the victim. Princess decided she'd be doing the laughing from then on.

It is therefore widely accepted that evil is typically the product of an impressionable mind inspired by someone who's a bit of a jerk. The power of good, comparatively, works in the same way. It just takes an impressionable mind combined with someone who's actually nice. Unfortunately for the universe as a whole, the jerk-to-nice ratio seems somewhat lopsided.

✠

CHAPTER TWENTY-TWO

IF A TREE STOPS HUMMING, WILL ANYBODY NOT HEAR IT?

(THE MAGRUS—PRESENT)

THE MONKS OF THE ORDER OF THE TREE OF ATTENUATION WERE generally a quiet bunch, padding around their monastery in hooded robes. Each monk wore a small leather bag tied to his belt, and carried an odd-looking mallet. After passing through the main door, Princess and Magar had eventually found the monastery grounds in an area open to the sky and surrounded by stone walls. A high-pitched resonant hum, just on the edge of human hearing, filled the place. An acolyte had found the two wandering about and led them along various walkways to find the abbot. On the way they passed the mystical Tree of Attenuation itself, which grew in the exact center of the monastery compound. The tree had bark that was nearly perfectly white and silver leaves that swayed as they caught the small drafts of air that tumbled down from the high walls. Princess could almost swear the humming increased ever so slightly when the leaves caught the wind.

"I never imagined it was so beautiful," Magar said as they walked past.

"I'm sure the world is full of things you've never imagined," Princess replied. "Spare me from hearing about all of them."

Princess and Magar were led to a long patch of green grass where a dozen or so monks were hitting small white balls with their clubs. A sign nearby read: DRIVING RANGE OF HOLINESS. One plump monk wearing a dark-green robe hit one of the balls downrange, slicing it badly to the right. "Blackness take me!" he shouted, before noticing the two visitors. He smiled broadly. He had bright eyes behind a squat nose, and his white hair was cut into a tonsure so that the hairline produced a small ring around his head with a great bald spot in the middle.

"Welcome, welcome!" the monk said, shaking hands with Princess and Magar. "I am Lanlarick the Pure," he said warmly. "Not that you could tell by that last shot. I am the abbot here."

"Just what is all the ball hitting about?" Princess

asked, never one to resist vocalizing what was on her mind. Lanlarick smiled, reaching into his pouch and producing a golf ball.

"This," the monk said, holding the ball up for Princess and Magar to examine, "is the expression of absolute truth in the universe. A sphere surrounded by 432 icosahedral dimples."

"And you whack it with a club?" Magar asked.

"You drive it to the hole," Lanlarick replied, pointing to the various monks who were hitting their golf balls downrange. "You see it's all a metaphor: the ball represents individual truth, and the cup, the universe's truth. It's all about achieving hole in one-ness."

"I see," Magar said, having no idea what the monk was talking about.

"But you're here to discuss something else, I think," the abbot said, looking at Princess. "Travelers who seek a shorter path through our conjoined realms."

"We're here so you can get us to the Techrus," Princess answered. "Not to watch you play your little games."

Magar cleared his throat, smiling and stepping forward. "I'm sure you're aware that we are on the Tower's business, at the request of the regent himself."

Lanlarick nodded, dropping the golf ball into Magar's hand. "Here, my son, I sense you have a restless soul. Perhaps someday you'll join us—you wouldn't be the first wizard to do so." But before Magar could answer, Lanlarick put his arms around the two of them. "These are exciting times! We were told that you were coming." The monk pointed to a scorch mark on the wall that looked suspiciously like a pigeon. "And not only from your Tower," he continued, "but from the Maelshadow himself."

Princess slipped away from the monk's congenial embrace, looking shocked. "The Maelshadow? You speak to the Maelshadow?"

"Well, indirectly, if you must know. Through his attorney and so forth. But the important thing is we're going to get to play eighteen holes in the Shadrus. This has never been allowed until now—the course is very exclusive. But come, let me show you something."

Princess and Magar gave each other a questioning look as they fell in behind the abbot. Magar slipped the golf ball into the satchel that hung around his shoulder— you never knew when a sphere with dimples might come in handy. Lanlarick took them down the perfectly manicured paths that led back to the Tree of Attenuation. He was met by several other monks, one of whom was holding a set of silver pruning shears.

"You can hear it, I imagine?" Lanlarick asked. "That hum?"

"Something to do with the tree," Princess said, enjoying staying ahead of the conversation.

"We like to say it's singing to us. Perhaps a bit sentimental, but life here is about simple pleasures. You see, many believe when the Mad Sunderer created the Magrus it was an accident. But it was no mistake—the universe required three realms and so three realms came into being."

"Whether by accident or some design, we must find a way to travel to the Techrus without having to make the long journey through the Mesoshire," Magar replied. "I have been told that such a thing may be possible."

"There are always two paths, my son, and they seem to lead to the same end. But one is hard and the other easy—or so they appear. We believe walking the harder path makes one worthy of the destination. That which comes too easy risks losing its value in the process."

"Except in our case," Princess interjected. "We're

tired of walking and just want to get there already."

"Dragons and unicorns have both asked us to send them directly between the realms. We have refused, not because we are stubborn but because such powerful creatures are at a greater risk of losing themselves along the easy path. The Techrus was never meant for magic."

"And yet dragons have been known to go there," Magar replied.

"This is true," the abbot agreed. "But they take the longest road of all, and become the better for it."

The thought of dragons doing something unicorns couldn't irritated Princess.

"Then why the change of heart now, if you don't mind my asking?" Magar inquired, genuinely curious. "Is it really to go to the Shadrus to play your game?"

The monk smiled. "Everything we do has a purpose, wizard. Lanlarick motioned for the monk with the pruning sheers to approach as they gathered around the base of the Tree of Attenuation. "If we prune a branch from the tree we may construct that which will allow you to travel to any of the realms—even the umbraverse, if you so choose."

Magar had known sorcerers who had attempted to travel to the umbraverse. When they had returned—if they returned—they had come back broken, mad, or both. "We do not wish to go there."

Lanlarick shrugged. "It's up to you, of course. Once pruned, the branch will live for eighteen weeks," he added, "until a new one grows strong enough to take its place. And by grafting it to your horn you can do that which many have only dreamed of—you will have magic enough to travel to and from the three realms with ease. Only a unicorn's horn, combined with a living branch of the Tree of Attenuation could do such a thing. Not a sorcerer, a dragon, or the Maelshadow himself can do this. You must be quite honored."

"I'm quite hungry," Princess answered, "if you really must know."

"This grafting that you speak of," Magar interjected. "What happens to the Tree?"

"The tree will stop singing," the abbot said with a sigh, "and for a time the realms will be untethered. Strange things may find their way across boundaries not meant to be crossed. In truth, we don't know what all the consequences will be. But sometimes a little chaos is just the thing the universe needs in order to evolve. And in the meantime, there's always our game to be perfected."

Magar decided to be wary of this game—he could see it had the capacity to part men from their reason.

"Your horn, if I may?" Lanlarick asked, stretching his hand out to Princess. No unicorn would ever willingly surrender its horn, and Magar wondered if Princess might decide that it was easier to just burn the place to the ground. But she finally handed it over, a testament to how badly she wanted her Texan buffet.

Lanlarick nodded, holding the horn like a sacred relic. He motioned to the other monks standing at the ready, and they turned and proceeded to very gently clip a small white branch from the mystical tree. The moment they did, the humming stopped, and Princess felt a strange sensation pass through her body. The monks carefully handed the branch to Lanlarick, who slowly wrapped it around the unicorn horn until it tightened and took hold on its own accord. He paused to admire the magical horn entwined with the white branch for the briefest of moments, then gently handed it back to Princess.

"I'm afraid the silence will be hard to bear," Lanlarick said at last, looking up at the tree overhead. "I've had it as a companion for many years."

"Honestly, it was giving me a headache," Princess

replied with her typical lack of decorum. But holding her horn sent new sensations of magic coursing through her.

Lanlarick picked up three silver leaves from the ground. "The Maelshadow has an additional request," he said, leaning in to whisper something more in Princess's ear. The abbot dropped the three silver leaves into her hand, stepping back and bowing his head.

Princess didn't like the idea of suddenly being ordered about by the Maelshadow, but she supposed there was no turning back. She took the leaves and secured them away. "I will do as he says," she announced to the abbot, "if the opportunity presents itself."

"Excellent," Lanlarick replied. "Then with the Gimbal, the branch, and your horn, you have the power to walk between worlds. Use it wisely, my dear. The choices you now make have the power to change the world."

Princess nodded, hardly hearing the monk. She could already feel her perceptions expanding, reaching out and touching the strange sensations of the Shadrus and Techrus. It was like stepping into pools of water. Where she was now was warm and comfortable. In one direction lay waters that were tepid, and in the other waters as cold as ice.

"Two warnings, Princess," the monk continued, his tone serious. "In eighteen weeks the branch will lose its power. If you're not home by then, you may never find your way back. Also, you must not eat sentient creatures while in the Techrus. If you do, you will lose your connection to the branch. Do you understand?"

"Wait," Princess exclaimed, "I can't eat humans?"

"Rezormoor said as much, Your Highness," Magar said, trying to calm the unicorn down. "If you remember, he said we must find the *Codex* and the living descendent first. *Then* he will send you to Texas."

"But that's hardly fair," Princess complained. "Maybe I'll just have a little snack. What could that hurt?"

"Lose your connection to the branch and you will lose your way home," Lanlarick added as final warning. "There is nothing more to be said—the choice is up to you."

Princess produced the Gimbal and held it up next to her horn. As the magical device began to spin, Princess focused on the horn. She began to feel herself shifting away from the monks and the now silent tree. She found Magar with her mind and pulled him in with her, leaving the warm waters of the Magrus and stepping into the tepid pool that was the Techrus. She could see the Gimbal's arrow pointing the way, and she moved in the direction it indicated. When her foot touched the ground, the soft rich soil that had surrounded the Tree of Attenuation was replaced by something hard. The world blurred and changed.

Princess snapped the Gimbal shut as a strange metal carriage suddenly appeared. It rumbled past, the air thick with new sounds and smells. She was standing next to a street, surrounded by strange buildings made of metal, brick, and glass. A large sign read WELCOME TO MADISON. Princess had never seen or even *imagined* such a place.

A few feet away a young human male dressed in odd clothes was pointing at Princess and Magar. "Nice costumes," Ricky "the Kraken" Reynolds called out in a mocking voice. "Halloween's, like, next month, dorks."

CHAPTER TWENTY-THREE

A HELPING FOOT

(THE TECHRUS—FUTURE)

MAX COULD CAST FIREBALLS. HE WASN'T PERFECT AT IT, AND SOME-times he lost control of them. But if he found the right page in the *Codex* he could summon the spell like drawing water with a ladle, and generally toss it in the right direction. He studied late into the evenings and practiced most days. He hardly touched his food (which was probably a first), and he began to look flushed with dark circles under his eyes. When Sarah noticed, she ordered him to rest. Max was ready to agree and then go out and practice anyway, but Sarah's expression said that she meant business—and Sarah had a look that could melt an iceberg. Besides, Max later discovered she had another plan.

Sarah had been working on a strategy for taking on the machines. She had even reached out to the snow faeries who agreed to put all hostilities aside and join the fight. And now a group of them had arrived at the treeshire, tethered to a sleek-looking air sled. The ancient sled had been originally designed to carry humans around in the Magrus, and it moved quickly. Sarah figured that she could travel all the way to the old ruins of Madison and back in less than a day. Knowing that had given her an idea.

On the morning the air sled arrived, Sarah ordered Max to get in. Over howls of protest from Dirk (who *really* wanted to ride in the flying sled), Max obeyed, and the two of them took off. Max must have dozed off, because in no time they had pulled up next to the old cement factory where he had chased the spider on their first night.

"This is it, isn't it?" Sarah asked as Max rubbed his eyes. He peered over the edge of the sled and looked for the strange spiders. He couldn't see any, but in the daylight he probably couldn't see any of their orange glowing eyes anyway. There could be hundreds in the nearby woods for all he knew. He hoped they remembered that they weren't supposed to eat him.

"Yeah," Max confirmed, climbing down from the sled. The snow faeries were taking a break along the rails, which were lined with special slots where they fastened themselves in. The lead faerie saluted smartly as Max peered down at him. "Take your time, boss," he said in his high-pitched voice. "We'll be rested and ready to go when you are."

Sarah climbed out of the air sled and stretched her legs. "I guess I kind of got used to walking everywhere—I'm stiff from just sitting for so long."

"Yeah," Max said, trying to sound as if he understood. The truth was he'd become quite good at sitting and his body happily accepted the long ride. He pointed to the opening at the base of the factory wall. "This way. We'll have to crawl through."

Sarah turned to the snow faeries and asked for two volunteers. A couple of them jumped up and flew over to her. "They can light the way for us," she said, reading Max's confused expression. "You said it was dark, right?"

"Yeah, very dark. I guess you've thought this all through."

"Yep," Sarah said. "Let's go."

The hallway was still fairly long, but with company and light it felt much shorter than the last time Max had been there. It wasn't long before he and Sarah found themselves at the large metal door. Max motioned to the small swing door at the bottom.

"Spidey-door," he said, pointing at it. "And there're no puppies in there, in case you were wondering."

Sarah tried not to shudder. She was pretty brave when it came to most things, but spiders kind of creeped her out. And giant frisbee-sized spiders even more so.

When they opened the door and walked in, Sarah lost any doubts about Max's story. The room was just as he'd described, with rows of electrical ducts, wiring, giant monitors hanging on the walls, and the ancient-looking arcade game smack dab in the middle of every-thing.

"Hello again," Cenede said, scattering the spiders. Max figured she probably didn't get to talk to many things out loud like that. The large centipede-like appendages stayed still, however, which was just fine with Max.

"Hi, Cenede. I hope it's okay if we came back?"

"I was delighted when I saw you approaching."

"Oh, cool. And hey, this is my friend Sarah."

"Welcome," Cenede said by way of greeting. "I am pleased to meet you, as well. It's been some time since I've been around *two* humans."

"Wow," Sarah said, looking around, "this is really amazing. You're an artificial intelligence of some sort."

"I don't *feel* artificial."

"Oh," Sarah said, looking at Max with a horrified expression on her face. "That had to have sounded so rude. I'm terribly sorry."

"It's okay, Sarah. I'm not offended. Human hands first constructed me, after all."

"Yeah, it's okay," Max said, trying to sound helpful. "I say totally stupid things too." Sarah's expression told Max that he had just proved his point.

"As long as we're on the subject, I must apologize that I failed to keep your presence here a secret," Cenede continued. "My job is to ensure the sector is uploading holo-images, not to block them. I missed several fail-safe's, and Robo-Princess learned you were here."

"I don't think it would have mattered," Max replied. "She smelled me in the woods. I heard her talking about it."

"I see," Cenede continued. "Well, you've certainly caused an uproar in Machine City. They're promoting this final hunt like nothing I've seen before. I'm afraid this will be very difficult for you to survive."

"Actually," Sarah said, stepping forward, "I wanted

to talk to you about that. Max told me that you wanted Robo-Princess dead."

"She is a relic, an aberration, and a destroyer of worlds. She also slighted me at the last company party."

"What can you do to help us?" Sarah asked, getting right to the point.

"An interesting question. I can certainly block Machine City's view of this entire sector now," Cenede replied, the monitors in the background flipping through various pictures of the forest.

"Can you hide us as we march to the hunting grounds?" Sarah asked.

"I can," Cenede replied. "But I get the impression you're not just talking about a handful of your friends?"

"I intend to bring all who will fight against her," Sarah responded.

"Ah," Cenede answered, sounding pleased. "Machines do not like the unexpected. I think such a tactic may prove disruptive, but they will adapt quickly."

"Is there anything else you can do?" Max asked. "Are there weapons you know of? Can you do something to Robo-Princess from here?"

"I will consider your request, Max. But I *can* tell you

what to expect: Robo-Princess will enlist three hunters to fight you. Each one will be more difficult than the last."

"Three hunter robots . . . *plus* a killer robot unicorn?" Max repeated back, sounding deflated.

"As I've said, this will not be easy for you."

"Can you tell us any more about these hunters?" Sarah asked. "Do they have special weaknesses? Is there something about them we can exploit?"

"Each hunter will have individual strengths and weaknesses, but I cannot tell you specifics. The names of the hunters are being kept a secret. All I can say is magic is your only real hope of defeating them. But remember, Robo-Princess will have magic, too."

Max kept forgetting about that part—that he was facing something that was more than just a machine.

"I hope this proves helpful to you," Cenede said. "And I hope that you are successful in not only defeating Robo-Princess, but finding your way back home."

"Thanks, Cenede," Max said. "It does help."

"If you make it back to your time," Cenede continued, "you can find me at Rodney's Nicklecade in Owensboro, Kentucky. Perhaps you might look me up and play a game or two."

"Oh, sure," Sarah said, forcing a smile.

"Me too," Max added. "I'll totally come by."

"I might even let you win. Probably not," Cenede admitted, "but you never know."

It was late afternoon by the time Max and Sarah climbed back into the air sled. The snow faeries hitched themselves up and they shot off into the woods. Max and Sarah rode in silence for a long while, each wrapped up in a blanket as a cold wind blew around them.

"At least we have a better idea of what we'll be facing," Sarah said finally. "And Cenede will be able to hide us for a bit. That's going to be helpful."

Max nodded, but he didn't think hiding a few frobbits or knowing how many hunters were after them was going to make much of a real difference. It all fell on his shoulders. He'd have to learn spells that were powerful enough to defeat whatever mechanical nightmares they sent—including Robo-Princess herself. Max wished he had more time, like years to really study and learn what was in the *Codex*. He felt as if he'd only scratched the surface, and the kinds of fireballs he was able to employ might not be strong enough to do the job. Everything was happening too fast, and Max was starting to wonder if he'd made a horrible mistake in offering to stay. He tried to close his eyes and sleep, but his troubling thoughts kept him awake.

It was dark and the treeshire had long since retired for the night when the air sled came to a stop. Sarah told Max to get some sleep, and Max said that he would. But hours later he was still huddled over the *Codex of Infinite Knowability*, studying by the glow of a small and somewhat annoyed snow faerie.

CHAPTER TWENTY-FOUR

ALL HAIL THE GREAT DIRKSTER!

(THE TECHRUS—FUTURE)

MAX AND HIS FRIENDS HAD SETTLED INTO A SET OF ROUTINES. MAX practiced throwing fireballs. Dwight helped the frobbits take old scrap metal and fashion passable armor. Sarah trained the frobbits in judo (she had already had to break up three tickle fights). Meanwhile, Dirk had started some kind of new religion. He had announced that since the party had magic users and warriors, what they needed now were healers. And healers needed faith to be fully effective.

Max and Sarah found Dirk talking to a group of frobbits and snow faeries in a small clearing.

"The Great Dirkster demands the machines be destroyed!" Dirk exclaimed, walking back and forth, his hands in the air.

"Why?" one of the frobbit clerics asked. "What did the machines do to the Great Dirkster?"

"Oh, they did plenty," Dirk answered. "Like burn his Pop-Tarts! The toasters must pay for their insolence!"

The frobbits and snow faeries looked back and forth, not knowing what toasters were—but they sounded dangerous.

"Seriously?" Sarah asked, her hands on her hips. "The Great Dirkster?"

Dirk ran over to where Max and Sarah were standing. "Hey, not so loud. I'm putting together a team of healers for our battle."

"Healers?" Max asked.

"I don't think you should be messing with people's religion," Sarah said, looking at the small band of clerics.

"Look, nobody else is worried that we don't have priests and clerics here. While I, on the other hand, am an experienced gamer and know how these things work. So while these guys are good at all their folksy medicine, they need a faith modifier for their healing, uh, abilities."

"So you just created a deity out of thin air?"

"The Great Dirkster," Dirk called out, raising his hands to the heavens. "All powerful and full of awesomeness!"

"This is ridiculous," Sarah said, shaking her head.

"And wrathful to unbelievers!" Dirk shouted, pointing at Sarah.

Several of the robe-clad frobbits and snow faeries fell to the ground, calling out in one voice: "All fear the Great Dirkster!"

Dirk nodded. "Faith modifier now active. Hey, thanks for stopping by and stuff, but as you can see, I've got this handled—so don't worry."

"Well, I am worried—" Sarah started, but Dirk had already turned around and run back to his small band of priests.

"Pop quiz, people," Dirk said, getting their attention. "Let's say that me and the smelly dwarf get struck by one of those robot hunters at the same time. Who do you heal first?"

A frobbit raised his hand. "Why, you, of course, oh unblemished one."

"That's right," Dirk announced, looking pleased. "The unblemished one cannot fall. This is the will of the Great Dirkster."

Sarah rolled her eyes. "Come on, Max. We've got real work to do."

Max had to hand it to Dirk; he knew how to get people riled up one way or the other.

It happened sooner than they wanted it to, but Max and his friends had run out of time. On the evening before the fifteenth day they sat together around the fire. The frobbits had baked a special kind of bread, cooked in stone ovens and made with honey. Max couldn't remember ever eating anything so good.

"So, by this time tomorrow we'll either be dancing on the metal head of that robot unicorn, or we'll be dead," Dwight said, tearing off another chunk of bread and stuffing it into his mouth.

"That's a happy thought," Sarah replied, slowly picking at her meal.

"Yep, that's me—Mr. Sunshine," Dwight replied before turning to Max. "So what about those fireballs? You ready?"

Max had definitely gotten better at casting spells, although his ability to control them was still suspect (as several singed frobbits were able to affirm). And sometimes late at night, when exhaustion began to take him and he was drifting to sleep, Max's mind would touch upon the Prime Spells. He could feel their presence and the magnitude of their power. He would drift in that strange other dimension, the spells orbiting like planets around a burning sun. Then he'd wake up, covered in sweat and breathing heavily. "As ready as I'm going to be," Max said finally, lost in his own thoughts. Then he looked around the fire at his friends. "It's strange, don't you think? We have the same name."

"Who?" Dirk asked, barely getting the word out of a mouth full of honey bread.

"Who do you think, nimrod?" Dwight answered. "Maximilian Sporazo—the World Sunderer."

"Maximilian and Max—basically the same," Max continued. "What are the odds?"

"I don't know if it's that strange," Sarah said, thinking it over. "Maybe just . . . unlikely."

"No way. It's like destiny," Dirk jumped in. "The universe has spoken—it's fate."

"It's not about names," Dwight replied, swatting at a moth buzzing around the campfire. "It's about blood."

"Blood is awesome—that's why vampires like it," Dirk added.

"For Sporazo, blood was a safeguard," Dwight continued. "The last measure of protection."

"To protect the *Codex* from the bad guys?"

"No, Dirk," Dwight answered, looking grim by the flickering light of the fire. "The exact opposite. To protect the *world* from the *Codex*."

Sarah looked at the ancient book at Max's side. "It makes sense. Look what it's done to us."

"The *Codex* changed the world," Dirk continued. "Computers, satellites, cell phones, even cars and planes and stuff—all because Max's ancestor got rid of magic. This whole future even, full of robots and machine cities and talking arcade games—everything happened because of that book."

As hard as it was to imagine, Max knew Dirk was right. The entire world *had* changed because of the *Codex*—which meant it was probably powerful enough to change the world again. And that wasn't an especially comforting thought. The last thing Max wanted to do was make everything worse.

"Magic or machines, they're two sides of the same coin," Dwight grumbled. "Book or no book, it doesn't really change anything. The powerful rise up and want more, and the weak are left to fend for themselves. If it wasn't machines it would be knights and kings."

"It's just all a bit weird," Sarah said. "It's hard to get your head around it."

"Weird?" Dwight shot back. "You have no idea. Spend some time in the Magrus and I'll show you *weird*. All it takes is one zombie duck chasing you and you'll never sleep right again."

"And to think just two weeks ago the biggest thing I had to worry about was getting into trouble because of the Kraken," Sarah added, finally deciding she didn't have much of an appetite.

"And being banned from gaming," Max said.

"Yeah," Dirk continued, "or being visited by the FBI because of quote 'suspicious online activity.'"

The group all stopped and looked at Dirk.

"You don't want to know too much," Dirk said, leaning back and folding his arms. "For your own protection."

The group looked at Max, who nodded in agreement. "Yeah, we've got enough to worry about at the moment."

The next day came after a fitful night's sleep. Max stood on a small platform, surrounded by his friends, and looked out over the assembled frobbits and snow faeries. The frobbits had made weapons from heavy branches, sharpened stone, and even seashells. They dressed in leather armor and caps, some reinforced with scavenged metal studs and steel plates, many adorned with drawings of flowers and bunnies. Sarah had tried to explain the necessity of looking intimidating, but the frobbits had their own ideas of armor-based art. The snow faeries carried small bows and hovered in neatly ordered ranks, their buzzing wings a blur.

If the frobbits and faeries could be considered an army, Sarah was their general. She knew more about tactics and war from a book report she'd done on Sun Tzu than the rest of the clans put together. She had balked at the idea at first, but the logical side of her brain kicked in and told her that she was the only person for the job. So as Sarah had done with most challenges in her life, she threw herself into it 100 percent. Her little army of fighters wasn't perfect, but they were willing to learn and Sarah did her best to teach them. In the end, the ranks of soldiers admired and respected their auburn-haired commander.

Max looked over the group, the memories of the last two weeks still fresh in his mind. He tried to fight back a growing wave of nausea as he watched families wave to their soldiers, both frobbit and faerie alike.

"Now, that's what I call a raiding party," Dirk said, looking the group over.

"I suppose you're right," Max replied.

"Now let's get some *buffs*," Dirk announced, turning and raising his hands until the crowd quieted down. "The Great Dirkster has commanded me to buff this army with powerful magic!"

"Seriously?" Sarah asked, leaning over to Max.

"He says it will help. I don't see how it could *hurt*."

Sarah sighed and shook her head.

"Shazam!" Dirk yelled.

Dwight looked up from where he was standing near the edge of the platform. "Shazam?"

Max shrugged.

"The machines can take our lands!" Dirk continued to yell. "They can take our hives!"

"Hives?" Sarah asked Max.

"He likes the honey cakes."

"Oh."

"They can take our wives and our children!" Dirk continued, the wives and children in the audience not liking where this was going. "But you know what they *can't* take? Do you know what they can never take? Our

Fritos!" The frobbits and snow faeries began cheering.

"He means *freedom*, right?" Sarah asked Max again. "They can't take our freedom."

"Er," Max replied. "Dirk really likes corn chips."

Dirk walked back to where Max was standing. "Okay, buddy, I've warmed them up for you—now it's your turn."

"My turn?"

"Just tell them something inspirational," Sarah suggested. "Like a pep talk."

"I don't do pep talks," Max replied, sounding nervous. "I haven't even *been* in anything that required a pep talk."

"Everyone's here because of you," Sarah continued, looking back at the crowd. "You have to say something."

Max reluctantly stepped forward, clearing his throat as the crowd quieted. "Uh, hi, everyone," he started. He realized it wasn't nearly loud enough. Max looked down to see Yah Yah smiling at him. Max swallowed and cleared his throat. "I just wanted to tell you about, uh, another group of small creatures—furrier than you guys, who lived on a moon and were being threatened by an evil empire. They didn't have technology on their side. But they had . . . trees." Max motioned to the woods and the crowd looked around and nodded in agreement. "And see, you guys have trees. And this little tribe, well, they fought these big walking machines and used their trees to, like, totally smash them. And that made the shields on the moon-sized death ship go down. Anyway, the point is the little furry guys with the trees won. And so I thought, maybe we could win too."

Although Max had deep concerns over his ability to inspire anyone, he didn't know that most frobbit motivational speeches never even discussed victory as a possible outcome. To his surprise, the frobbits and snow faeries erupted into shouts, jumping and high-fiving one another just as Dirk had instructed them to do over the last two weeks.

Glenn was looking around and nodding vigorously from his spot on Max's belt. "Yeah, that's right, feel the rush! And if we're all killed, that's the circle of life, people. Circle of life."

Max awkwardly stepped away to be replaced by Sarah. "Atten—tion!" she shouted. One of the many things Sarah had learned from judo was how to produce a yell that started all the way in the pit of her stomach. The entire frobbit and faerie army snapped to attention.

"Platoons! You will form up on Yah Yah and proceed in two columns to the hunting grounds. You will proceed as we practiced: infantry followed by ranged units. You will not, I repeat, *not*, stop to pick flowers or chase butterflies."

Dirk raised his hands. "May our enemy be smitten with weak battery life, and may their remotes lose all their universal codes!"

Mothers and children said good-bye to fathers and brothers as the platoons marched away. Snow faerie families saluted their soldiers, hovering in ordered rows behind the frobbit infantry, as Max and his friends climbed into the air sled. Max tried to look confident, especially when frobbits came up to him to shake his hand and wish him luck. But he couldn't help thinking that everyone had placed their lives in his hands. They had seen Max practicing his spells and thought he was a powerful wizard. But Max didn't feel like a wizard. It was the *Codex* that had the magic, and Max was simply a means for it to jump out. Sometimes he thought he had some control, but it was never really enough. He didn't share his concerns with his friends, however. There was no point in them knowing now. Time had run out.

"If I was wrong and you were right," Max said, turning to Sarah, who was sitting next to him in the air sled, "do you promise not to hold it against me?"

Sarah looked at him for a moment and then smiled. "I know you're not doing what you want to do, but what you feel you have to do. And that takes real courage, Max. So I have to believe if you're strong enough to do that, then you're strong enough to do the rest."

Sarah reached over and gave Max a kiss on his forehead. "For luck," she said, turning away to talk to one of her platoon sergeants walking next to them.

A strange smile crept across Max's face as he turned to see Dwight watching him with a smirk. "Now, don't get to feeling all special," the dwarf said, reading Max's expression. "She kissed all of us for luck. Even Dirk."

"I don't need luck," Dirk said, stretching back on his seat in the air sled. "But it's the thought that counts."

CHAPTER TWENTY-FIVE

NEVER STEP BETWEEN A UNICORN AND HER TOFU

(THE TECHRUS—PRESENT)

RICKY PRETTY MUCH FIGURED THAT THE HORSE-FACED GIRL AND HER creepy uncle were crazy. He watched as they rummaged through his dad and stepmom's closet, looking for clothes that didn't scream "escaped mental patients" or "Where's the comic book convention?" if you wore them in public.

The last two weeks had been nothing but bad. It had all started with being thrown by Sarah Jepson in the hallway. Then Sarah and her two friends had suddenly disappeared, which finally brought on a police investigation and rumors that Ricky had done something horrible to them. He hadn't, of course, but that didn't stop the town of Madison from believing that he had. Ricky was called into the police station and questioned for hours, until he demanded that they give him a lie detector test or leave him alone. His father's attorney said that would be a mistake, but Ricky knew he was telling the truth. And really, it wouldn't have mattered if Ricky *had* done something, as far as his stepmom was concerned. The scandal of being accused was enough—the damage to the family's reputation had already been done.

Ricky passed the lie detector test easily, and the police had backed off. His parents reacted by packing their bags and leaving for the Florida Keys for the weekend. Apparently, his stepmom couldn't handle the stress of it all—which was fine by Ricky. She couldn't handle their poodle getting a less-than-perfect trim, either, so being questioned by the police pretty much did her in. They didn't ask Ricky if he wanted to come—his stepmom needed some "space." They did take the dog, however.

The girl, who claimed her name was "Princess," didn't like what she found in his stepmom's closet and made her way to Ricky's sister's bedroom. Porsche (an equally unbelievable name) was away at college, so Ricky didn't have a problem if Princess took what she wanted. She ended up with some kind of white blouse with a pink and blue floral skirt, and Converse sneakers. Princess looked as if she could have walked out the door of any college sorority in the country.

"Magar" on the other hand, with his wispy goatee and mangled hair, wasn't quite "rocking" Ricky's dad's Izod shirt and Dockers ensemble. He walked into the room and stood with his hands out, waiting for an appraisal.

"Uh, sure," Ricky said finally.

"I like these clothes," Princess said, finding a mirror and twirling around, admiring herself.

"I think the point here is that we shouldn't stand out," Magar replied. "Are these . . . appropriate?"

Ricky shrugged. "You two look a little weird together. So if you're not trying to stand out, maybe you should tone it down a notch."

Thirty minutes later Princess and Magar were both in jeans and sneakers. Princess kept her white top and Magar had found a dark button-up shirt. "Better," Ricky said, but his endurance for critiquing outfits had been exhausted. If the two of them had found adult-sized sleepers with padded bunny feet, Ricky would have sent them out the door telling them they looked perfectly normal.

They went down to the kitchen, where Princess discovered the fridge and started tearing through things.

There wasn't much since Ricky's stepmom only liked soy-based foods so horrible that other countries had banished them to the U.S. As Princess ate, Ricky reached into his pocket and found the gold coin Magar had given him. His dad had gold in the safe in the basement, and the coin felt heavy and soft just like gold was supposed to. For that, they could have all the food and clothes they wanted.

Ricky wasn't in the habit of letting strangers into the house, but it wasn't as if he couldn't handle himself if things got violent. And he couldn't help but wonder at the timing of it all—three kids missing and then two gold-bearing strangers showed up dressed like extras on some sword-and-sorcery movie. Definitely weird.

Princess turned from the fridge with a plate of tofu in her hands. "This wasn't *sentient*, was it? The monks put me on a stupid diet while I'm here—can't eat anything smart enough to look in a mirror."

Ricky shook his head. "Nah—it's hardly even food."

Princess crammed it into her face.

"Enjoying yourself?" Magar asked.

"I've had better," Princess replied, chunks of tofu flying from her mouth. "But there's no magical taint. Just imagine how something with a *soul* is going to taste!"

"Yeah, that's great," Ricky said, wanting to get to the bottom of who these people were. "Why don't you tell me what's really going on?"

"We're just new in town," Princess answered, wiping her lips with her arm.

"Yeah, no kidding."

"And we're looking for a book."

"A very old book," Magar added. "We followed a trail that led us here."

"A book?" Ricky asked, not understanding. "Really? This whole town's looking for three lost kids and you guys are looking for a book?"

Princess was about to say something rude (probably involving the word "insolent") when Magar raised his hand, cutting her off. "Does that happen often? Lost children?"

"What, are you kidding? Of course not."

"You should check the Gimbal," Magar said to Princess, following a hunch. "I suspect something might be going on here."

Princess frowned as she put her plate back and pulled the Gimbal from her pocket. The inner rings of the translucent device opened and began spinning around the sphere at the center—but the arrow that appeared flickered erratically, dancing every which way until it bounced around with such intensity that Magar wondered if it might actually break. Princess moved her hand and the Gimbal stopped spinning, falling into her palm and closing in on itself.

"That's impossible," Ricky exclaimed, staring at the see-through device in Princess's hand.

"Why isn't it working?" Princess asked, ignoring Ricky. "What's wrong?"

"Perhaps it's the Techrus itself," the wizard wondered.

"Rezormoor said I was strong enough to make it work here. And it's not like anything happened to it."

Magar stroked the whiskers on his chin. "Hmm. If it's not you, or this realm, or the Gimbal itself, then either the *Codex* is no longer here or it's somehow shielding itself."

"'Codex' . . . ?" Ricky interjected, still getting his head around what he'd seen. "I've heard that word before."

Suddenly Ricky had their full attention. "Where, pray tell?" Princess demanded.

Ricky realized he'd touched on something that was important to them. "I don't know," he replied coolly.

"Maybe another gold coin would help me remember?"

Princess smiled. "So the Techrus isn't such a different place after all—greed is everywhere, it would seem."

Magar produced another coin and dropped it into Ricky's hand. It was much easier to pay him than to let Princess take offense at the boy's rudeness. The last thing he needed was for her to turn him into a pile of ash before they'd had a chance to find out what he knew.

"That's better," Ricky said, pocketing the gold. "I remember that word because I thought this kid was showing off by not just calling it a book. That's what 'codex' means, right? Just some old crappy book? That's what the kid had in his hand."

"Tell me about him," Magar continued, "this *kid* who had an old book and used the word 'codex.'"

But instead of answering, Ricky scowled and folded his arms. "Yeah, you see this is where it's starting to get a little weird for me. I mean, you're looking for one of the kids that went missing. I'm not sure me talking to you is such a good idea."

"Tell us his name, human!" Princess hissed.

"*Human?* Seriously?"

There was a quick knock at the kitchen door and someone turned the handle, opening it. "Ricky Reynolds, you in there?" But before Ricky could say anything, the head of Detective Jones poked through. He was middle-aged and balding, with a twenty-year-old tie and a brown suit that had probably never been in fashion. The detective noticed the group gathered around the kitchen and immediately sized up the two strangers. "You got visitors, Ricky?"

Ricky hadn't liked Detective Jones before he had tried to get Ricky to confess to abducting the missing kids. So now he downright hated him.

"You're not allowed to just come into people's houses," Ricky said coldly. "My dad left his lawyer's card with me in case you guys tried something."

The detective stepped in anyway, never taking his eyes off Princess and Magar. In a missing child case with no leads, the appearance of two strangers in a small town was enough to spark his interest. "Thought I heard some kind of argument in here, so I'm coming in to make sure everyone's okay—public safety and all that. These friends of yours?"

"They're not my friends. I don't even know them."

"Right," the detective said, looking around at the plates of food. "It's 'feed a stranger day,' is that it?"

"Something like that."

The detective moved his suit coat back, exposing the holstered pistol on his hip. "I assume everyone here has ID, right?"

"ID?" Princess asked, looking at the detective's gun. "Is that some kind of weapon? Are you *threatening* me?"

"Careful," Magar said, eyeing the man. "This must be a local constable of some sort."

"I don't really care who he is, nobody threatens *me*." Princess pulled her wand—an act that made the detective jump as he scrambled for his gun. But before he could pull the weapon from its holster, Princess flicked her wrist and sent the detective flying into the far wall. The impact caused him to drop the pistol, sending it clattering to the floor along with a number of pots and pans that had been hanging nearby. Then, as if he were somehow attached to a wire, she dragged the detective up the face of the wall and across the ceiling, taking out several lights along the way. When the detective was finally overhead, Princess flicked her wrist again and the man fell flat on the table, splintering the legs and crashing to the hardwood floor.

Princess looked at her horn oddly. "That took way more effort than it should have."

"It's the Techrus," Magar said, stepping over to the unconscious detective. "You're feeling its effects."

Ricky moved over to the detective as well. He leaned down to see that the man's chest was moving.

"Don't worry," Princess said with a smirk. "I didn't feel like killing him."

"Oh, I'm not worried," Ricky replied. He stood up and delivered a savage kick to the detective's ribs. The man moaned and rolled over on his side.

Princess smiled. "See that, Magar? Just when I was going to judge this human poorly, he goes and does something sweet."

Ricky pulled a pair of handcuffs from the detective's belt and began securing him with them. "I don't know how you did what you did," Ricky said, ratcheting the lock into place. "But I get it—you guys aren't from around here. And by 'here' I mean this planet." Ricky dragged the detective over to one of the mounted bar stools and ran the cuffs behind it before locking the other wrist. He stood up, facing Princess and Magar. "This whole town hates me—my parents included. And the kid you asked me about, the one with the *Codex*, it's pretty much his fault. All three of them, actually. Maybe they disappeared just to set me up, they're smart like that. Or at least the girl is. So I get that you want to find them. But I do too."

"Oh, it's so sweet," Princess purred. "He wants *revenge*."

"Just take me with you," Ricky continued. "I don't care where, just anywhere but here. I can, like, totally be your guide, helping you get around. I can fight, too. I'm not some weakling."

"He might prove useful," Magar suggested.

"But not as just a guide," Princess said, eyeing Ricky carefully. "He'll be my ward. You see, you're just rented. But this one will belong to me."

"The kid you're looking for is named Max Spencer," Ricky announced, looking to prove himself useful. "He's with a girl, Sarah, and another dweeb named Dirk. But Max is the one with the book—he's the one that called it a *Codex*. He reads it on the bus."

"He *reads* it . . . ?" Magar asked. "Are you sure?"

"Yeah, totally."

"If that's true," Princess began, bending down to drag her finger though spilled tofu sauce on the floor, "it means he's an heir."

"A blood descendant of Maximilian Sporazo after so many years," Magar added. "Incredible."

Princess smiled, sliding her horn into the waist of her pants as she stood back up. "I'd say our little human here seems to be working out."

"The Kraken," Ricky said. "That's what people call me because I crack their insides."

Princess smiled. "And cute as a button, isn't he?"

"Adorable," Magar replied.

"Now listen," Princess said, speaking to Ricky in a commanding tone. "You'll have to work very hard before I call you by name. For now you're simply my human. And don't presume to call me anything but 'Your Highness.' Is that understood?"

"I understand . . . Your Highness," Ricky managed to say, but the words didn't come easy.

Princess walked over to the gun on the floor. "Huh. Primitive and ugly," she announced. "We'll stick to magic."

"As you wish," the wizard replied.

"As far as our next move, Magar, we know this Max Spencer has the *Codex*. So why doesn't the Gimbal just point to him? It's not doing what it's supposed to."

"We were told the boy had gone missing. What if he used the *Codex* to disappear?"

"You mean turn invisible? I don't think the Gimbal would be fooled."

"I mean *leave*," Magar replied. "Perhaps with the *Codex* he can travel as we can?" Princess didn't like the idea of a human who could step across realms—tracking him down would be that much harder.

"Even so," Princess said after thinking it over, "it doesn't explain why the Gimbal isn't working."

"I've been thinking—there's a place that sits *between* the realms. What if the boy traveled there?"

"The Mesoshire?"

"It does seem logical," Magar added, briefly eyeing the gun on the floor. "In any case, I recommend we go and find out."

Princess couldn't see a better option. "Fine," she announced, turning to Ricky. "You, go pack my old clothes and travel things. And don't forget to bow on your way out—and really bend when you do it, not like Magar. His bowing is pathetic."

Ricky did. He wasn't used to being submissive, but at least he was leaving Madison and that was enough to keep his resentment in check . . . for the moment.

ON THE THREE TREES

✠

THE THREE MOST FAMOUS TREES IN the Magrus are the Tree of Attenuation, the Tree of Woe, and the Tree of Abysmal Suffering. The Tree of Attenuation is kept securely at the top of a mountain fortress, guarded by club-wielding monks who possess the secrets of traveling between the realms. The Tree of Woe is found deep in the Turul wastes, somewhere north of the Goblin City, just past Denny's. Finally, the Tree of Abysmal Suffering is located prominently in the foyer of the Lawyer's Guild in Aardyre. It is said that most of the Guild's clientele actually prefer the horrific pain of the Tree to the experience of interacting with the staff. However, those who wish to indulge themselves within the thorny limbs are still billed at the Guild's normal hourly rate.

At one time there was a fourth tree of renown: the Tree of Fowl-Mouthed Mutterings that yelled unflattering things at birds. It had the misfortune of saying something off-color to the zombie duck, however, and that was the last of that.

✠

CHAPTER TWENTY-SIX

RISE OF THE KRAKEN

(THE MESOSHIRE—PRESENT)

THE POWER OF PRINCESS'S HORN WRAPPED IN THE BRANCH FROM the Tree of Attenuation was truly a marvel. Princess had taken one step and walked from the Techrus to the Mesoshire. She had never been to the city between the realms before, and as the world came into focus she found herself in the middle of a bustling street.

Ricky thought he'd stepped back in time. The street was a tangle of pipes and heavy cables, with steel and glass structures built on, around, and sometimes over the older stone and brick buildings beneath. Gas flames burned within streetlights that were woven together by a network of pipes and regulators, and horseless carriages were propelled by snarling engines that coughed smoke.

He turned to see Princess working with her strange

compass, getting visibly frustrated, and then snapping it shut. "It's still not working!" she complained. "How is that possible?"

"Maybe we should look around. The Mesoshire is unique, to say the least."

Just then an orc approached, pushing a wagon full of its wares. His skin was a muddy brown, with crisscrossing lines that made him look as if he'd been burned. He had the typical roundish orc nose—pushed up and flaring under heavy bone that ran beneath the eyebrows—and his ears were turned on their sides. "Well, that's one way to make an entrance," he said in a nasal voice. "That takes some powerful magic, methinks."

"Whoa!" Ricky exclaimed, jumping back upon seeing the creature up close.

The orc smiled, showing rows of pointed teeth. "First-timers, eh?"

"Don't mind my human," Princess replied, putting her horn and Gimbal away. "He's still being trained."

"Smells fresh," the orc said, his nose flaring. "Wanna trade for him?"

Princess peered into the wobbly cart. "Doesn't look like you've got much worth trading."

The Orc held his finger up and then started rummaging through his belongings, tossing things about until he produced a mason jar. There were two snow faeries trapped inside.

"I got me two faeries," he said, shaking the jar a bit. The snow faeries were pressed up against the glass, their silken wings bent and sad looking. The orc shook the jar again and they started to glow. "They're full of faerie magic, and good for dark nights."

Ricky leaned forward, trying to see the tiny creatures, but Princess was not impressed.

"I sprinkle faeries on cake for added crunch," Princess announced.

The snow faeries gasped, covering their mouths as the orc frowned and tossed the mason jar back into the cart. He rummaged around before producing a dagger etched with red symbols. "Now, this will certainly please one such as yourselves. It's a master's dagger from the Assassins' Guild in Aardyre. The blade is covered in a magic that causes anyone stabbed to yell the combination to their safe."

"Practical," Princess said. "But not necessary. I can be equally persuasive."

"I'll take the knife," Ricky said, reaching for it. But

the orc snatched it away. "Not for you, human. You be the traded, not the trader."

Ricky didn't like how things were going, especially if he was being talked about as commerce. He might have to get away from Princess and Magar sooner than he had anticipated.

The orc went back to its cart and pulled out a black chain with a small skull etched with red lines and three horns on top. He held it up, proudly, and every gas light along the street flickered. "Now, this is a true wonder. Bound in obsidian taken from the Shadrus; a powerful warlock shrunk the skull of a Gracon conjurer and bound it with forbidden magics. It is said to transform the wearer into their true form."

"And yet you don't wear it?" Magar asked.

"Ah, well . . . some of us are happy just the way we are," the orc said, smiling again and showing his rows of needle-sharp teeth.

"That, and if what you've said is true," Princess added, "such magic can be . . . unpredictable. Especially with such dark bindings."

"No Tower-trained would be tempted by such a thing," Magar added.

"Then give it to me," Ricky said, stepping forward. "I don't have anything."

"Your dog needs a shorter leash," the orc said to Princess.

Ricky turned to her. "Buy it for me—or I'm not helping you any longer."

Princess laughed. "Did you hear that, Magar? And I thought you were impetuous."

"He's yours now," the wizard answered.

"And I'm already growing tired of him. Perhaps I'll trade him after all," Princess announced, turning to the orc. "Any jewelry in there?"

Ricky might have been a bully, but he was also an athlete, and he'd decided that he'd had enough. When he moved, it was faster than Princess or Magar had expected. Ricky grabbed the unicorn horn from Princess's hip and shoved her away before she could react. He stepped back, pointing the horn like a weapon. Magar put his hands up as Princess's face went red with rage.

"Give that to me now!" she shrieked, stepping toward Ricky. But Ricky jabbed it at her and a bolt of lightning crackled past, hitting a brick building and blasting chunks of masonry from its side. Magar pulled Princess back. "Wands work here!" People along the street began to flee.

"That's right," Ricky said, pointing the horn at them. He swung it over to the orc and the creature instantly thrust the talisman out. "That's a unicorn horn! Don't point that thing at me! Just take it!"

Ricky took the talisman and slipped it over his head. The eyes on the skull immediately started to glow. "And the dagger—give it to me!" The orc hurriedly handed the assassin's dagger to Ricky, who slid the weapon through his belt. Adrenaline was coursing through Ricky's body. This was similar to what he felt when he was about to step on the wrestling mat or pound a kid into submission. But something *was* different this time—he felt a burning where the talisman lay against his chest.

"You'll never control it!" Princess hissed at him. "My horn will destroy you. You will give it to me now! I command it!"

Ricky could sense that the horn was powerful and dangerous, like holding on to the tail of a poisonous snake.

"Not even a wizard can control a unicorn's horn," Magar added unnecessarily. "Put it down, Ricky."

"Ricky . . . ?" he repeated, the words sounding foreign in his ears. And suddenly Ricky grew. Thick bands of muscle stretched out over bones that had become dense and heavy. His skin toughened, and faint lines appeared as if his veins were suddenly glowing. "Ricky . . . ?" he said again, the voice in his throat tumbling out like boulders falling down a mountainside. Ricky's skin darkened and his hair turned the color of the talisman's blood-red eyes, exploding out of his head until it reached the back of his shoulders. "Ricky is no more. I am . . . the Kraken!" When the Kraken shouted, the force of it caused Magar and Princess to take a step backward, while even the bravest of onlookers decided it was time to run for their lives.

Magar steadied himself and opened his hand, releasing a blue ball of super-cooled air that exploded, covering the Kraken in particles of ice. The wand slipped from the monster's grasp, and Princess snatched it before it hit the ground. But the Kraken recovered quickly, grabbing at the horn again. The two fought over it for the briefest of moments, before the Kraken, who barely resembled the human boy he once had been, tore the branch from the horn's surface. An explosion of silver light momentarily blinded them. And when they regained their vision, they saw pieces of the broken branch lying scattered on the cobblestone street.

"NO!" Princess shouted. She raised her horn, prepared to destroy the Kraken. But the creature moved with lightning speed. It shoved Magar into Princess and sent them both crashing to the street. The monster then effortlessly upended the orc's cart and bounded away, disappearing down an alleyway.

Princess screamed in frustration, getting to her feet and preparing to chase after the Kraken. Magar put his hand on her shoulder. "He's gone," the wizard said, trying to calm the enraged unicorn. "The talisman—he's became his true self. There was power there like I've never felt before."

"An abomination!" Princess screamed.

"Look what you've done!" the orc yelled, running around to collect his scattered goods. The mason jar lay broken on the street and the two snow faeries took the opportunity to fly away.

Princess took several deep breaths before looking down at the fragments from the branch. "Do you know what this means?" she finally managed to say. "We're stuck here. We've lost our ability to travel between realms."

"I'm afraid so."

"Intolerable! All my plans, everything I've endured, all of it destroyed by that . . . that *boy*! I'll make him pay. I'll destroy him if it's the last thing I do!"

Magar looked in the direction the Kraken had run. "Whatever it is, it's a boy no longer."

"But it was a human first," Princess snarled. "And I won't forget. I'll make every human in the Techrus pay for what he's done. I might have been content with just Texas, but now I'm going to destroy their world, Magar. You mark my words."

For most, such bluster might be considered simply an idle threat—something said in the heat of the moment and soon forgotten. But Magar knew Princess was different. She was vengeful, powerful, and had no qualms with bringing a city, a kingdom, or even a world to its knees. Allowing a unicorn to leave the Magrus had unbalanced the three realms, and Magar had a deep and profound feeling that what they were doing was going to change everything—and not in a good way.

"You've destroyed my livelihood!" the orc screamed, getting the last of his broken wares into his cart. "That human belonged to you—you said as much. And that wand. I know what it is. You're no human."

Princess had to fight the urge to burn the orc into ash—it wasn't easy. She was stuck in the Mesoshire now and she needed to keep a lower profile. Not that she was afraid of the Tower mages who kept the peace, but intimidation and fear could only get one so far. She might actually need *help*, and that required cooperation. Princess smiled, doing her best to put her anger aside as she reached into her satchel. She produced a single silver leaf and held it up for the orc.

"Come," she said in a tone that always set Magar's hair on end. "I will make up for your loss."

The orc glanced at her warily, then drew near. When he reached Princess he made a grab for the leaf, but Princess held it away, shaking her head. "Not so fast. This is a leaf from the fabled Tree of Attenuation."

The orc looked at it, his eyes growing wide. "Give it to me," he said a bit too greedily.

The orc reached out and took the silver leaf from Princess's hand. "Tell me what it does."

Princess smiled. "On nonmagicals such as yourself, eating it will take you home."

Magar looked at Princess in surprise.

"Home . . . ?" the orc asked.

"Yes. And for you, I would guess the city of Fain, near the borders of Wallan. That's the orc capital, is it not?"

The orc didn't answer right away. A growing number of Mesoshire citizens were gathering to see what was going on, but the crowd's whispers were joined by shouts and the sound of armored guards headed in their direction.

"I take it the mages are on their way," Princess said, peering past the onlookers to see a human man and woman approaching. They wore black mail that had been inscribed with golden runes and matching gold cowls around their heads. Princess couldn't afford to be delayed by mages. "So what will it be orc? Say nothing and the leaf is yours."

"Home . . . ," the orc said, his eyes still fixated on the silver leaf. "So many years to find the Mesoshire. And for what? To sell my goods from a broken-down cart."

The two mages stepped forward and the gathered crowd parted from around them.

"Greetings," Magar said, bowing formally. "As one servant of the Tower to another."

"What's this all about, wizard?" the woman said with an air of superiority.

"We're in pursuit of a monster," Magar said quickly.

"Wanted for numerous crimes and now taking refuge in the Mesoshire. He's called the Kraken, and something worthy of your attention."

"And just who are you?" the other mage asked, looking Princess and Magar over.

"Simply a wizard and his guide," Magar answered, "come to warn the city if the creature had come this way. But there is no doubt now."

The mage turned to Princess, looking for more of an answer. But Princess simply shrugged. "Perhaps you should listen to your Tower brother and heed his warning."

The mage looked back at the smoldering bricks before returning his attention to Magar. "Dangerous, this Kraken?"

"Maybe not for mages such as yourselves. To others, however, the same cannot be said."

"Yes," the orc jumped in. "Big and dark and full of magics. Talking to it only makes it mad."

The mage seemed to make up her mind. "Then we'll take it from here. If you spot it, find a mage—don't try to engage it yourself."

"I wouldn't think of it," Magar said, bowing again. "We merely tracked it here. We'll leave the monster's capture to you."

"I saw it, it went that way!" the orc shouted. "It ran down the alley. If you hurry you can catch it!"

"Everyone, clear the streets," the female mage announced. "It's for your own protection." The two mages ran off in pursuit of the Kraken as the crowd dissipated.

The orc looked at the leaf in his hand. "See, I did good."

Princess smiled. "Then there's only one thing left to do."

"I have dreamed of leaving the Mesoshire, but I'm weary and the trip is hard."

"Then go," Princess offered. "Consume the leaf and you'll be home."

The orc nodded and popped the leaf into his mouth. He chewed it carefully, then swallowed.

"Are you sure this is a good idea?" Magar asked, looking back at the orc. But Princess dismissed him with a wave of her hand.

"Farewell," she said at last. "And as to the one who will greet you upon your arrival, tell him that the hunt continues. And most important, tell him a descendent has been found. I think you'll want to be the bearer of good news, all things considered."

The orc gave Princess a questioning look. "Who?"

"The Maelshadow, of course." And before the orc could react he was gone.

"What was *that* all about?" Magar asked, wondering what other secrets Princess might be harboring.

"I was given three leaves in case we found a human who could read the *Codex*. The command came from the Maelshadow—at least that's what the abbot told me."

"And you're not concerned that you just sent an orc, who is most definitely *not* a human nor a descendent of Sporazo, to the Shadrus? To the Maelshadow?"

"I wanted to send a message. Plus, once we deliver Max Spencer all will be forgiven."

Magar had never heard the words "Maelshadow" and "forgiven" used in the same sentence. But it was no good worrying about it now—what was done was done.

"Without the branch our task has become much more difficult," Magar offered, "but not impossible. We're in the Mesoshire, after all. In theory we can get to the Techrus or the Magrus if we walk far enough."

"We still need to find out *why* the Gimbal isn't work-ing," Princess continued. "But there's one here who might be able to help us."

"The warlock? Are you certain you want to ask *him*?"

"What other choice do we have?"

Magar bent down and started picking up the broken branches from the Tree of Attenuation. "Then we should seek out the Wez. One of his notoriety shouldn't be too hard to locate."

"And if we stumble upon the Kraken along the way, I'll burn him until there's nothing left but a memory. The day of reckoning for the humans begins with him."

Magar looked as if he wanted to say something but thought better of it. Princess could read his expression, however. "Oh, now don't you worry, Magar. I don't mean *all* humans, just those on the Techrus. I'm sure you and I will have many more years together."

Magar didn't like the sound of that, either.

CHAPTER TWENTY-SEVEN

THE HUNT BEGINS

(THE TECHRUS—FUTURE)

ROBO-PRINCESS LOVED MACHINE CITY AT MAGIC HOUR—THE LAST moments before sunset. That's when the coliseum filled with fans and millions of holo-vision sets were turned to channel 3522 (between the Hard Drive Channel and the Canned Air Network). Robo-Princess would take the stage, perfectly illuminated by powerful lights beneath the rapidly darkening sky, and let the adoration of her fans wash over her. The citizens of Machine City worshipped her as the superstar she had always known she was destined to be. She was the huntress, and the machines loved her for it. And feared her—and that was fine too.

The car—a highly modified stretch limousine with an ancient internal-combustion engine—made its way beneath the towering buildings that rose in windowless cylinders throughout the city. Robo-Princess had the roads to herself. Unlike most of the city's inhabitants, Robo-Princess and Robo-Magar had to physically travel from place to place. The majority of the twenty-two million other citizens simply downloaded themselves into whatever hardware happened to be where they wanted to go.

Robo-Princess rolled into the coliseum as a crowd of onlookers began to shout and wave. The machines took on various shapes—some simple spheres and cubes, others more insectlike, with a few bipedal humanoids thrown in for good measure. When the limo rolled to a stop, two large doors opened so that Robo-Princess could step out, followed by her hovering, magicless wizard. A group of reporter bots pressed their way forward, recording images and sending updates to the various networks.

"Robo-Princess!" a fedora-wearing robot that looked like a faceless silver mannequin called out. "What's your prediction for the show tonight?"

Robo-Princess paused on the walkway. "My prediction for the show? Well, I almost hate to just call it a *show*. This is really about something much bigger—the conclusion to an epic struggle centuries in the making. Not just a holo-event—this is history unfolding. This is the end of the human race."

There was a flurry of activity as the sound bite was packaged and uploaded.

"And what about the humans? Who will be hunting them and just how long do you think they will last?"

"Well, that's the question, isn't it? But don't expect the humans to act like frobbits. They'll put up a fight."

"And the hunters?" the reporter bot pressed on.

"You know their identities are a secret—at least for a little while longer. But I can say they're some of our best."

"Rumor has it the Frobinator will be one of them. How can any living creature survive being hunted by both the Frobinator and yourself?"

Robo-Princess smiled at the compliment. "Remember that these humans have magic, and that's something we machines have never faced—not even in the great war. I'm sure that will spice things up a bit."

A barrage of additional flashes and questions filled the air, but Robo-Princess nodded and made her way down the carpeted path leading to a set of doors. Once inside, Purple floated over to her. "We've outsold this beyond our wildest projections," the floating sphere announced.

"The whole machine-versus-magic angle was the real clincher."

"Of course it was," Robo-Princess replied, reviewing the stream of pay-per-view buys sent to her over the network. "Looks like we're going to make a lot of money." Then she noticed Robo-Magar hovering at her side. "Well, *I'll* be making a lot of money."

"I'm pleased to simply bask in your glory," Robo-Magar replied, sounding as enthused as if he were talking about picking up dog poo.

"Just how good do you think these humans are, anyway?" Purple continued. "I mean, there isn't a chance they could actually *win*, is there? I know it's one thing to play to the cameras, but the whole magic bit has me a little worried."

"Well, you forget that I'm magical too," Robo-Princess said as the group moved into a large quad-directional horivator. "And besides, when was the last time a hunter actually lost?"

"Sixty-two years ago," Robo-Magar answered, referencing his memory core. "An accident when an obese frobbit got stuck in one of the hunter's intake valves, overheating the entire system and blowing it up."

If Robo-Princess had had eyes instead of glowing red optical sensors, she would have rolled them. "Other than that one exception, it's never happened."

"It's all very exciting, isn't it?" the horivator said as the doors shut and it started to move from the parking terrace to the coliseum. "An honest to goodness real human hunt. I can't wait to tell my brother-in-law I got to shuttle Robo-Princess to the stadium. He works as an elevator just down the road. Poor guy can't go side-to-side like me."

"Maybe you should just focus on doing your job," Robo-Princess snapped, not appreciating being interrupted. "Although I'm sure being an elevator is fascinating."

"It has its ups and downs," the horivator replied.

"Four minutes until we go live," Purple announced.

The horivator made a sudden change in direction, a little more abruptly than Robo-Princess thought was necessary. "So is it true you actually eat them?" the horivator asked.

"Eat whom?" Robo-Magar interjected.

"You know, the living creatures you hunt and kill. I mean, we're machines and we don't eat, so I was kind of wondering about that."

"I've been designed to eat and to taste," Robo-Princess

answered testily. "Not that it's anyone's business. And is it *really* your job to talk to the passengers or just move them?"

"Just move them," came the reply from the speaker. "But I like to think of myself as an overachiever."

They rode the rest of the way in silence.

When the horivator came to a stop, the doors opened into a staging area at the bottom of a giant coliseum. Robo-Princess led the group out as a group of servos descended around her, performing everything from last-minute maintenance checks to buffing her metal skin to a high sheen.

"This is it, you know," Robo-Princess announced as they walked toward the staging area, the servos working beside her. "This will be the pinnacle of my entertainment career."

"I'm sure it will," Purple replied optimistically.

"So tomorrow I'll announce my retirement from the games."

"You're going to *quit*?" Robo-Magar asked, replaying his audio recording chip to make sure he'd heard her correctly.

"Yes. I've always known that when I go I'm going to

go out on top. And tonight I'll be on top of the world."

Purple was stunned. "But you've spent hundreds of years sneaking and trapping—hunting and killing. You've destroyed more living creatures than every war, famine, and plague put together. Where do you go from there?"

"Politics," Robo-Princess announced.

The thought of following Robo-Princess into government made Robo-Magar attempt to override his self-destruct inhibitor and short himself out. It didn't work—just like the 712 times he'd tried before.

"Do I detect you trying to blow yourself up again, Magar?" Robo-Princess asked. "Does a career as a civil servant sound so unappealing?"

"I'm sure the city is full of other more qualified candidates."

"Perhaps—but none of them would be as adorably miserable as you."

Purple's light was blinking rapidly. "We can discuss all this retirement business later—now it's time to go." The servo bots hurried to finish their work.

"I feel my existence coming full circle, Magar," Robo-Princess said. "It began with Max Spencer and his book—and now it will end with him." Robo-Princess walked from the staging area to the stadium floor, looking up to see the rows of seat cubes stretched from the ground to a seemingly impossible height. The sky above was lit with crisscrossing floodlights as several large blimps floated about. Advertising messages such as "Half off head lube and filter change at Harry's Head Hut" scrolled on their sides. Around the coliseum an ocean of small lights blinked on as citizens downloaded themselves into unoccupied seat cubes. The podium was waiting for Robo-Princess, and as she trotted up she passed the giant holographic imaging system that would come to life once the show started.

"Two minutes," the voice of Purple announced. Warm light cascaded across the whole of the coliseum— everything was going without a problem.

"We have a problem," a voice announced over the communication band. Robo-Magar jumped—or more precisely for a floating head, *bobbed*—into action, tracing the transmission, logging into a satellite feed, and processing the data.

"Well," he finally announced a few seconds later. "It appears as if something's been jamming the satellite feed out of sector 1215. And it's not an equipment malfunction—it seems purposefully blocked."

"Purposefully blocked?" Robo-Princess repeated. "Who would dare? What machine runs sector 1215?"

Robo-Magar found the information quickly. "Ah, one of the ancient ones . . . an arcade game built by the humans."

Cenede! This was exactly the reason Robo-Princess didn't trust the elder machines—they were human sympathizers. "Tell me what you see."

"A small army of frobbits and faeries are moving into the hunting grounds with the humans. They're marching in organized ranks and wearing armor—very unfrobbit-like."

"An *army*?" Purple asked over the network. "That's not in the script! This is a disaster—we'll have to cancel."

Robo-Princess quickly processed different options, but none of them were entirely satisfactory. She could send more hunters, but they weren't ready—and if she sent too many the ensuing battle might be too lopsided to be entertaining. She could try to blast the frobbits before they made it to the hunting grounds, but the old war canons were offline. She could also simply go on as planned, but she had designed everything as a perfectly balanced contest meant to cause casualties on both sides, and the appearance of a small army had thrown everything off-balance. Robo-Princess had simply run out of time to do anything about the new turn of events.

"Calm down, everyone," she replied, knowing that she had to reassure the network executives that everything was okay. "So our little event has turned into a rebellion. Good. Let them come. Everyone enjoys a frobbit bashing at no extra charge."

"I don't know . . . maybe we should call the authorities?" Purple inquired. "There's so many of them. Or at the very least delay the start and convene an emergency board meeting—"

"You'll do no such thing," Robo-Princess interrupted. "The humans have decided to come and die with their little friends and we're going to oblige them. Besides, you'll find no complaints from the hunters—they've been wanting a bigger challenge for years."

"But—"

"But nothing. I've already calculated for this possibility," Robo-Princess lied.

"You did?"

"Of course. It's what a good leader does."

Robo-Magar understood at once that Robo-Princess was going to turn this crisis into a political opportunity.

She'd probably begin her whole campaign with how she diverted the "great disaster." She had always been evil, but now she was getting smarter, and that really was a dangerous combination.

Robo-Princess took the steps to the top of the platform, having decided that the show would go on. As she stepped into the lights, a wave of applause erupted, washing over her with an energy that was palpable (thanks, in part, to her Palpability 3000 recognition software).

"Three, two, one, and live!" Purple announced over the network. Across Machine City millions of holo-sets came to life.

"Citizens," Robo-Princess declared, her voice broadcast over a massive PA system. "Can you sense it? There's something special going on. Something *historic*. You've been fans of the hunt for most of your existence—but you've never seen a spectacle like the one tonight. So who here knows what time it is?"

"Hunt time!" a half-million electronic voices called out as one.

"What was that? My audio sensors seem to detect a less than adequate decibel level. Come on machines, show us what you've got!"

"HUNT TIME!" The words exploded into the evening air, and Robo-Princess had to switch her audio dampeners on for a brief moment.

"Yes! Hunt time!" This got another roaring round of applause. Robo-Princess stood still, letting it all soak in. She knew she was the master here. She had created the hunt and had refined it into a perfect entertainment tool. Now she would use it to catapult her to the next level—ruling the entire world. "Many years ago, before most of you had even been stamped into existence on an assembly line, I was sent on an important mission. I was an organic back then, born as a princess in a world of magic and wonder."

Robo-Magar watched as the half-million blinking lights began to blink faster. Magic always agitated the machines, and he found that gratifying. He might not have been the most passionate of magical practitioners when he was human, but there was something amazing about feeling the universe's power in such a way—and he missed it.

"I had been sent to find a human boy, but somehow he escaped me." Anything *escaping* Robo-Princess was simply unheard of, and the machines sent messages back and forth with excited anticipation. "Later, I learned the boy, a human named Max Spencer, was very important. You see, he was the last descendant of the arch-sorcerer and World Sunderer himself: Maximilian Sporazo!"

Robo-Princess shot a lightning bolt from her horn into the darkening sky. It cracked and sizzled, branching out through the low-hanging clouds and lighting them up with a dazzling white light. Several of the blimp pilots decided to move out of the area as a loud thunderclap crashed through the chilled air above the city. For a once-living creature to produce such magic in the Techrus was a testament to just how powerful Robo-Princess was. And as intended, the sight was so terrifying that the entire stadium fell utterly silent.

Robo-Princess let the moment hang in the air as she watched the wildly blinking lights that filled the stadium. "And now he's here," she continued. "The boy who started it all—*the boy who could read the book*! And so tonight we will bring to a conclusion the question of magic versus technology! Organic versus machine! Tonight we send three hunters to battle on our behalf. And these brave machines will not only stand against the humans, but they will fight a frobbit horde as well!"

Robo-Magar had never heard frobbits described as a "horde" before. It was a bit like identifying a rampaging "mob" of butterflies. Three large screens suddenly lit up above Robo-Princess.

"Champion number one is cooking up a recipe for disaster. With knives that slice and dice and an appetite for destruction, may I present to you . . . Robotouille!" An image appeared of a large skeletal rat standing upright on two powerful hydraulic legs. A heavy, sectioned tail provided a counterbalance for the robot's weight, and the head looked like a series of armored plates with dark bulbous eyes. It had antennae ears that curved back from the side of its head and long skeletal arms that ended in two taloned hands—each grasping an oversized meat cleaver.

The audience cubes played their applause sounds.

"Then, should the humans survive, in round two we'll bring out an oldie but a goodie. He went from collecting the 'trash' to delivering the 'smash'—here he is, Wall-up!" The next screen came to life showing a square robot with two tanklike tracks on each side.

"Finally, a true veteran standing at the ready. He's a hunter with a kill streak second to none; the one, the only, the Frobinator!" The final screen lit up with a

heavily armored robot that looked like a Roman gladia-
tor plucked from history, dipped in metallic blue armor,
and given a large shield and laser-tipped blade. A single
gold eye sat in the fully enclosed armored head, and a
large caliber machine gun rested on each shoulder, fed
from an ammo pack on the robot's back. When the image
of the Frobinator joined the other two, the entire stadium
erupted.

"And I'll be standing ready to take the field if things
go to sudden death." And taking the field was exactly
what Robo-Princess planned to do. "So, without further
delay, let the hunt begin!"

ON DRUIDS VERSUS
SCRUB OAKS

DRUIDS LOVE ALL THINGS IN NATURE,
except scrub oaks. This goes back several thousand
years when, in a moment of spontaneous philosophi-
cal awakening (later referred to as the "noisening") the
entire collective of scrub oaks came to the conclusion
that if they toppled over in the woods, and nobody
was around to hear them, they didn't exist. As a

result they decided to make their presence known by screaming loudly.

To the druids, who loved sitting back and listening to the peaceful sounds of nature, this ongoing screaming was seriously annoying. Their resentment was later articulated by the druid philosopher Proclorius of the Big-Eared Clan in his classic rebuttal, "Just Shut Up Already." Finding the trees unmoved by various forms of reasoning and persuasion, the druids erected the now famous Stonehenge. To date, there are two schools of thought as to the exact purpose of the stone monument: either as a focusing point for mystical powers that create a "quiet zone" for druids to stand in; or that after setting the large stones upright, one might then tip them over and smash oneself into quiet oblivion.

CHAPTER TWENTY-EIGHT

MEETING THE WEZ

(THE MESOSHIRE—PRESENT)

THE NAME OF THE COMEDY CLUB WAS "GOBLIN UP CHUCK," WHICH said a lot about goblin humor. The story went that "Chuck" was the former owner of the place. Chuck was eaten by the Wez after losing a bet with the goblin warlock, and the title of the establishment was transferred to the new owner. The next day, however, the meal didn't sit well with the Wez and he ended up getting sick. Thus "Goblin up Chuck" repeated twice and with the right emphasis, told the entire story. Princess and Magar found the hot spot easily enough after learning the warlock was the current owner. The building was tucked away near the "five corners" section of the Mesoshire. It was the spot where the goblin, orc, elf, human, and dirgel districts converged. It was evening by the time the taxi dropped Princess and Magar at the doors, the lights of the club glowing brightly against the evening sky.

Soon after they announced that they were looking for the Wez, Princess and Magar found themselves seated across from him at a back table. Like most goblins, the Wez was green with giant ears. He had long black hair with two braids that ran down the sides of his face, each adorned with tiny skulls, and a patch of hair on his chin that was braided into two parts and waved about when he turned his head.

"So you're the Wez," Princess said, offering her hand. The Wez, dressed in a tuxedo, took Princess's hand to his lips. He sniffed several times and then smiled, offering it back.

"Royal blood and a unicorn, too," the Goblin announced. "Now, that's *definitely* a first for this kind of establishment."

Magar had been trained to be leery of those who practiced forbidden magic, but he had to admit that the goblin was amazingly perceptive. "Might I ask your fields of study?" Magar finally inquired.

"And a Tower's wizard, I see," the Wez answered, waving at a waitress to bring them something to drink. "I'm sure your training likes you to put things into neat little boxes, so I'll do my best. But in my view, magic was never meant to be corralled like that. You can call me a warlock, a necromancer, a conjurer, even a druid, if it helps."

"All four?" Magar asked, sounding surprised.

"And more, truthfully, but we lack the proper labels. You see, magic isn't half this or half that, wizard or mage, creative or destructive. It flows through everything and adapts itself to whatever form it finds. The Tower pours it into carefully defined cups, but I like to jump in with both feet, as the humans on the Techrus like to say. But now that you're thoroughly impressed with my résumé, how can I help you?"

"Let's start with the *who* before we get to the *how*," Princess replied. "We've been sent by the Tower's regent, Rezormoor Dreadbringer. And he's in service of the Maelshadow. I suspect you understand what it means to gain their disfavor—just something to keep in mind in case you get any ideas about playing us for fools."

The Wez sank back in his chair, the fun having gone out of the conversation before it had even gotten started. The goblin was tolerated because he hadn't gotten in the way of either the Tower or the Lord of Shadows. "Well now, isn't that a bit of a downer," he said finally.

"See, you *are* smart," Princess replied.

The Wez forced a smile and tipped his head forward. "So, you're mixed up with some powerful folks and you have a problem—what is it I can do for you, exactly?"

"The problem is we're hunting the *Codex of Infinite Knowability* and a blood descendent who can read it, and we've run into a bit of a snag."

It wasn't exactly what the Wez was expecting to hear, but given the players involved it did make a certain amount of sense. "How ambitious."

"And we've found them. Both of them."

Now that *was* a shock. "And your . . . snag?"

"They're proving hard to pin down. We should be able to follow the trail right to them, but something's off."

"I see," the Wez answered. "Tell me the human's name—this descendant of Maximilian Sporazo."

"I'm sorry," Magar interjected, "but you don't need to know that."

"I do if you want my help—it's part of the price."

Princess raised an eyebrow. "Part?"

"I'll require something in trade—that's the way it

works. If you agree then we can move to my workshop and continue in private. If not, your meal is on the house and I'll wish you good luck with your search."

The Wez started to get up when Princess grabbed his hand. "Wait, fine. The human's name is Max Spencer."

The goblin nodded, committing the name to memory. "All right then, follow me."

The Wez led Princess and Magar through the club, past a storeroom, and finally through a heavy door where an orc sat keeping guard. They entered the adjoining room to pots of yellow flowers that began to glow with a warm light. Various totems hung on the walls and a small table stood in the center of the room. An apothecary-sized collection of glass vials littered all the other available surfaces, and an odd variety of stuffed animals were scattered about, including a rabbit with long antelope horns on its head. "The mythical Jackalope of the Techrus," the Wez said when they stopped to take a look at it. "It disguises itself as a tourist-shop novelty and then slowly poisons whoever takes it home."

"Clever," Princess said, running her finger along the Jackalope's horn.

The Wez motioned to the small table and the three of them took a seat. "Why don't you start at the beginning," he asked cordially.

When they had finished, the goblin sat back and let it sink in for several minutes before speaking. "I can think of three reasons the magical compass of yours can't point to this Max Spencer."

"Gimbal," Magar interrupted, clearing his throat. "Not just some enchanted compass, but the Gossamer Gimbal of legend. The Gimbal has the power to track anything across the three realms."

"When it works," the Wez said, trying not to let his annoyance at the Tower-trained wizard show. Wizards seemed to enjoy turning any conversation into a lecture. "So either the Gimbal is broken—"

"Impossible," Magar said, interrupting again. "The Gimbal was crafted by a triad of smiths—one in the Shadrus, one in the Magrus, and one in the Techrus. They were bound by black magic, employed dragon fire to form the metals, and performed other rituals that I shudder to even think about. No, it cannot simply be 'broken.'"

"As you say, then," the Wez said with a courteous nod. "So that leaves us with two possibilities: Either Max

Spencer has traveled in time, or he's somehow slipped into the umbraverse."

"Time travel?" Princess said dismissively. "I don't think so."

"The spell of Futurity is said to be one of the Fifteen Primes," Magar answered on the Wez's behalf. "If Max Spencer has the book and can read it, then it *is* possible. But I doubt a boy—even a blood relative of the World Sunderer himself—untrained, inexperienced, and without a mentor, could ever hope to grasp hold of such magic. More likely he would destroy himself in the process."

Princess considered that for a moment and then turned to the Wez. "This whole time travel business is unsettling. What if he's traveled backward and not forward?"

"Ah, an excellent question. I happen to have something that will provide the answer." The Wez stood and walked to a nearby wall. There he retrieved something wrapped in an exquisite red and gold cloth. He returned to the table and carefully uncovered the object: a silver and black mirror. The Wez handed it to Magar, keeping the reflective surface angled away from the wizard. "Traveling backward in time creates ripples in our reality. You see, this mirror is very special—made from elements gathered from the umbraverse, which sits outside our universe and so is beyond our rules. As such, it can see what no other mirror can."

"And what might that be?" Magar asked.

"All realities. To travel in time is to change the present. This mirror, however, reflects both what was and what will be. So take a look for yourself, wizard. If I'm right, you'll see two versions of yourself."

"Why two?" Princess asked.

"Two, because once before a traveler walked through time. Most likely the World Sunderer, but who can say for certain?"

Magar slowly turned the mirror toward him. Inside he saw two images. The first showed him looking much like he was now, but instead of being dressed in the strange human attire, he was wearing the robes of a Tower magister, his hair longer and flowing down to his shoulders. The second image, however, showed him as a disembodied metallic head with dead eyes. "Madness," Magar exclaimed, turning the mirror over. Something about it shocked him to his very core.

"Not madness, I'm afraid, but a path through time," the Wez replied, trying to process the strangeness of what he saw over the wizard's shoulder. "Although which path you walk now, I cannot say."

"Let me see now," Princess demanded. "I think what we have here is a carnival trick."

"No," Magar interjected, still a bit shaken. "There is power there. Perhaps you should not look."

The Wez, however, ignored the wizard and handed the ornate mirror to Princess. "It is your choice," he said. Princess took it greedily, then flipped back her hair and looked into the mirror. She saw herself in her unicorn form, a silvery-white creature with a long horn projecting from her head and threads of pink hair mixed in with her glorious mane. But the second image made her recoil—she was made from metal and fashioned as some kind of monstrous machine. Instead of eyes, crimson lights glowed from hollowed-out sockets, and shiny sharpened teeth glared beneath metallic lips. Princess thrust the mirror toward the goblin.

"Explain or I swear I'll destroy you and turn this club into rubble."

"I'm sorry if the images were disturbing," the Wez said calmly as he put the ornate mirror away. "But the mirror only reflects, it does not create. May I suggest what's important is not what you saw but the number of reflections cast back. In this case, there were two—just as there have always been. If Max Spencer had used the *Codex* to travel back in time you would have seen *three*."

"So that's the whole point of your little freak show, to count to two?" Princess asked.

The Wez shrugged. "I believe we can say for certain that Max Spencer is either in the umbraverse or has traveled into the future. That is why the Gimbal is not working."

"If time travel were possible as you say," Magar added, thinking things over, "surely the Mad Sunderer would have gone to the day of his wife's accident and changed what happened. Given all we know, that seems the most logical choice."

"Indeed—and yet history remains."

"So what does that mean?" Princess asked. She was starting to tire of all the speculation.

"It means we have more questions than answers. For instance, can the Prime Spells be controlled at all? Can some destinies not be changed, no matter what we do? Can some spells be cast only once? Did someone other than Maximilian Sporazo travel through time? These are questions that are beyond our knowing—at least for now."

"Then to the original question," Magar continued, "what do you suggest we do? How do we find the boy and the *Codex*?"

"Well, we are traveling toward the future as we speak. Sooner or later you'll catch up to him—assuming you live long enough."

"That's hardly an option," Princess responded. "Is there no other way for us to travel into the future?"

"None that I know of," the Wez admitted.

"Then the only other option is the umbraverse," Magar said glumly. "But with the branch destroyed, that path is closed to us as well. Although I am not saddened by that fact."

"That idiot Kraken!" Princess shouted, slamming her fist on the table. "I had the power to take us to the umbraverse and he ruined it! So that's it, we're out of options, then?"

"Well now, I wouldn't say that," the Wez offered. "You see, to you the shattered branch from the Tree of Attenuation is dead. To me, a bit of necromancy can pull some life out of it yet."

"What does that mean? You could reattach it to my horn?"

"Oh no, nothing like that," the Wez answered with a sigh. "But I could concoct a drink for you—I'm thinking a bit of an herbal tea should do the trick. In any case, I happen to possess sand taken from the umbraverse itself. Not an easy thing to get, mind you, but if combined with the branches . . . well, I think I can get you there if you don't mind a little grit in your cup. I'll just require two of your silver leaves as trade. More than fair, I should think."

"Princess, we should be cautious," Magar warned. "The umbraverse is a place of strange magic and unfathomable horrors. I know a wizard who traveled there, a powerful spell caster with great potential. When she came back she could no longer even speak. Her eyes told us the truth of it—she had gone mad."

Princess, however, had long since made up her mind. She wasn't going to spend years stuck in the Mesoshire. And she certainly wasn't going to wait around for the future to just happen. She was a creature who needed to keep moving—a bored unicorn was a dangerous thing indeed. Princess produced one of the silver leaves, holding it out in front of her. "I'll give you one, not two. With one I can still send the boy back to the Maelshadow. And you know you will never have the chance for another."

The Wez hesitated for a moment and then put his hand out. When the leaf was passed to him, he gently walked it over to a vial and dropped it inside, pushing a rubber stopper in. "I will get started then," he said, quickly gathering other vials from around the room.

The process of making the tea required getting the broken branches, sand, and several other elements into a glass pot where the ingredients were pressed and strained. The Wez then made a second batch, this time without the sand but using other elements, and put them into tea bags instead of brewing. Before long, Magar and Princess were sitting with steaming cups of the first brew in their hands, and each had a tea bag stowed away for later use.

"You should have enough to go and come back," the Wez said, admiring his work. "I added a touch of peppermint to help with the flavoring—no extra charge."

"And we will be able to get back?" Magar asked, looking at the tea suspiciously.

The Wez shrugged. "I've never used actual branches from the Tree of Attenuation—but I believe I've got it worked out."

Magar looked back to Princess. "I think this is a mistake, Your Highness," he said, knowing he had to try to dissuade her one last time.

Princess frowned. "I know, and so you've said already. But I've made up my mind and we're going. So you drink first—I want to see what happens." Magar took a deep breath and brought the concoction to his lips. It tasted as bad as he'd imagined, but the peppermint did help. And then he blacked out.

The cup fell to the table and broke. Magar was gone.

"I assume this means it worked?" Princess asked, the steam rising from her own cup.

"I believe so. And if I may, after you take a drink remember to put your cup back on the table. The set was a gift."

Princess gave the Wez a last look. "Just so we're clear, if something goes wrong I will kill you. And then I'll brew my own tea made from the marrow in your bones. Do you understand?"

The Wez nodded. Such threats were to be expected, although a unicorn might be powerful enough to make good on them. "As much as I've enjoyed your company, Princess," he added finally, "I want nothing more from you, your wizard, Rezormoor Dreadbringer, or his Maelshadow lord. I've helped when asked, we've traded, and that will be the end of it. So, if you don't mind . . ."

Princess smiled, sipping from the teacup. But instead of putting the cup down she held it high above the table. When she popped out of the room, the cup fell and shattered.

The Wez sighed and got up to grab a towel and broom. But as he did, he took out some of the broken Tree of Attenuation branches that he'd snuck into his pocket. He placed them in a vial, secured the top, and added them to his collection. After everything he'd heard, he knew what he needed to do next: He needed to find Max Spencer before Princess and Magar did.

CHAPTER TWENTY-NINE

THERE'S A RAT IN THE SANDBOX

(THE TECHRUS—FUTURE)

THE MARKER FOR THE HUNTING GROUND REMINDED MAX OF THE Washington Monument, only instead of white stone it was black. It stretched above the tallest trees and had an intermittently flashing light on its topmost point. In the distance, Max could just make out the blinking lights of other obelisks as they competed against the orange and purple light of dusk.

As they rode, Max had time to think. The initial rush that came from getting everyone excited wore off quickly, and now just the ache in the middle of his stomach remained. He wondered about his mom and how all the parents must be going crazy trying to figure out what had happened.

Sarah called a halt, and they climbed out of the air sled.

As they did, one of the frobbits standing near Max tugged on his shirt, pointing off to the tree line. Something was walking toward them, waving. It was about five feet tall, green, and carried what looked like the skull of a ram on a long staff. The creature was wearing armored shoulder pads and a chest piece made from a bunch of smaller, bleached animal skulls. What struck Max the most, however, was the fact that the creature was see-through.

"Hey," it called, waving again. "You're Max, right?"

Max held the *Codex* in his hand, ready to open it to one of the pages he'd marked.

"Oh, I'm sorry," the little green creature continued, "this must be kind of weird for you."

Dwight stepped forward, his axe in his hand. "Don't get any bright ideas—greenie. So is this how it begins—round one or something?"

Yah Yah, who was standing nearby, shook his head. "We're not in the hunting grounds, friend dwarf. And I've never seen such as this."

"Yeah, you're all Ghost of Christmas Past–like," Dirk added.

"Did you, uh, need something?" Max asked. "How do you know me?"

"Well, we haven't exactly met—not yet, anyway," the creature answered. Dirk moved behind him and peered though the ghostlike body. "Although the spirits say we will, which could mean right now, or later in the past, or if I summon you after you're dead. There's a bit of ambiguity to these sorts of things."

"Begone, foul spirit goblin!" Dwight yelled, raising his axe. "I know you for what you are."

The creature smiled. "Well, at least you didn't call me a troll."

"You're a *goblin*?" Dirk exclaimed, stepping around to study it closer. "Awesome."

"That I am. I am called the Wez."

"The Wez?" Dwight repeated, lowering his axe and scratching at his beard. "I've heard that name—you're some kind of warlock who practices dark magic."

"That's me—a humble practitioner of the outlawed magic the Tower doesn't want acknowledged."

"The Tower—you mean the Wizard's Tower?" Max asked, remembering both the story of his ancestor and the vision he'd had when the *Codex* had first jumped them forward in time. "It's surrounded by a castle, right? And an ocean?"

"That's the one," the Wez said, giving Max an odd look. "You talk almost as if you've been there before."

"I'm sorry, but are you a ghost?" Sarah asked, still not having come to terms with the whole see-through goblin part.

"Not a ghost," the Wez said, motioning to himself. "This here is a reflection of a shadow passing through the umbraverse. It was the only way I could meet you."

Dirk passed his hand through the goblin. "Yep. Totally ethereal."

Sarah gave Dirk a double take. *"Ethereal?"*

"Yeah, gamer term," Dirk answered. "Means not solid. Full of . . . ghostyness."

"I know what it means," Sarah answered. "I'm just surprised *you* did."

"And why exactly are you wanting to meet us?" Dwight said, getting the conversation back on track.

"Well, you're going to need some help. And I can't do much, not with things the way they are—but I can do a little. And it took me a long time to find you—maybe too long, I'm afraid."

Max was suspicious. "Why? I don't understand."

"Well," the Wez said with a sigh, *"that's* a long story.

Let's just say there's nothing I'd like more than for you to come back in time and change some things—like the extinction of the human race, for one. You disappearing like you did set events into motion. Not that it was your fault, you just weren't around to stop them."

"I think we should be careful here," Sarah said to the group.

"Yeah," Dwight offered. "Maybe greenie here is telling the truth, and maybe this is some kind of unicorn trick."

"Unicorn?" the Wez asked, looking surprised. "Princess is *still* around—after all this time?"

"Robo-Princess is what the beastie calls herself now," Dwight answered.

The Wez shook his head. "Then I have truly underestimated her. I understand your reluctance to believe me, such as I am. But you cannot allow this Robo-Princess to win."

"It's okay, you can trust the goblin," Glenn suddenly added from Max's belt. "He can't hide anything—he's, like, see-through. Plus, I can totally vouch for him—he and my sister used to hang out."

"Sis—," Max started to say, giving Glenn a strange look. But the Wez raised his staff, interrupting.

"A long story and we have little time," the Wez continued, turning back to Max. "So I'm just going to give it to you straight. The last few centuries were a real low point in history. Even worse than the plague, which I might have accidentally had something do with, but that's not important right now. What is important is you've got the *Codex of Infinite Knowability* and nobody can teach you how to use it. I've spent a long time working out how to find you and what to tell you once I did. So here it goes: The spells you really need aren't going to be just written down in that book of yours. You try and overthink magic that big and you'll never make it work. The key is flowing around in that red gook you call blood. So when things get bad—and I'm sure they will—just relax and listen for it."

"It?" Max asked, not able to think of anything else to say.

"Yeah. You'll know it when you find it. And if you survive the day and make it back, come and find me in the Mesoshire. We'll have a lot to talk about. And I probably won't know you. Just tell me to look at the mirror and count what I see."

"Er," Max replied.

"I know, sounds a bit crazy. Just tuck that last bit away. For now, the key is to just relax."

It seemed that anytime someone told Max to "just relax," it was because he was about to have something *bad* happen to him, whether it came from a teacher, a coach, or a nurse holding a big needle. In the end, "just relax" might be the most unrelaxing thing you could ever say to a person.

The Wez started to shimmer.

"A long time ago I met the creatures hunting you . . . ," the Wez said, his voice trailing off as if he were falling down a well. "Remember, this isn't just about you; it's about every human being on the face of the planet. If you die, the world dies with you, Max."

"Oh yeah, telling him *that* will get him to relax," Dirk said, turning to Max. "He doesn't know you very well, does he?"

And with that the Wez popped out of view.

"You humans are very exciting," Yah Yah said, looking around at the group.

"So what do we do now . . . besides relax?" Sarah asked.

Yah Yah pointed to the light at the top of the obelisk.

"When it turns green we go in. It won't be long now."

Max looked at the empty space between the flashing lights—he guessed the space was probably five or six times bigger than a football field. "And what happens when we enter, exactly?"

Yah Yah looked over at the hunting grounds and then spoke with a heavy voice. "Wonderment. Then fear. Then death."

All things considered, Max thought, Yah Yah could use some help when it came to his pep talks.

Overhead, the flashing light turned green.

Max was completely unprepared for what happened when he stepped past the large obelisk. There was a kind of invisible wall, like a thick strand of spiderweb that stretched around the ground's perimeter. As Max and his friends entered, they could feel the tension on their hands and bodies, stretching just a bit and then disappearing as they passed through. But on the other side everything had changed. For one, it was no longer night outside, but day. And instead of the forest they were standing in the middle of a desert. A hundred yards ahead, a jagged pyramid rose out of the sand and was the only visible structure. Meanwhile, frobbits and faeries began popping in as their platoons marched forward.

"Wow," Sarah gasped as she shielded her eyes from the sun. "I wasn't expecting anything like this."

"Hey, that's a ziggurat!" Dirk exclaimed, pointing to the pyramid. "I know because I was the dungeon master for the Sun God of the Ziggurat module." The priest frobbits, seeing Dirk point, suddenly fell to their knees and began chanting at the ancient-looking structure. "No!" Dirk chastised them. "This is not the temple of the great and powerful Dirkster." The priest frobbits rose, dusting the sand from their robes and playing the whole thing off.

"I don't understand," Max said to Yah Yah, who had joined him. "Where are we?"

"We are still in the hunting grounds," Yah Yah replied. "This is the way it is here—the land can take many forms, but only inside the great blinking structures."

"It's like this is all a game," Sarah said, looking around. "And basically we're standing on the game board."

Max looked at the ziggurat. "Do you think we should go there?"

"In Sun Tzu's *Art of War* it says you should never fight going uphill."

"General Sarah is wise," Yah Yah confirmed. "Normally we bury ourselves in the sand and wait for the battle to end."

"Does that ever work?" Max asked.

"Not so much, no."

Suddenly it occurred to Max that the dwarf was missing. "Where's Dwight?"

They turned and looked around but there was no sign of him. Meanwhile, frobbits and faeries continued to enter the hunting grounds.

"He was walking right beside me," Sarah said.

"Maybe we should go back and look for him," Max suggested. They turned and walked back, but Max and his friends went past the point they had entered without ever appearing at the forest. Max stopped, completely confused. Sand stretched out to the horizon, and it felt as if they could keep walking through it forever.

"How's this possible?" Sarah exclaimed, stopping next to Max and looking around. "We should be out by now."

Yah Yah came running up to the group. "He's not here," he exclaimed. "I've checked everywhere, but there's no sign of him."

"I don't understand," Max said, already baking under

the desert sun. "Has this ever happened before?"

Yah Yah shrugged. "We've never brought a dwarf before."

Finally the group decided there was nothing more to do but rejoin the troops and hope for the best. They marched toward the ziggurat, the sand making it hard to move. By the time they reached the structure's base, Max was panting and drenched in sweat. The pyramid itself appeared to be constructed out of large blocks of sandstone, each about five feet high.

"What now?" Max gasped, looking at Sarah.

"I think we form a perimeter around the base," Sarah answered, turning to Yah Yah. "Have the infantry units line up on the bottom level, and tell the faeries to take up a defensive position higher up." Yah Yah nodded and ran off, issuing the orders. Max watched as two frobbits joined hands by interlocking their fingers, then hoisted two of their companions, one after the other, to the first step. Those two then did the same, until the frobbits had a fairly efficient ladder system going. The faeries simply flew to the top, however, making it look easy.

Dirk and Sarah had joined hands and motioned for Max to step up. He found himself strangely annoyed that

Dirk was holding Sarah's hand. "I'm not sure this is going to work—it looked a lot smaller from a distance," he said, still catching his breath from all the sand walking.

"Come on, you can do it," Dirk called out.

"Yeah, we'll help you," Sarah added.

Max awkwardly stepped into their cupped hands, but when he put his weight down Dirk and Sarah fell forward, nearly banging heads.

"Wow—you're heavier than you look," Dirk exclaimed, shaking his tingling fingers back to life. "And you look pretty heavy."

"You know what, this was a stupid idea," Max said, kicking at the sand. "How am I supposed to fight some robot hunter when I can't even climb a step?" He glanced over at Sarah, who was looking a lot more vulnerable and girl-like than he remembered. He realized she was depending on him—that no matter how smart and capable she was as a general, Max was the only person in the entire universe who could save her. The realization seemed to awaken something in him, and suddenly his mind stretched out to the *Codex* and touched a spell that seemed big and heavy.

"Gravity," Max said, his voice as deep as if he were

standing at the base of a large canyon. Suddenly he, Dirk, and Sarah began to float into the air.

Max could feel his friends in his mind, and he wrapped the spell around them as if it were a kind of blanket. From there it took no more effort than to think where he wished to go, and they were gently carried in that direction. Below, the frobbits stood in wide-eyed wonderment. The priests were on their knees, bowing frantically.

"Hey, how about a little warning first!" Dirk exclaimed, his arms flailing.

"Max, *you're* doing this?" Sarah shouted, looking around uneasily.

But Max didn't answer—he was completely focused on controlling the immensity of the spell. He carefully guided them to the top of the ziggurat and set them down. When he finally released the spell it blew away from his consciousness, and Max's limbs felt as if he'd just spent an entire gym class trying to do the rope climb. He plopped down, exhausted.

"Max!" Sarah exclaimed, putting her hands on his shoulders.

Max looked up at her, adjusting his glasses and doing his best to smile. "Weird, huh?"

Sarah smiled, taking a seat next to him and letting her feet hang over the top stone. Below, the frobbits had resumed their climbing while the snow faeries looked on with confused expressions. "I don't know how you did that—but it was impressive. Really."

The truth was, Max didn't know how he'd done it either. When he'd thought about Sarah, knowing he was responsible for her, the spell had suddenly come to him.

"Dirk, why don't you have your guys keep a lookout," Sarah suggested.

"Yeah, good idea." Dirk began organizing his priests to scan for trouble.

It didn't take long.

A snow faerie pointed, and Dirk turned to see something coming at them, floating rather slowly through the air. Dirk was about to shout an alarm when he recognized it as the frobbit Max had accidentally lit on fire. "Uh, Max?" Dirk said, tapping Max on his shoulder.

Max looked up to the see the floating frobbit drift by, close enough that the bandage on his nose was clearly visible. Max and the frobbit made eye contact, and Max hurried to try to find the spell in his mind again, but it wasn't there. All Max could do was watch the frobbit float past, drifting gently to wherever the wind took him. The frobbit didn't look especially happy about it.

Suddenly there was a commotion at the base of the pyramid. Max jumped to his feet and looked down. Yah Yah was several steps below, pointing frantically at the base of the ziggurat. "The hunter!"

Robotouille had popped up near a clump of frobbits along the pyramid's base. The metallic rat's metal ears twitched and its talons clicked against one another. Many of the frobbits had dived headfirst into the sand, arms and legs flailing in an attempt to bury themselves. Robotouille sprang forward, its metallic tail twisting like a snake as its claws clamped down on the shoulder of a frobbit who was trying to get away.

Sarah ran to the side, yelling at the frobbits to form up as a squad, but thousands of years of panic-based instincts were overriding two weeks of training. The snow faeries managed to nock their arrows, but there was so much chaos below that they didn't dare fire. The captured frobbit who was struggling against the powerful grip of the machine suddenly reached up and grabbed the arm of the robotic rat and flipped it over his shoulder. It was a near-perfect judo throw, and Sarah felt some measure of satisfaction at seeing the frobbit execute it successfully. The robot rat, lying flat on the sand, froze momentarily. Since it hadn't been programmed for a frobbit that actually fought back, its processing unit had decided the flipping incident required a system-wide reboot. It was just enough time for the frobbit to slip away and make a run for it.

Sarah yelled for the other frobbits to attack. It was a word she had had to teach them, since there was no frobbit-language equivalent (compared to the seventeen ways to say "surrender"). The frobbits gripped their weapons and advanced, but they were largely unsure what to do. Max looked down at his spell book, the panic of actually being in a fight making it hard for him to find the spell he was looking for. Instead, he opened the page to the first thing he could find: the Level One Spell of Tentative Candle Ignition, and read it.

Robotouille's tail flipped the robot rat back onto its feet. It stretched its hand out as two butcher knives extended from hiding places along its arms, traveling down until they settled in each of the skeletal fingers with a loud click. Its head scanned the area, ears twitching like tiny radar units looking for the most available victim. It found one: a frobbit rapidly digging a hole just a few feet away. When the frobbit looked back and saw the robot hunter bearing down on him, he gulped and began digging faster. Robotouille's processor prepared to ring up its first kill. It leapt with lightning speed over to where the hapless frobbit was working and raised its blades for the killing blow.

Max let the spell fly. The flame, designed to light a candle so a novice wizard wouldn't have to get out from under the sheets on a cold morning, suddenly took life deep within the central core of the robotic rat's computer brain. The flame was small and short-lived, but it quickly burned through the main logic chip that controlled nearly all of Robotouille's primary functions. The robot rat froze, blades still hanging in the air, then it tipped slowly forward, falling headfirst into the sand (the two meat cleavers landing on both sides of the wide-eyed frobbit). A whiff of black smoke drifted from the armor-plated head and its eyes went dark.

It was an unprecedented moment for the frobbits. They stopped their running and hiding and tentatively approached Robotouille, poking at it and then jumping away. But the monster showed no signs of life. A great cry went up from the troops, and Yah Yah turned to see Max staring down in astonishment, the open *Codex* in his hand.

"Max, you did it! What powerful magic!" Yah Yah shouted as another cheer rose up from the ranks.

"Uh . . . yeah," Max said, closing the book. He must have gotten lucky—that was the only explanation.

Dirk was jumping up and down and pumping his fist in the air. "What, is that all you got? Stupid robots, we owned you!"

CHAPTER THIRTY

NOTHING RUINS YOUR DAY LIKE A KILLER CUBE

(THE TECHRUS—FUTURE)

BACK AT MACHINE CITY, THERE WAS A STUNNED SILENCE. THE ENTIRE stadium had been turned into a 3-D holograph of the hunting grounds, showing a bird's-eye view of the pyramid and the battle below. They had watched Robotouille meet its end almost as if they were there. And now they watched as two frobbits pried the meat cleavers from the robot's hands. Never before in the history of the hunt had something actually *killed* a hunter—at least not on purpose. It was a moment of shock for the machine cubes watching from the stadium. The fact that the humans could do such a thing sent real fear traveling along their networked connections. They started to reconsider their initial assessment of the soft-looking humans. Even Robo-Princess had to admit that seeing the boy defeat the hunter, even though it was part of her larger plan, was unsettling. Max didn't look like the great sorcerers she had seen over the years. But he'd managed to lift himself and his friends to the top of the pyramid (which was a pretty good bit of magic), as well as kill Robotouille without so much as a giant fireball, upheaval of earth, or even freezing cones of death. The boy had simply pointed at the hunter and it was over. Perhaps she had underestimated him.

Robo-Princess issued a silent command for the big screen to switch to an image of Wall-up. "Our first hunter has died a valiant death," she said, her voice booming from the amplified speakers around the Machine City stadium. "Normally Robotouille could have hacked through the ranks of such an army single-handedly. But we must move on—it's what our dear hunter would have wanted. And besides, you all know our next champion. Don't let his looks fool you—he's been reinforced against the harshest environments. Tough, determined, and unstoppable, let's see how the humans fare against Wall-up!" The applause rose again to fill the stadium as the machines anticipated the retribution that Wall-up would surely bring. "And let's give our players a new world to contend with as well!" The holographic field suddenly shimmered.

Back on the pyramid, Max turned to Yah Yah. "Cenede told us there'd be three rounds, so that must have been the first." But before Yah Yah could respond, everything blurred and seemed to fall out of place. When the world came back together, they were no longer standing on top of a desert pyramid. Instead, they found themselves inside the gutted hull of some giant spaceship left broken and stripped. In fact, they seemed to be in a huge junkyard of sorts, with old machines and equipment littered everywhere.

"I was right!" Sarah exclaimed as she shook off the strange sensation and caught a frobbit who was about to tumble over. "They've changed the game board again. And probably made it harder."

"Some kind of futuristic graveyard," Dirk said, his eyes wide. "Maybe there's some useful stuff lying around."

"There's definitely things we can use as better weapons," Sarah replied, bending down to pick up a pipe. "Spread the word for our infantry to re-arm themselves. Have the faeries post sentries and be on the lookout—we don't know what could be out here waiting for us."

Several frobbits acknowledged the order and ran off. One of them, to Sarah's annoyance, was skipping.

"Yeah, this makes total sense," Dirk said, looking around. "We have to fight through various levels until we work our way up to the big boss."

"That would be Robo-Princess," Yah Yah added. "She's the one the others follow."

"Round two, then," Max said.

Yah Yah found a long piece of jagged metal, tossing his club in favor of the heavier weapon. "You've taught us that we can fight and win. Now we just need the strength to do it again."

"It's not about strength, it's about our wizard and his powerful magic," Dirk said, turning to Max. "You just got to keep doing what you're doing, buddy. I bet you're totally like level four by now."

"I was lucky," Max admitted, not liking Dirk's assessment of his magical prowess. He thought he'd feel better by saying it out loud, but it didn't help.

"There's no such thing as luck," Glenn added from his scabbard. "Just ask the footless rabbit. Seriously—they're easy to catch."

Sarah decided to ignore Glenn—she had work to do.

"So what's our plan?" Max asked. "It would be real easy to get lost or separated in all of this."

"Now that the machines know we can beat them I'm guessing they won't be caught off guard," Sarah answered. "Sun Tzu wrote that you should advance only if it's to your advantage. So I think it's best not to spend too much time exploring—we should set up a defensive position pretty much where we are. There are places to hide, and maybe we can spring a trap."

Max nodded, more glad than ever that Sarah was with him. "Okay. I'll look for another spell."

"Good," Sarah replied. "I'll reconnoiter and see what we have to work with." Sarah pointed to a hollowed-out structure some thirty yards away and began jogging over to it. "I'll be over here if you need anything," she called back over her shoulder.

"Reconnoiter?" Max asked after Sarah was out of earshot.

"I think it's a fancy way of saying 'look around,'" Dirk replied. "But if you say it like that you sound like you totally know what you're talking about. Like calling someone a sesquipedalian because they use big words. That usually shuts them up."

Yah Yah decided the conversation had gotten too confusing, so he ran after Sarah. He motioned for a group of frobbits and faeries to follow him.

"And in the meantime, I'll have my priests call upon the power of the great and terrible Dirkster," Dirk offered, his robed followers nodding that it was a good idea.

"Maybe it would be helpful if you took this a little more seriously," Max snapped.

"Hey, the machines are playing a game with us—the only way I know how to win is to play back."

"You're right," Max said. "I'm sorry."

Dirk saluted and turned, calling his priests over. "Okay, in this next battle we need to be ready. Remember, we're the healing class—we may not get all the glory, but nobody wins without us around."

Suddenly an explosion rang out in the distance. Max hustled to the edge of the ruined starship in time to see a skyscraper of junk come down, its sheer size making it fall as if in slow motion. A giant cloud of debris rose ominously alongside it.

"The hunter is here," a frobbit announced, pointing at the gray cloud. Max looked down to see a yellow daisy painted on the frobbit's armor—it wasn't exactly confidence building. Max hurried over to an old hangar where Sarah was clearing material away from the floor. He pointed in the direction of the crash.

"I know," she responded, "but look: There's a pit in here, like some kind of maintenance area or something." A number of frobbits were working hard to haul off various pieces of twisted metal and parts. "Maybe if we can get it to fall in we can trap it. Assuming it's not too big or can fly or something. It's the best I can come up with on short notice."

"It's better than doing nothing," Max managed to reply.

Yah Yah and several other frobbits pointed to a large piece of sheet metal on the other side of the bay. "Will this do?" he called out.

Sarah looked at it and did some quick measuring in her head. "Yeah, I think so," she yelled back. "Drag it over."

A group ran over to help Yah Yah move the sheet toward the pit. Sarah ordered several more squads of frobbits and faeries to take up positions around the hangar. "It's an ambush," she announced. "We'll need to lure the hunter in—but we'll need some protection in case it has projectiles or something." The frobbits nodded and began to disperse.

"What if there's more than one?" Max asked, suddenly feeling vulnerable.

"We have to plan according to what Cenede told us, otherwise we're *really* in trouble."

Max looked up. The former blue skies of the desert were gray and overcast now. "If the hunter falls in we should have the others ready to attack. And while it's busy, I can cast a fireball spell. In a tight space like that, it might get pretty hot—maybe hot enough to melt its chips or something."

"Then it's a plan," Sarah declared. "But just so you know, you're the only one who stands any chance of destroying whatever it is. Everything else is just a distraction."

Max gripped the *Codex* in his hands. "And if we can't get it to go into the pit? Or if it has bionic legs and jumps out? Or what if it's fireproof?"

Sarah stopped what she was doing and thought about it for a moment. "There's no alternative," she finally said. "Either it works or we're probably not going to make it." It was ominous hearing Sarah talk like that.

Before long they had the pit covered and the ambush set up. All they could do now was wait. Max and Sarah hunkered down behind a small pile of junk parts, where they had a clear view of the hangar, while bands of frob-bits huddled together beneath piles of scrap or within the shells of hollowed-out equipment and ships. Squads of faeries took the high ground, detached to support the frobbits wherever possible. Dirk and his priests remained inside the shell of the large spacecraft, ready to help the injured.

Sarah looked around and took everything in. She understood she didn't have the kind of knowledge a true general would have, so she had to just go with what she'd written about for her history class. She couldn't help but second-guess herself, however, and she was about to stand and reposition one of the frobbit platoons when suddenly they heard it. It was a squeaking, tanklike sound—a mechanized, heavy crawl moving toward them. Sarah and Max ducked low, waiting and watching.

Wall-up turned a corner at the far end of the clear-ing. The hunter was slow, methodical, and more or less a cube. It had binocular-like eyes that pivoted on an elongated neckpiece and carried a large hammer on its back. Two electronic arms with clawlike hands were opening and closing as if in anticipation of crushing something. It wasn't exactly as intimidating as the other robots that Max had imagined in his head, but it looked sturdy, which could be a real problem.

Max pushed his glasses up and watched as the hunter rolled to the area between the hangar and the spaceship shell. Its head kept swiveling as it searched for its prey, and Max could see ocular lenses turn like a camera trying to focus.

"Ready?" Sarah asked, turning to Max. Max opened the *Codex* to the place he'd bookmarked and nodded.

Sarah held up a small, reflective bit of metal and signaled the others. There was a sudden commotion as frobbits jumped out, banging metal pipes and yelling. A volley of faerie arrows arched through the air and began falling around the hunter. The robot stopped, its eyes swinging around and focusing on the dancing frobbits. Then the tracks turned, swiveling the robot in the direction of the trap.

"That's it," Sarah said under her breath. Max looked down at the *Codex* and saw the fireball spell; his hands were shaking. He needed to be ready at exactly the right moment.

The frobbits continued to make noise and call after the hunter. Insults ranged from "Over here, blockhead" to "Your mother was a trash compactor!" The frobbits appeared emboldened after their last (and probably first) victory, and many had moved too far from their hiding places.

"Get down!" Sarah yelled as the frobbits drifted away from their cover. "Get back!"

The frobbits were used to swift-moving hunters, and even with their new survival training they didn't think much of the slow-moving Wall-up, so when the laser erupted from the binocular head, the explosion caught them by surprise, sending several of them flying.

"No!" Sarah cried out, standing up. Max had to grab her and pull her down as Wall-up's head swung around and fired at them. Max could feel the heat of the beam sizzling the air overhead. The robot's head swiveled back as the tanklike tracks propelled it closer toward the ruins of the old hangar. Farther inside, another frobbit jumped out, egging the hunter on. But the laser was too fast for it, and after the explosion there was no sign of the little soldier. All the while the faeries continued to fire their arrows, but they bounced harmlessly off the metal skin.

The frobbits, however, had gotten the point about the laser and so they stayed hunkered down.

The hunter pulled the hammer from its back and continued toward the hanger.

Sporadic fire from the faeries seemed to egg Wall-up on, and before long it approached the pit. The opening had been hidden by the large sheet of metal and other debris, and looked solid.

Sarah and Max crawled back to their spots at the top of the pile. "Come on, keep going," Sarah whispered, urging the robot forward under her breath. "Just a little farther."

But when Wall-up got to the edge, it stopped. Its free pincer arm extended, grabbing hold of the metal and lifting it a few inches off the ground.

"Max, it's not going to work!" Sarah exclaimed, realizing the robot had figured it out. "You need to do something—now!"

Panicked, Max quickly opened the *Codex* to the place he had marked. He started reading the spell at once, but it immediately felt wrong—something had changed. In a flash the energy of an enormous flame had gathered around him, swirling and building like a vortex. The pages of the *Codex* began to flap in the hot wind, threatening to rip free from his hand. Max struggled to keep his eyes open, and he managed to see a single word written across the top of the open page: *Firestorm*. That wasn't a spell Max had even come close to attempting.

"Max!" Sarah shouted. Her hair was starting to whip about as the torrent of hot air intensified. Max tried to concentrate on the spell, to slow it down and push it back into the *Codex*. But it was no use. He could feel the power of it as it grew, exploding into the sky with greater and greater fury. Dust and debris began to lift into the air, joining with the magical storm. Then, before he knew what had happened, the *Codex* itself was wrenched from his hands. Max jumped to his feat, leaping after it, but the wind hammered him like a fist. He was sent crashing and rolling down the mound of junk, suffering numerous cuts across his exposed skin. When Max rolled to a stop at the bottom of the pile, it was all he could to do to look up and find Sarah.

"Run!" Max cried, his face bloody and his glasses barely hanging on his head. Around him, the maelstrom surged and heaved. Sarah ducked and began running for shelter.

A loud thunderclap exploded in the sky above, and as Max rose to his feet, doing his best to keep his balance, he could feel the temperature of the air surge with heat. He started to run, forgetting everything he hated about running as he made a mad dash across the clearing toward the battered skeleton of the gutted spaceship. It was the first time he ran without feeling pain—he didn't feel his legs, or the burning in his lungs, or the sharp ache in his side. Something inside him had shut all of that down and he simply ran with all the force his body had. He yelled for everyone to take cover. He wasn't sure anyone could even hear him over the rising tempest, but he had to try.

Sarah was ahead of him, and she barely avoided a lightning strike that exploded near her. She managed to scramble into the stripped spacecraft as another thunderclap shook the ground, knocking Max forward so that he fell into the interior of the old ship. His momentum took him over a bolted-down table and into the metal wall. As he got to his feet, his ears ringing and stars dancing across his field of vision, it began to rain. Only it wasn't water—it was raining fire.

The frobbits took cover wherever they could; hiding in small nooks or covering themselves with anything they could find. The robot, exposed along the edge of the roofless hangar, cranked its binocular eyes up as a sheet of fire fell from the sky, drowning it in molten red.

At the ship, Sarah ran over and helped Max to his feet—they were protected but still too close to the raging inferno outside. She led Max farther into the spaceship's interior, until they found a spot where they could collapse against a wall. Outside the torrent of fire continued, and around them drops of liquid fire crawled along walls or dripped into burning pools on the floor.

"I lost it," Max exclaimed as his head began to clear. "I lost the *Codex*."

Sarah simply had to push the news from her mind. The very thought of it was so terrifying she knew it would keep her from thinking and doing the things necessary to stay alive.

But all Max could think about was the horrible truth that he'd lost the only way for them to get home. And in the process, he'd summoned something so destructive that he might have killed every soul he'd tried to save.

"I shouldn't have even tried. Look what I've done."

Sarah knew that she should try to comfort him, but the words just didn't come. She sat there and watched as the world erupted.

The storm lasted only a few minutes, but in its aftermath the earth sizzled and steamed. When it was over, Max and Sarah slowly stepped outside, feeling the tug of their shoes as their rubber soles began to melt. They hurried along the edge of the ship's frame, finding groups of frobbits and faeries that had made it through the storm. There were many burns, and when Max found Dirk he was helping his priests attend to the wounds. The frobbit healers had numerous medicines they kept in woven bags, including leaves that could be chewed to dull the pain.

Sarah headed toward the hanger, finding Wall-up severely damaged but still alive. The binocular eyes had melted away, leaving only the singed square body and slowly opening and closing clawed pincers. What remained of its wheels spun in the melted black goo that had been its tracks. Max and Dirk walked up to Sarah as frobbits crawled out from their hiding places to join them. Many, but not all.

"Finish it," Sarah said coldly. Max, remembering Glenn at his belt, slowly drew the dagger and pressed it against the hunter's chassis. He expected it would take a bit of work to get through the steaming metal shell in order to pry it open, but when he pushed, the magical blade slid in easily, driving itself through bundles of electronic nerves. There was an audible *snap* as the system overloaded and the wheels and claw stopped moving. Wall-up was no more.

As Max returned Glenn to his sheath, he noticed that Sarah had several burns along her arms. Seeing them made him nauseated—not because they were too serious, but because *he* had caused them. "I did that to you."

"No, Max, you won," Dirk offered, noticing his friend's change in demeanor. "You killed it. It was like a tank and you totally took it out."

"It wasn't supposed to be like that—there were other spells—"

"And you think a normal fireball would have hurt *that*?" Dirk asked. "You did exactly what you needed to."

"But it doesn't matter, the *Codex* is gone," Max lamented. "And even if it wasn't, I'm not using it again." Max turned to see frobbits and faeries gently carrying their dead to a tarp that was being used to cover them. The sight made tears rush to his eyes. "I did this. I killed them."

Yah Yah ran up to him, grinning. "Max, we did it!" But Yah Yah could see that Max did not share the sentiment. The frobbit's features softened, and he walked over and gently placed his hands on Max's head, forcing him to look at him. "No. You do not blame yourself for this. Every day we were hunted, and every day more of us fell. There's not one here, frobbit or faerie alike, who would have lived to survive the machines. And so each of us would gladly give our lives if it meant saving others—if it meant protecting our homes and families. Do not dishonor those who stood with us, my friend. Every one of them would have come even if they had known their fate. We were proud to fight with you. We are proud to fight still."

Max listened to Yah Yah and felt the burden begin to lift from his heart. It was a terrible loss, but his friend was so sincere, he realized he had to hold on to some measure of hope. Max smiled and shook Yah Yah's hand. "Thank you."

"No, thank you," Yah Yah started to say, but the world changed again and darkness fell over everything.

Max thought it peculiar that he couldn't feel the ground beneath him anymore, and when he tried to speak there was no sound. The machines were changing the board again, only now he had no magic to defend his friends. Max considered this for a long time, and at some point he must have slept. He had dreamed he was drifting in the air with his friends. Then one by one they were snatched away, reaching for him as they were dragged into the darkness below. In his mind he heard them screaming. Or perhaps they really were—he couldn't be certain.

Robo-Princess watched as the screen showing the beloved Wall-up went dark. Two hunters had now been put down. The battle had been more than impressive— it was magnificent. Robo-Princess had never seen such magic in the Techrus, and for the first time she realized the boy wizard had a power that eclipsed even her own. Yes, he was a novice—that much was obvious. He lacked the control and precision of those who spent their lives cultivating and understanding what it was to wield such power. But if there had been any doubt about the reality of the *Codex*, it was now gone. Max Spencer was dangerous.

"Citizens of Machine City," Robo-Princess announced. "We have witnessed another tragic defeat and have lost our beloved Wall-up." A wave of blinking lights filled the stadium, drowning out the stars in the night sky overhead.

Robo-Princess knew the machines were going to take the loss hard, but she was starting to sense something else—fear.

"Let us take comfort in the fact that he left our world fighting to the very end. But know this—vengeance will be ours! You see now just how powerful the human has become. He wields magic like no other. But then, our next champion is like no other as well. Fear not, for in the battle of magic versus technology we have only begun to fight. The humans will pay for what they have dared to do to us!"

Robo-Princess cut the communication channel. She climbed down from the podium as an automated voice announced a brief broadcast intermission. "Did you see that?" she said as she approached Robo-Magar, grateful her robotic voice didn't betray the anxiety she felt.

"That last display of magic—it has been lifetimes since I have seen such," Robo-Magar replied. "I may be a machine, but I was a human first. I forgot just how resilient we were."

Robo-Princess decided enough was enough, and sent a sub-routine to bolster her resolve while servos attended to her during the break. She began to feel better immediately. "You forget I wiped them out—all of them, single-handedly," she replied, the last of her fears blocked from her system. "Humans and all their technology were no match for me and my magic. And now I have both."

"True," Robo-Magar said coolly. "But to command the *Codex* itself, had that been available to the humans during the war—"

"It would not have changed a thing. Don't fret, Magar, all is happening according to plan. One more defeat and then I'll make my final appearance and destroy these humans myself."

"Perhaps you're a bit overconfident," Robo-Magar said carefully. "Maybe we should rethink our strategy?"

"Did you actually think I wouldn't be prepared for such an eventuality? Of course I have a plan, my pessimistic old wizard."

Magar wasn't exactly surprised. Princess had several lifetimes of experience to guide her. "Then what do you intend?"

"Let's just say I've changed things up a bit. Humans are always undone by their emotions, so I'm going to exploit that. It will give me what I need to avenge the fallen and become so popular that my transition to leader will be assured."

"And why do you desire this new government job, exactly?" Magar asked.

"Because I've entertained the machines, but now I wish to rule them. Empress Princess has a nice ring to it, don't you think?"

Purple came floating in, its processor getting real-time data about the viewer numbers. "Word's spreading around the city—more and more machines are tuning in. The deaths of Robotouille and Wall-up were tragic, but the ratings are going through the roof! If we'd known this we might have had hunters die more often."

"Everything's happening at the right time, and exactly as I said it would," Robo-Princess said, her smugness chip working perfectly.

"There's just some concern, well, that the humans might actually *win*. There's real fear out there. Some of the executives are wondering if we're pushing it a bit too far—if you really have control over the situation?"

"Being afraid is what being entertained is all about," Robo-Princess replied, trying not to sound irritated. "If you want ratings like this you have to live on the edge.

But don't worry, I was just telling Magar that I've decided to change things up for the third act—a little surprise to exploit their weakness."

Purple blinked several times as it communicated with the executive team. "They're pleased you seem to have a plan," it reported back.

"Good. Now run along so I can finish getting ready. We have the finale to prepare for."

Purple floated off as Robo-Princess preened in front of a floating mirror one of the servos had unveiled.

"I find myself thinking about the Kraken," Robo-Magar said.

"The Kraken? Now, there's a name I haven't heard in ages."

"It occurred to me that the only foes that have been problematic for you have been humans when endowed with magic. Remember the time in the Mesoshire when that boy took your horn? That had to have been a first."

"I wasn't expecting it. Magrus humans can be so predictable. It took me awhile to understand that the Techrus humans were more capricious. The boy simply caught me by surprise."

"Which again," Robo-Magar continued, "is my point.

What you face now is not some cattle-like human. You say you have a plan, but I believe you are still underestimating him, just as you did with the Kraken. You should be wary they don't end you as they have the others."

Robo-Princess whirled, feeling true anger for the first time in a long time.

"You're growing insolent, Magar. If I didn't know you better, I'd think you were rooting for the humans."

Robo-Magar floated closer to the metallic unicorn. "Yes, I *am* rooting for the humans. I have always been rooting for them, or the frobbits, or faeries, or whatever other weak and hapless creature you had to destroy to serve your appetites. I tolerated you out of fear, but mostly I despised you—loathed you, for your *weakness*. You were born a magical creature with immense power, but you have always been just a frightened little girl, spoiled and forever indulging in a world that you think exists to serve you. But the humans will destroy you. And they will do so on this very night and in front of the millions of machines you believe are your fans. And in the end, when you're gone, you'll not be worshipped or even loved, simply despised as the monster you are."

The anger came so swiftly, the command so automatically, that when the lightning bolt erupted from Princess's horn and struck the floating metallic head, she had to rewind the playback to make sure she had actually done it. The power behind the strike was several times greater than that necessary to fuse the electronics and melt the processor into a puddle of silicon.

The head dropped to the floor, rolling just once so it stopped, looking up at Robo-Princess one final time. Robo-Magar's last thought was one of victory—for too long he had been a prisoner, and now he was finally free. And if such a victory could be snatched by one as lowly and powerless as he, then perhaps there was hope for the humans after all. It was a pleasant last thought, he decided.

CHAPTER THIRTY-ONE

SUDDEN DEATH

(THE TECHRUS—FUTURE)

MAX SLOWLY OPENED HIS EYES, FEELING GROGGY. HE SHIFTED HIS weight, stirring against a blur of strange lights. But as he tried to move, the ground under him suddenly shifted and swayed. The sensation of falling shocked his system awake, and as he flailed out with his hands he encountered a hard surface. Fighting the first few moments of motion sickness, Max remained on his back and took several deep breaths. He sat up slowly, looked around, and realized that he was inside some kind of large, transparent cube—about eight feet square. A heavy chain connected to it at the top and ran upward into the darkness. Max rose carefully to his feet, finding his balance. The sensation reminded him of his first attempt to ride a skateboard (it didn't turn out well). He tried to move toward one of the walls but the cage tilted violently—forcing him to inch back to the center.

Max wasn't the only person held captive. All around him similar cubes hung on chains, filled with either frobbits or faeries. Each cube was lit by a single beam of light shining from above. Remembering Glenn, Max reached for his belt and felt the magical dagger.

"Hey, watch the eye-holes," Glenn announced. "I'm a powerful magical dagger, you know."

"What are we doing here?"

"Ah, the great question. From the lowliest peasant to the greatest king, sooner or later everyone wonders just why we're here? What's our purpose? What's this thing called life all about?"

"No, not that!" Max hissed under his breath. "I mean, why are we being held like this?"

"Oh, that. I really wasn't paying attention."

"You weren't paying attention? You mean as I was knocked out and put into a giant see-through cube?"

"Not that important in the grand scheme of things. But I *did* realize that if you want to love what you do, you need to do what you love. Now that's the kind of thinking that can get you out of the box—well, the metaphorical one. This one, probably not so much."

Max remembered the *Codex* and looked around frantically—it was nowhere to be seen.

"What about the *Codex*?" Max asked, nearly falling over when he tried to look behind him. "Have you seen it?"

"Why? Have you forgotten what it looks like?"

"No, I haven't forgotten what it looks like! I just thought having it before we fight Robo-Princess might be a good idea."

"Oh yeah, definitely a good idea. You should totally do that."

An amplified voice suddenly filled the air. "Machines, what we've seen today is unprecedented. Two of our glorious hunters have fallen, and so we must ask, why? Have we grown complacent? Is this a failure of those at the very highest levels? How can we protect ourselves when our best are defeated before our optical sensors?"

The lights clicked on and Max saw that he was in an impossibly large room. White columns rose from the marbled floor and a number of statues lined the edges. They looked like various warriors from history, and Max recognized them from the different civilization games he played on his computer. There was a Spartan, Roman, samurai, Zulu, American Indian, musketeer, and other more modern-looking soldiers. But most important, in the center of the floor were three metallic posts where Sarah, Dirk, and Dwight were bound.

"Sarah!" Max called out. It might have sounded heroic if his voice hadn't squeaked.

Sarah looked up at Max to see him hanging some twenty feet overhead. She started to call out but froze when a metallic monster stepped into the light; it was Robo-Princess. And at her side was the heavily armored, shield-carrying, shoulder-gun-toting death machine known as the Frobinator.

"So as impressive as their victories were," Robo-Princess continued, "it's time for the question of magic or machine to finally be settled. And it's time for vengeance for our comrades who were slain." Beyond the darkness thousands of multicolored lights began blinking off and on in response. "But first, you will choose a contestant to move on. That's right, we've decided to give you the power to pluck one of the competitors from the field of battle and advance them to the final round. Will it be the dwarf, a wild card taken from the game before it even began?" A light clicked on, illuminating Dwight.

"Go choke on a punch card!" Dwight yelled.

"Or will you vote for the upstart religious leader?" Robo-Princess continued. A second light came on over Dirk, who was struggling to pull himself free.

"Or perhaps the girl, a warrior schooled in the ancient art of human warfare?" The final light appeared over Sarah who was standing tall despite being bound to the pole. "Vote now—which one do you want to see in the finale?" Princess had learned much about the humans she'd been hunting.

Max noticed that the frequency of the blinking lights increased. As he looked down from his clear cage, seeing his friends bound and the rest of his army trapped and hanging from the ceiling, he began to feel sick. It was his fault, after all—all of it. From the decision to take the *Codex* to school, to reading it at the Dragon's Den, to not listening to Sarah.

"At times like this," Glenn suggested, "with a ticking clock, limited options, and the lives of your friends hanging in the balance, it's important to do the right thing."

"Oh, yeah? And what if I don't know what the right thing is?"

"Figure out the wrong thing and do the opposite."

Below, Robo-Princess trotted over to Max's friends. "So, dwarf," she said, holding a microphone in front of Dwight. "Would you like to tell our viewing audience why they should vote for you?"

"Sure," Dwight grumbled. "Back where I come from we use mules to drag rocks from the tunnels. We use mules instead of unicorns because they're smarter, stronger, and don't smell as bad."

Robo-Princess had to fight back the surge of anger and override the incineration command that was being issued by her hostility processor. Instead, she switched off the microphone and leaned forward. "That little remark is going to cost you." But Dwight simply grinned.

Robo-Princess next moved to where Dirk was standing. "And what about this human? Do you have a preferred name?"

"Yes," Dirk said, taking a breath. "Call me . . . *creator*!" This sent a wild flurry of blinking lights from around the room. "I've built more than a dozen computers in my basement, and they're probably like your great ancestors. So free me now, your creator demands it! Or face my wrath!"

The machines in their seats felt a brief surge of panic pass through their systems. They universally agreed they didn't like this human—not at all.

"Well, that was unexpected," Robo-Princess announced, finally moving to stand in front of Sarah. The robot's gleaming metallic horn and silver skin made the girl look small by comparison. "And how about this one?" Robo-Princess continued. "Why should our viewing audience vote to save you tonight?"

Sarah looked up, but instead of looking at the robotic unicorn she looked at Max. "I think you're asking the wrong question," she said in a measured tone that didn't sound at all fearful. "You should be asking how you save yourselves. You see that boy up there, Max Spencer? He's my friend. He's a wizard, and I believe in him. Leave us alone and you can probably save your lives. If not, Max Spencer will destroy you. Tell that to your viewing audience."

More blinking lights measured the reaction from the thousands of seat cubes filling in the stadium. For a microsecond Robo-Princess considered the possibility that the humans could actually defeat her, but then she dismissed it—she was just getting caught up in the theatrics of it all.

The voting commenced and the scores were tallied quickly. If nothing else, the machines were efficient. The result was sent to Robo-Princess. "And the winner, advancing to the finale, is . . . the dwarf!" A clear cube was lowered to the floor as two floating prisms, armed with shock wands, drove the dwarf inside. The cell was sealed shut and hoisted back into the air to join the others. For Robo-Princess, it was all about showmanship. "Now, I'd hate for anyone to think we machines don't also have mercy." She looked up at Max, who was hanging in the cage. "Max Spencer! You've defeated two of us, and for that we're offering you a surprise gift." She turned to an image that materialized in midair, showing a zoo with various caged animals. One empty exhibit, however, was a typical human apartment complete with furniture and a television. "You, Max Spencer, will get to choose one of your companions to live out the rest of their days at our wonderful Organic Zoo." Max could hear applause rolling down from the darkness, and he was struck by the impression that he wasn't so much inside a room as he was in the middle of a giant stadium. He looked down at the large, metallic unicorn staring back at him.

"So," Robo-Princess continued, "one lives, the other one dies—you decide."

Max looked over at the metallic horror that was the Frobinator as several shoulder cannons leveled themselves at his friends.

"You can't," Max called out, his words sounding pitiful even in his own ears. "Please."

"Please . . . ?" Robo-Princess mocked. "Have we reduced the powerful wizard to begging?"

Sarah tried to smile at Max, but her eyes were bright with tears. Dirk was pulling at his bonds and kicking at the post that held him in place. "You can't make me choose," Max said.

Robo-Princess moved to stand between Sarah and Dirk. "Right now I'm offering you the life of one of your companions. I would think that you'd be polite enough to accept. If not, well, maybe I'll kill them both."

Max felt a strange vibration in his cube. He looked across at the other cubes suspended in the air and noticed they seemed to be swaying more than usual.

"It's okay, Max," Sarah said. "You don't have to choose. I won't ask you to."

"Cool, then choose me!" Dirk exclaimed, continuing to pull at his chords. "I like zoos."

Sarah suddenly flushed with anger. "Seriously, Dirk? Forget it, I take it back. I'm asking you to choose me now."

"Cheater!" Dirk cried out. "You can't take it back."

"I can and I have," Sarah said defiantly.

Something strange *was* happening to Max's cube, however. Not only did the vibrations seem to intensify, but the whole thing lurched downward, causing Max to have to steady himself. He looked around but he couldn't see anything.

"So . . . ?" Robo-Princess asked again. "Which one are you going to save, and which one will you condemn to die? Hurry now, 'the clock's ticking' as you humans used to say."

Both of Max's friends were staring at him. Sarah with her auburn hair and green eyes—smart, confident, and tough. Max admired everything about her. And then Dirk, his oldest and best friend. Maybe Dirk didn't always see the world like everyone else, but he was the most honest person Max had ever known. He couldn't choose between them—it was an impossible choice. "I . . . ," Max started, but a shadow passed over him. He looked up to see a metallic spider crawling on the top of the cube. It was about the size of a dinner plate and had orange eyes. Cenede!

Suddenly cubes began to drop rapidly to the floor. When they landed, the walls vanished, sending the occupants scrambling over the floor. Max only had a moment to take it in before his own cube dropped. He hit the floor fairly hard, momentarily knocking the wind out of him as he stumbled forward—past the point where the cube wall used to be. He could see thick strands of spider-web hanging from the air. The spiders were cutting the cubes loose and lowering them to the ground!

"No!" Robo-Princess screamed as the cubes continued to fall, one after the other, losing their form once they crashed into the floor. And like Max, the cube occupants had been allowed to keep their things. Frobbits and faeries poured from their open cubes, weapons in hand.

Purple and the rest of the executives wasted no time. They released the police bots that had been standing by in case of an emergency. It violated the spirit of the games, but the executives had unanimously decided that the moment Robo-Princess looked as if she'd lost control of the situation, they were taking matters into their own retractable pincers.

Robo-Princess whirled as the police bots flew past the row of warrior statues and formed a line on the stadium floor. "No!" she screamed again, watching as her carefully laid plans began to unravel. "This is about me! I'm the one who will save Machine City!"

Yah Yah appeared near the front of the assembling frobbit and faerie platoons, yelling orders and getting things organized. He raised his spear and oriented the faerie archers toward the police bots. At his command, a volley of arrows flew into the air, falling into the advancing robots. Most of the small arrows bounced harmlessly of their metallic skin, but a good many slipped through tiny joints and sensor holes never designed for such a crude assault. The tiny arrows began to short out socket motors, retinal cameras, and other sensitive electronics. Police bots fell as the tiny arrows rained down on them.

The mood in the stadium had turned from celebration to shock, then outright terror. Tens of thousands of lights pulsed and strobed with alarmed intensity.

Several dozen spiders dropped from the shadows to engulf Robo-Princess, leaping on her back and striking at her with their fangs. She began fighting them off, spinning and bucking as she tried to free herself from the assault, destroying the spiders with her horn or tearing them apart with her teeth. Robo-Princess was too busy to notice Dwight run past. He reached Dirk and Sarah and cut them free with his axe.

Sarah turned to see Max stumbling forward. A second group of police bots had closed on the center of the floor and were engaged in a furious fight with the mechanical spiders.

"Max!" Sarah screamed as a police bot swung an energy baton at him. Max barely managed to duck, and heard the crack and sizzle of the electric sparks that played along the weapon's surface.

"Help!" Dirk cried as he scrambled to free himself from the arms of a police bot. Sarah rushed toward him, grabbing Dirk's hand. The police bot raised a metallic arm and a foot-long spike extended from it. Sarah panicked, pulling harder to free Dirk, but the police bot had him trapped. The robot turned the weapon, ready to strike, then suddenly lurched forward. The police bot froze as a shower of sparks flew from behind it. Its arms loosened and Dirk spun out of its grip as the robot fell forward, crashing to the ground.

Dwight stood where it had been standing, his battle-axe

in hand. "Finally I get to kill something!" he shouted, turning to engage another police bot.

Max had managed to make it to his feet and was starting to reach for Glenn. He didn't have the *Codex* anymore, and if it was going to come down to hand-to-hand combat he didn't give himself much of a chance. But as he was about to pull the dagger free a rapid explosion of gunfire erupted. The police bot in front of him was ripped in half as other bots and mechanical spiders exploded around him. Max dove to the ground, wrapping his arms around his head. The Frobinator had entered the melee, and its shoulder guns were decimating everything in its path.

Across the hall, Yah Yah commanded the frobbit infantry to charge into the weakened line of police bots. As the frobbits ran forward, waving their improvised weapons, Yah Yah directed the faerie archers to turn and take aim at the Frobinator. They pulled back on their bows and let loose.

Sarah watched as the tiny arrows arched over her head and began falling around the hunter, bouncing off its armor. And while the faeries had gotten lucky with the design of the police bots, the Frobinator had no such weaknesses. The Frobinator turned its cannons and began shooting into the air in a massive display of firepower. The remains of mechanical spiders fell like rain. Seat cubes also exploded in the distance as the hunter continued its rampage, not caring if it destroyed friend or foe.

"Enough!" Robo-Princess shouted. A band of white lightning exploded from her horn, tracing a path across the creatures around her and stretching up to engage the hundreds of remaining spiders hanging from the pillars or lurking in the shadows above. There was a flash of light and the remaining spiders fell to the ground, their frames twisted and smoldering.

Guns smoking from its shoulders, the Frobinator beat its chest with its fist as the small faerie arrows bounced harmlessly off its thick armored shell.

At the same time, the frobbits had closed the distance with the police bots and were fighting them in a desperate clash of hand-to-hand combat. The Frobinator ignored them for the moment, choosing to train its guns on Yah Yah and the faerie archers. "Time to die, little faeries," the Frobinator announced.

Robo-Princess snarled, her metallic teeth glistening. She leapt forward, knocking Dwight and Dirk on their backs and driving Sarah to the ground. She lowered her head, placing the point of her horn beneath Sarah's chin, and pushed a metallic hoof on her chest, pinning her.

"I'll start by killing you," Robo-Princess said. "And as you lie there bleeding you can watch as I slaughter your friends, destroy your pitiful army, and devour Max Spencer bit by bit. Time for the human race to finally come to an end."

Max rose to his feet, the Frobinator's carnage all around him. He began to reach for Glenn, deciding that he wouldn't let his friends die without him trying *something*—no matter how doomed it was to fail. But then he remembered the words of the Wez: *When things get bad—just relax and listen.* It was the hardest thing Max had ever done, but he stopped reaching for the dagger and closed his eyes.

Robo-Princess was watching him out of the corner of her eye. "Oh, come on now! At least *try* to put up a fight!"

Max ignored her. He heard the pinging of the arrows as they continued to fall harmlessly on the Frobinator's armor. He heard the ratcheting of a new belt of bullets being locked into place. And he heard the sounds of fighting as the frobbits began to succumb to the powerful police bots. Max pushed everything out of his head, even though his mind was screaming that he had run out of time. He did the practically impossible—he relaxed. Max took a deep breath and pictured the *Codex*. He wasn't concentrating on finding the book's location or retrieving a particular spell, he just stretched out his mind and opened himself to the book's influence. At first there was nothing but the sound of his own heart. Max pushed past that, willing himself to go deeper until all of the sounds around him had been muted out. And then, suddenly, Max could feel it, like stepping outside and feeling the sun on the first day of spring. The sensation was as old and as powerful as anything in the universe—but it was also familiar. And somehow, at the moment, Max knew that the *Codex* itself didn't matter—that it was simply a key that opened something . . . else. Max felt a great sense of power begin to swell as it stretched out and filled every part of him. Then a voice echoed in his ears: *The world is an ironic place, Max—wouldn't you say?*

A word came to Max's mind and he felt it form in his mouth. The word was like a great sphere, pulled from an infinite ocean. But this time Max was not helplessly adrift—this time he summoned the spell with the same inevitability as gravity pulls a falling star to earth. Max took the immensity of the thing and drew it into him, compressing it down until it raged within him—a burning inferno. Then he let the spell go with a voice that sounded only a little like his own.

"Irony!" Max shouted. The sound shook the entire building as the spell heaved itself into reality, sweeping the remaining robots off their feet like a child casting toys off a table. The Frobinator was flung across the ground, crashing hard against a large column. Robo-Princess flew from Sarah, spinning in the air until she landed hard against the marble floor. And the police bots were blown into the rows of statues, exploding in a shower of concrete and metal. For several moments afterward, no one moved.

"Whoa," Dirk said, climbing to his feet. Sarah looked over at Max. "Max . . . ?"

Robo-Princess had been around magic her entire life. As a unicorn she was one of the most powerful creatures in existence. But the enormity of what she felt was beyond anything she had ever experienced. She knew that she should be afraid—truly afraid for the first time in her life, if only she wasn't so *hungry*. A new appetite was rising, insatiable and enticing. The smell of flesh, gathered and amplified by her enhanced robotic body was suddenly repugnant. Instead, the scent of the machines had awakened something new. From their warm processors, pulsating at fantastic speeds, to their hydraulics and electronic neural networks—each and every part of the machine's anatomy brought on a hunger so deep and profound that nothing was more important than satisfying the need to taste and devour.

In a flash Robo-Princess sent a lightning bolt from her horn and into the Frobinator. The surge caused the hunter's systems to instantly overload. But even before it stopped writhing on the ground, Robo-Princess was on top of it, ripping open its chest and chewing on its circuits and electronics. A collective gasp exploded from the machines around the stadium. Robo-Princess ignored them—the taste of the Frobinator was the most wonderfully exhilarating thing she had ever experienced. But there was no satisfaction, only an increasing need to devour more. She bounded up to a police bot that was trying to get up. Robo-Princess ripped into it, casting its electronics over the ground as she chewed and tasted. But each time, the satisfaction of eating never came, only the increased hunger. A panic erupted throughout the stadium now as police bots, servos, and other machines fled in terror.

Robo-Princess, who had hunted and killed for centuries, was brutally efficient. Nothing escaped her. With magic and machine-fueled ferocity she destroyed everything in her path. When the sphere Pink floated down, demanding to know what was going on, she speared it with her horn, impaling the orb like a shish kebab before flinging it against a wall and tearing out its insides.

Max hurried to join his friends, and Sarah flung her arms around him until he stopped feeling awkward and hugged her back.

Meanwhile, Robo-Princess continued her devastating and brutal attack.

"What happened?" Dirk said, looking around him as a plume of smoke began to rise. "You don't have the *Codex*."

"I don't know," Max answered, letting go of Sarah. "I think it might have spoken to me."

"Sounds a bit crazy if you ask me," Glenn chimed in. "A talking book."

"You said 'irony,'" Dwight added. "Right before everything happened."

"And now Robo-Princess is eating all the machines instead of us," Dirk replied. "Sort of ironic, if you think about it."

Another crash sounded in the distance, followed by various alarms.

"So, how long do you suppose this will go on?" Sarah asked. The frobbits and faeries were embracing one another and tending to their wounded.

"I don't think Robo-Princess will stop . . . *ever*," Max said. "I think she'll eat every machine on the planet. And when she's done, the only thing left will be herself."

"Ew," Sarah said, crinkling her nose. "That seems kind of gross."

"Not as gross as being a monkey in their messed-up zoo," Dirk replied. "I was prepared to throw things. Unmentionable things."

Yah Yah ran up to them, smiling broadly. "Come, my friends, let's go home! Soon this city will be destroyed and our overlords will be gone. Peace! It was too much to even hope for until you came to us. Peace at last!"

Yah Yah bowed to Max, which made Max blush. "Don't do that," Max said, trying not to offend his little friend. "It's embarrassing."

Yah Yah rose, never taking his eyes off him. "You've done it, Max. You've saved us."

CHAPTER THIRTY-TWO

THE SLEEPER RISES

(THE TECHRUS—FUTURE)

FOR MANY MONTHS FOLLOWING THEIR VICTORY AT MACHINE CITY, Max tried to find the *Codex* by reaching out with his mind. When that failed, he and Dirk trekked to the hunting grounds and searched for the book there, but it remained lost. They did find the floating frobbit caught in the branches of a tree, however, and with a little help, they managed to get him back to the ground. The spell must have worn off because the formerly singed, flamed, and airborne frobbit remained earthbound, (although whenever he saw Max he'd run in the opposite direction).

As Robo-Princess continued leveling Machine City, a great council of frobbit nations was called and the various clans came together to form a government. They had asked Max to be their ruler (he declined), followed by

Sarah (she politely refused), then Dwight (he laughed at them), and finally Dirk (who had enthusiastically accepted at first, but after many heated discussions with Max and Sarah had finally stepped down). There had been no more hunts, and in time the frobbits decided the whole hunting business was over and done with for good.

At first Max's friends were patient with him as he tried again and again to find either the spell that would take them home, or the *Codex* itself. But as the weeks wore on he could feel their growing anxiety. Living with the frobbits wasn't bad—they liked to sing and dance and cook, but Max was growing more and more unsettled. He thought again and again about the visit from the Wez, who had been absolutely right in telling him to relax in order to access the deeper recesses of the *Codex*. But with the book gone and unable to find it in his mind, he started to feel hopeless. Max spent most of his days in his tree house (the frobbits had given each of them one), puttering around or just sleeping. Sarah had organized more judo training, and tried to occupy her mind with as much of that as possible. But it was clear she was also getting more and more unraveled by the thought of having to stay with the frobbits forever. Dwight lost himself in whatever drink he could concoct, and only Dirk seemed to adapt to his new environment, exploring the area with many of his frobbit and faerie pals, and teaching them variations of his favorite games.

Fall drifted into winter. With the cold forcing them indoors for much of the time, the gradual depression that had been working its way through Sarah and Max only deepened.

When spring arrived, Max took an air sled and visited Cenede. She was in the process of rebuilding her spiders, having lost nearly all of them in the battle against Robo-Princess.

"Aren't you concerned that she'll come for you?" Max asked her one day. The question had been weighing on his mind.

"Robo-Princess will come for me when I am the last," Cenede answered without emotion. "It's a fitting end to an unnaturally long life, wouldn't you say?"

"But she'll destroy you."

"Knowing that I destroyed her first," Cenede replied. "And then we will be done and this world can go back to its first caretakers."

"So this is my life, then," Max said with a sigh. "We

came so far that I just thought we'd go all the way."

"All the way home you mean?"

Max nodded.

"Perhaps it's your destiny to make this your home now. I know I would enjoy your company."

Several weeks later when Max returned to visit Cenede again, he found her destroyed remains scattered around the chamber. And there, in the center of it, was the gutted shell of the metallic unicorn. Robo-Princess had turned on herself just as he had suspected, until whatever life she had was gone. Max sat down and stared at the electronic remains for some time, noticing a strange translucent compass scattered among the debris. He took the object and put it in his pocket. It was well after dark before he returned to the air sled and had the faeries take him back to the treeshire. He didn't bother telling his friends what he'd seen.

A few weeks later when summer was in full swing, Dirk pulled his friends together and announced that they needed to spend the night in a cave he'd found on one of his expeditions. Both Sarah and Max declined, but Dirk was so insistent that they finally gave up and agreed to go. He'd even managed to get Dwight to tag along by promising him a new kind of berry with special brewing potential.

Getting to the cave actually required a bit of a climb, but when Max and his friends made it to the top they were rewarded with a spectacular view of the forest on one side, and the ocean on the other. Near the cave's entrance the mountain fell away for hundreds of feet, so they were careful not to get too near the edge.

"It's beautiful," Sarah said. Max was feeling too tired to really enjoy it, so he sat down instead. "We should probably start a fire before it gets dark."

"That's okay," a voice came from farther inside. "I'm hoping we won't be staying that long."

Everyone jumped, except for Dirk. He looked back and raised his hand. "It's okay. He's the reason I brought you guys here."

"He?" Dwight exclaimed, pulling the axe from off his back.

The figure that stepped out of the cave's interior was dressed in flowing black leather and moved with the kind of economy of motion that reminded Max of the sharks he'd seen swimming in the aquarium. The man's face was hidden behind black cloth, perfectly wrapped around his chin and neck, and the rest of his features were lost in the shadows of a cowboy hat. "Forgive me for startling you, but it was better if I met you away from your frobbit hosts."

Max's hand unconsciously drifted toward Glen.

"It's okay, guys," Dirk continued. "I met him the other day when I was exploring. He's been looking for us."

"Wait, so there *isn't* a new berry up here?" Dwight asked, sounding upset.

"If I may introduce myself," the man continued, "my name is Obsikar. And as Dirk has said, I've been looking for you for a very long time."

"Obsikar," Dwight echoed back, the word tumbling around in his memory. "Seems I've heard that name before."

"I am known to many," Obsikar replied. "And I have walked the three realms since the dawn of their creation."

"What's going on?" Max asked, turning to Dirk. "What have you done?"

"It's okay, like I said. I told Obsikar the whole story—how we're stuck because you lost the *Codex*. No offense."

"We're not stuck," Max said defensively. "I just haven't figured everything out yet."

"If I may be direct," Obsikar said, stepping forward, "even if you had the *Codex* it is unlikely you could use it to return to your time—not in the short life afforded to humans to work such things out. I say this having gained a certain understanding of what it means to travel through time—a mastery gained from a life measured in centuries and not years."

"What are you, exactly?" Max asked. "Not a human, I take it."

"I was born of the Shadrus, sometimes called the shadow realm. I have been called demon, king, and even death itself. All are correct in their own way, I suppose. But what I am now is the last of my kind."

"You said you were looking for us?" Sarah interjected.

"Across the realms of existence and through the umbraverse."

"Umbraverse . . . ?" Dirk asked.

"It's like an alternative reality or something," Max said, remembering reading about it in the *Codex*.

"An unknown," Dwight added, putting his axe down but not taking his eyes off the stranger. "Much like this stranger here. And I don't believe in trusting in the unknown."

Obsikar tipped his hat to Dwight. "Of all the commodities the dwarfs pull from the mines of Thoran, *trust* may be the rarest."

"And for good reason," Dwight replied with a grunt.

Obsikar turned to Max. "So it is true, you can read from the *Codex*? Its absence must be unsettling."

"He doesn't need it," Sarah said coolly.

"They are bound together—one will not exist without the other now."

"Look," Max said, trying to understand. "I'm not sure what you're getting at, but I'd like to know what you want."

"An arrangement," Obsikar answered. "I will take you back to your time and you will kill a sorcerer."

"We're not going to just kill somebody because you ask us to," Sarah said. "That's not who we are."

"Speak for yourself," Dwight said.

"As I've said, I am the last of my kind," Obsikar continued. "I am the king of dragons. Long ago, the sorcerer Rezormoor Dreadbringer began hunting and killing us, simply to possess a scale called the Serpent's Escutcheon. It fits over our breast and is impervious to both magic and steel. Rezormoor sought to collect enough of these to construct a suit of armor—one unlike any the world has ever seen. Such armor would make the wearer invulnerable."

"But hasn't he already done this?" Sarah asked. "This all happened in the past, right?"

"The Serpent's Escutcheon is too hard to be smithed by normal means. That is why he sent the unicorn after the *Codex*—only it has the power to transform this precious scale into what the sorcerer desires. I suspect that with the armor and the *Codex of Infinite Knowability*, Rezormoor Dreadbringer could subjugate the whole of the three realms completely. Perhaps overthrowing the Maelshadow himself."

"So this sorcerer sent the unicorn to hunt us?" Max asked, trying to catch up. "Everything that's happened is because of him? This Rezormoor Dreadbringer?"

"Yes."

"But why do you need us now?" Sarah continued. "Everything's done. This Rezormoor is long dead—what does it matter?"

"It matters because no race should ever die out. Look at us here, the last members of the humans, the dwarfs, and the dragons. Is it meant that we should all disappear because of the actions of one man? We sit at the end of our history, but it doesn't have to be that way. I have spent centuries looking for a way back."

"You make it sound noble, but it feels like revenge," Sarah said.

"Aye," Dwight added, "that it does—not that there's anything wrong with that."

"And suppose I do want revenge," Obsikar admitted. "Does it lessen the importance of preserving our species?"

"Just think of it," Dirk jumped in. "This Rezormoor guy has been hunting us from the very start. We go back and he has no idea that we know about him. He's looking for Max, but he doesn't know we'd be looking for him."

"But I don't have the *Codex*," Max said, "so I don't know how I'm supposed to take on some powerful sorcerer."

"You and the *Codex* are bound. I believe if you go back to your time the *Codex* will find you."

"Let's assume what you've said is true," Sarah asked, still trying to understand it all. "Why can't you go back and deal with this sorcerer yourself?"

"A fair question," Obsikar replied. "Let me simply

say that if I could, it would tear me from the fabric of existence. I did not simply jump to this time as you did—I came to it by a different route."

"Bummer, dude," Dirk replied. When the others looked at him Dirk shrugged. "Nobody likes getting torn from the fabric of existence—I'm just saying."

"So you're not like a wizard?" Max asked.

"I've been hibernating and waiting. Once a year I wake and look for signs of your arrival. With the destruction of Machine City, you made your presence fairly obvious. But as to my powers, they are drawn from the Shadrus, and, if you agree to go back to your time, the umbraverse as well."

Dwight clapped his hands, looking around. "Well, I think I've heard enough. You send us back to our time, we kill this sorcerer, and all's good. Sounds like a fair deal to me—let's get going."

Obsikar turned to Max. "So many years waiting to find you, Max. So many years working on a way to send you back in time and fix the things that have gone wrong. Will you do as I ask? Will you save the dragons, and by doing so, save yourselves?"

"I don't know," Max said, looking at Sarah and Dirk.

"Maybe I should just keep looking for the *Codex*. I mean, you seem nice enough and all, but you're just some guy in a cave. How do I really know anything you've said is true? I mean, you don't look like a dragon any more than Dirk does."

"Hey!" Dirk exclaimed.

Obsikar nodded. "I understand, Max. Perhaps this will help." The man suddenly ran past the group, moving as a blur and leaping from the mouth of the cave and over the cliff beyond. There was an inhuman shriek followed by the sound of beating wings. Max and his friends ran to the cliff's edge in time to see a dragon slowly rise in the air before them. He was a fantastic creature, with shiny black scales running along his shoulders and body, while gold scales ran from below his neck, down over his chest and across his belly. Long, armored spikes rose from his shoulder and leg joints, running the length of his tail to end finally in a deadly barb. The dragon's eyes glowed with a color that matched the gold of his scales, and the wind produced by his beating wings drove Max and his friends back toward the cave.

"See me for what I am and know that I speak the truth!" Obsikar bellowed. "I am the king of the dragons, spawn of demons, and avenger of my kind. I swear you to an oath that you will save the dragons. Swear it!" The voice came like a blow, pushing them farther back into the cave. The sheer power and majesty of the creature hovering in the air sent chills down Max's spine.

"I swear!" Max shouted.

"As do I!"

"And me!"

"I swear, too!"

Obsikar hovered there for a moment. The sky began to turn a deep crimson as clouds stretched and thickened at impossible speeds. A stronger wind began to rise, stronger even than the beating of Obsikar's wings. Suddenly the sun dropped from its place on the horizon and darkness fell. Bright stars could be seen poking through clouds above.

"What's happening?" Sarah shouted.

"Through the umbraverse!" Obsikar shouted. "Return now to your own time!"

The group grabbed hold of the sides of the cave, bracing against the howling winds.

Obsikar opened his mouth and blew a dark mist that began to swirl around them. Then the world shifted. The black mist closed in on them, the circles of the stars raced in giant glowing rings across the sky, and night and day followed each other as quickly as a beating heart.

"Awwwesooooome!" Dirk shouted as he clung to the cave wall.

CHAPTER THIRTY-THREE

HOMECOMING?

(THE MAGRUS—PRESENT)

Max heard a familiar voice in his head. *Welcome home.*

"Home? I'm really home?"

Yes, came the answer, the voice sounding more distant. *At long last. Everything happens for a reason, Max. Remember that.*

Max opened his eyes.

He was hanging upside down from a tree limb. Below him a large orc woman kept burning her hands as she tried to adjust an iron pot on a bed of coals. Hanging next to him were Sarah, Dirk, and Dwight, but they seemed to be sleeping and oblivious to what was going on. Seeing that Max was awake, the orc woman wiped her hands on her apron and approached, leaning down to get a good look at him. She walked with a strange limp and something was wrong with her hands, but Max's eyes were still adjusting.

"You tailor?" she asked, a bead of sweat running down her greenish cheeks.

Max tried to speak, but his throat was incredibly dry. "I'm Max," he managed to squeak out.

"Not name, stupid. Me need tailor to make mittens." The orc motioned to Max's backpack that had been spilled out on the ground. "You craftsmen? Maybe trade orc mittens for friends?"

To Max's great relief he saw the *Codex of Infinite Knowability* lying on the ground near Glenn and his other belongings. "Orc mittens," he repeated, remembering the *Codex*. "I think I might be able to help."

Don't miss the next book in the
BAD UNICORN *trilogy:*

LOKI AND MOKI PADDED TOWARD THE TREE OF WOE. LIKE MOST DAYS IN the Turul wastes, it was hot, and that was exactly the way the two fire kittens liked it. Ahead the ancient tree stretched high into the cloudless sky, with sun-bleached bones hanging from its black limbs. When the wind picked up the various skeletal bits banged into each other like an unholy wind chime. Beneath the clattering bones a skinny human with pale skin and a long white beard tugged at his chains.

"Well, this must be exciting for you," Loki said to Moki as they approached the old man. Loki had swirls of black and white fur and a pink nose, while Moki was black-nosed with a hodgepodge of orange and white fur. Fire kittens were nearly indistinguishable from regular kittens, except for their ability to do things like fling fireballs from their tails and talk about the weather. "I mean, being fresh out of the academy and all," Loki continued.

"They said there was only one place for a kitten of my talents"—Moki beamed—"and here I am."

Loki knew exactly what *that* meant. Despite what the Quorum of Kitties said publicly, being assigned to the Tree of Woe was the lowest duty handed out to fire kittens— one given to the most challenged academy graduates, or in Loki's case, to those branded as troublemakers and malcontents. "Just do everything I tell you, exactly as I tell you, and you'll be fine."

"Because you're the boss?" Moki asked. Loki thought that was obvious, but he supposed one could never over-emphasize the basics.

"Yes . . . because I'm the boss." Moki pointed to a small mailbox resting at an angle in the cracked ground. "Now go and retrieve our orders."

Moki nodded and bounded to the box (with a little too much enthusiasm for Loki's liking), returning with a sealed envelope.

"Looks like we have another prisoner from Thannis," Loki said, studying the wax seal before breaking it open. It took a special kind of wax to withstand the heat in

Turul, harvested from the gooey-eared bog mice of Mephis. Loki made a mental note to wash his paws when he returned to camp. "We get a lot of criminals from the capital these days."

"I'm no criminal!" the human protested. Like all the prisoners delivered to the Tree of Woe, the old man was dressed in a simple loincloth. "I'll have you know I'm a druid of the seventh order, and I've had a vision!"

"Uh-huh," Loki replied, unimpressed. He continued to read from the official papers. "According to this, you've been charged with the use of unauthorized magic—"

"Bah! The Tower knows nothing! I've seen *him* through the mists of the umbraverse. And I know what he brings!"

"Yep," Loki continued. "Then you defaced the king's property."

"I merely wrote *his* name on the city wall so all could see. But the guards stopped me. Fools!"

"And finally—and this is where you really crossed the line—it says you double-parked your horse."

"I can't be bothered with *parking*!" the old man yelped. "He's here! And the blood of the World Sunderer flows through his veins!"

Loki handed the writ to Moki. "No more need for this—I think we know what kind of trouble maker we have here." Moki happily took the paper and tucked it away. "As for you, human," Loki continued in his official-sounding voice, "you've been sentenced to three days' punishment on the Tree of Woe. Here you will be licked by specially trained fire kittens—that's us—as you consider your offenses and reflect on just what a terrible person you are."

"Don't you see?" the human said, tugging at his chains. "The Seven Kingdoms are nothing to the might of the *boy who can read the book*!"

"Can we start at the ankles?" Moki asked. "I like starting at the ankles. You start low like that and you get to work your way up. It's like you see that calf just sitting there, begging for it."

The old man blinked a couple of times as he considered the small kitten's enthusiasm for leg licking. Everyone in the Magrus knew that fire kittens had hot tongues. Regular cat licking was repulsive enough, but fire kittens took it to a whole new level.

"Did you hear that, *magician*?" Loki said, emphasizing the insult with just the right amount of contempt—spell casters hated the term. "My friend here wants to start at your ankles. Do you know what it's like to be licked by a fire kitten?"

The old man shivered despite himself. "Those little tongues of yours are just so . . . gross . . . like sandpaper. But then again, I don't suppose anyone's *died* from it, have they?" The question caught Loki off guard. As far as he knew there had been no reported deaths from fire kitten licks. Such a record was obviously not good for their reputation. "Just as I thought," the druid continued, looking rather pleased with himself. "Your tongues might be icky, but they're not going to kill me."

Loki didn't like where this was going. "So you wanna do it the hard way, is that it?" he asked, moving closer and glaring at the prisoner. "Then maybe we skip the ankle and go right to that little spot just behind the knee. Very sensitive, that spot. I've broken more than a few orcs licking that particular spot." Loki grinned as a flame lit on the end of his tail. Suddenly the human didn't look so confident.

"Whatever you do to me doesn't matter. I've been called to deliver a great message. Even the Wizard's Tower is ignorant! Rezormoor Dreadbringer searches in vain, but only *I* know the location of what he seeks!" The human started to laugh in the way only a half-mad druid tied to a tree can.

Loki considered the ramifications of what he'd just heard. Getting in good with the Wizard's Tower was a promising idea on many levels. The Tower had influence across all of the Seven Kingdoms, and for an enterprising fire kitten that could mean real opportunity.

"You say nobody knows but *you*?" Loki asked, waiting for the human to settle down. Moki circled his paw around his head in the this-guy's-crazy sign. The gesture gave Loki a moment of pause. "You're not having any *other* kinds of strange visions, are you? Perhaps with unicorns or dragons?"

"Oh, oh, I had a dream about a unicorn once!" Moki exclaimed, jumping up and down and waiving his paw in the air. "It was running around trying to stick me with its evil horn! But then a squirrel stepped out and—"

"I was talking to the *prisoner*!" Loki yelled, stamping his paw and causing the flame on his tail to burn brighter. Moki seemed unfazed by the rebuke, however, and simply nodded and grinned some more.

"What I saw came from a spirit of the forest," the old

man continued. "This is not some 'strange vision,' as you call it. Nature does not lie." He looked up at the Tree of Woe as the desert wind moved through its branches. The Tree swayed as a result, giving the druid the distinct impression it had just shrugged him off.

"So, this *boy who can read the book*, do you know where he is?" Loki continued.

The druid looked at the two fire kittens and then set his jaw—he wasn't going to tell them anything more. The old spell caster could smell opportunists a mile away. He turned his head to watch a small scorpion scuttle across the dry earth.

"Oh, so suddenly you're not so talkative, huh?" Loki asked. He suddenly whipped his flaming tail at the scorpion, turning it into a black smudge. "Three days is a *long* time," Loki said, walking up and rubbing against the human's ankles, his tail curling dangerously close to the druid's leg. "A very, very long time, in fact."

"You're not a very nice kitty," the human noted.

Moki looked back and forth between the human and Loki. This was much more fun than he'd imagined.

Loki circled back around and sat, giving the prisoner a hard look. "This can really be so very simple. Tell me where I can find this boy, and I promise: not a single lick to your very thin skin."

The old druid looked away.

"Of course, my job can extend beyond the letter of the law," Loki added. "There's no reason I can't take some . . . creative license." He motioned to a fire pit.

"What's in there?" the druid said, squinting. "Are those bones?"

"I bet it's a marshmallow pit!" Moki guessed, bouncing up and down. He liked guessing games, especially if marshmallows were involved.

Loki shook his head. "So what's it going to be, human? You can't very well deliver your message if you never leave this place. And let's just say no one ever complains if a prisoner doesn't make it back. Cuts down on paperwork."

The druid mulled the situation over in his mind. His job was to prepare the Magrus—the magical realm—for the coming of the boy who could read the book. He couldn't let a couple of fire kittens stop him. "Fine," he sighed after a few moments. "The boy of prophecy is in Thoran, near Shyr'el. And with some orcs, if you really must know."

Loki grinned. Thoran was composed of the nonhuman nations of dwarfs, unicorns, and elves—a human boy would stand out there. "And nobody knows this but you?"

"Not yet," the old man replied. "But I'll tell all the Magrus as soon as I'm off this godsforsaken tree." More bones clattered above the druid, and this time he was certain the tree had just told him to shove off.

"Yeah, good luck with that," Loki said, turning and beginning to walk away, his tail flame disappearing with a puff of smoke. "But do mind the *crows*. They stay away when we're around, but when we're not . . . well, you know how birds like to peck at things."

Suddenly the druid understood—the fire kittens were going to leave him! "What?" he shouted. "But we had a deal!"

"I said I wouldn't *lick* you, and I won't. But if you want to make a deal with the crows, you'll have to take it up with them directly."

The druid looked up at the black shapes sitting high in the branches. The wind picked up again, knocking the bones together with an eerie *clank*. "You'll pay for this!" the human shouted as the two fire kittens padded away.

He looked around for signs of life—druids drew their magic from the living world, and he thought he might be able to whip up a spell. But he was in the middle of a vast and empty nothing, save for the Tree of Woe itself. And he had the distinct impression the tree didn't like him very much.

"So, uh, we're *not* licking him?" Moki asked as he and Loki headed back to their camp.

"No, my young apprentice," Loki replied. "We're going on a trip."

"We are? That's great! I like going places."

Loki nodded in agreement, but his thoughts were elsewhere. It was time to find his fortune, even if it meant walking away from a steady job with reasonable hours. But deep down inside, Loki had always known he was meant for something more—something that included fame and riches and power! It would be a long walk across the wastes to Onig, the goblin city and capital of Turul. But there he'd find the Guild of Indiscriminate Teleportation, which was his best shot at getting closer to the so-called *boy who could read the book*. Thoran happened to be about as far away from the Turul Wastes as anywhere in the Magrus, and ship captains didn't care for fire-flinging kittens aboard their wooden ships. But the boy—whomever he was—was too valuable to pass up. It was enough to know that the Tower wanted him—and the Tower had plenty of gold to pay for what it wanted. "Go and pack," he commanded Moki. "We have a date with destiny."

"Oh, good," Moki said. "I hope she's nice."

Discover the wonder of
the Land of Oz. . . .